IT'S GREAT
TO BE A
SUPER STAR

HEAD
BEAGLE

PEANUTS CLASSICS

Dr. Beagle and Mr. Hyde
Fly, You Stupid Kite, Fly!
How Long, Great Pumpkin, How Long?
It's Great to Be a Superstar
Kiss Her, You Blockhead!
My Anxieties Have Anxieties
Speak Softly, and Carry a Beagle
There Goes the Shutout
Summers Fly, Winters Walk
Thank Goodness for People
The Beagle Has Landed
What Makes You Think You're Happy?
And a Woodstock in a Birch Tree
A Smile Makes a Lousy Umbrella
The Mad Punter Strikes Again
There's a Vulture Outside
Here Comes the April Fool!
What Makes Musicians So Sarcastic?
A Kiss on the Nose Turns Anger Aside
It's Hard Work Being Bitter
I'm Not Your Sweet Babboo!
Stop Snowing on My Secretary
Always Stick Up for the Underbird
What's Wrong with Being Crabby?
Don't Hassle Me with Your Sighs, Chuck
The Way of the Fussbudget Is Not Easy
You're Weird, Sir!
It's a Long Way to Tipperary
Who's the Funny-Looking Kid with the Big Nose?
Sunday's Fun Day, Charlie Brown
You're Out of Your Mind, Charlie Brown!
You're the Guest of Honor, Charlie Brown
You Can't Win, Charlie Brown
Peanuts Every Sunday
The Unsinkable Charlie Brown
Good Grief, More Peanuts
You've Come a Long Way, Charlie Brown
The Cheshire Beagle
Duck, Here Comes Another Day!
Sarcasm Does Not Become You, Ma'am
Nothing Echoes Like an Empty Mailbox
I Heard A D Minus Call Me

IT'S GREAT TO BE A SUPER STAR

Cartoons from *You're Out of Sight, Charlie Brown*

by Charles M. Schulz

An Owl Book
Henry Holt and Company / New York

Henry Holt and Company, Inc.
Publishers since 1866
115 West 18th Street
New York, New York 10011

Henry Holt ® is a registered
trademark of Henry Holt and Company, Inc.

Library of Congress Catalog Card Number: 90-81562

ISBN 0-8050-1477-2 (An Owl Book: pbk.)

Henry Holt books are available for special promotions
and premiums. For details contact: Director, Special Markets.

Originally published as *You're Out of Sight, Charlie Brown* in 1970
by Holt, Rinehart and Winston. Published in an expanded edition
under the title *It's Great to Be a Super Star* in 1977 by
Holt, Rinehart and Winston, which included strips from
You've Come a Long Way, Charlie Brown, published in 1971 by
Holt, Rinehart and Winston.

First Owl Book Edition—1990

Printed in the United States of America
All first editions are printed on acid-free paper.∞

3   5   7   9   10   8   6   4   2

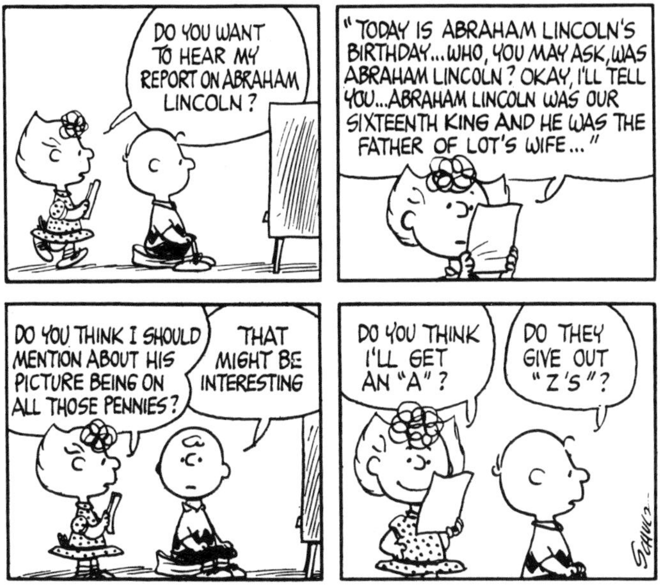
DO YOU WANT TO HEAR MY REPORT ON ABRAHAM LINCOLN?
"TODAY IS ABRAHAM LINCOLN'S BIRTHDAY...WHO, YOU MAY ASK, WAS ABRAHAM LINCOLN? OKAY, I'LL TELL YOU...ABRAHAM LINCOLN WAS OUR SIXTEENTH KING AND HE WAS THE FATHER OF LOT'S WIFE..."
DO YOU THINK I SHOULD MENTION ABOUT HIS PICTURE BEING ON ALL THOSE PENNIES?
THAT MIGHT BE INTERESTING
DO YOU THINK I'LL GET AN "A"?
DO THEY GIVE OUT "Z'S"?
SCHULZ

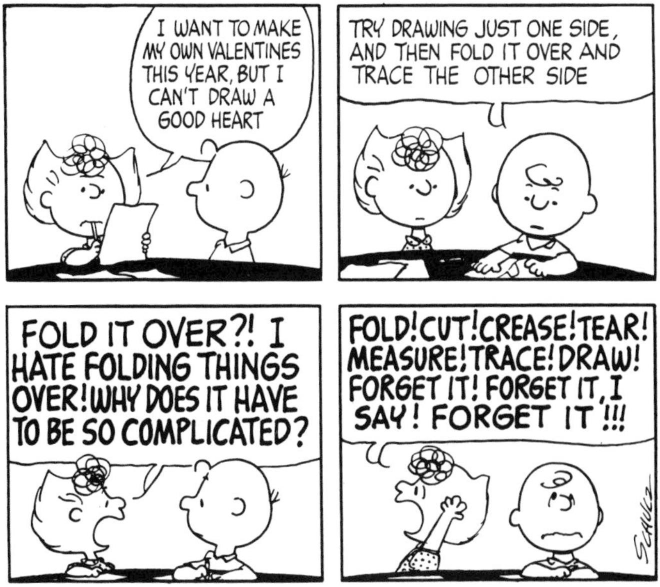
I WANT TO MAKE MY OWN VALENTINES THIS YEAR, BUT I CAN'T DRAW A GOOD HEART
TRY DRAWING JUST ONE SIDE, AND THEN FOLD IT OVER AND TRACE THE OTHER SIDE
FOLD IT OVER?! I HATE FOLDING THINGS OVER! WHY DOES IT HAVE TO BE SO COMPLICATED?
FOLD! CUT! CREASE! TEAR! MEASURE! TRACE! DRAW! FORGET IT! FORGET IT, I SAY! FORGET IT!!!
SCHULZ

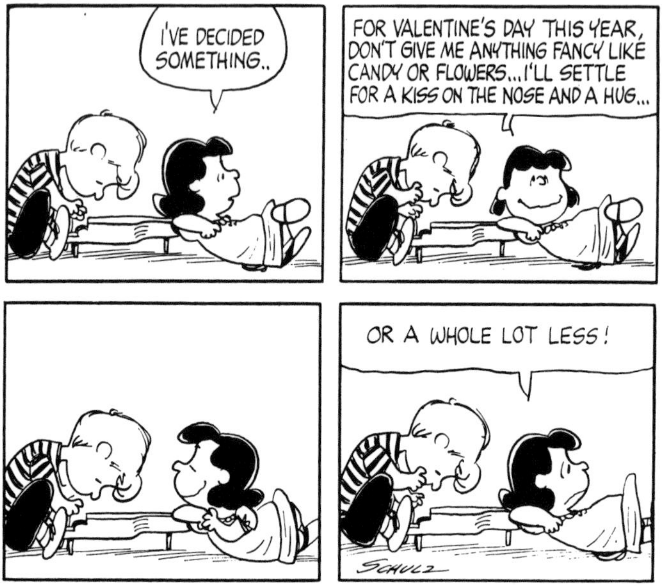
I'VE DECIDED SOMETHING..
FOR VALENTINE'S DAY THIS YEAR, DON'T GIVE ME ANYTHING FANCY LIKE CANDY OR FLOWERS...I'LL SETTLE FOR A KISS ON THE NOSE AND A HUG...
OR A WHOLE LOT LESS!
SCHULZ

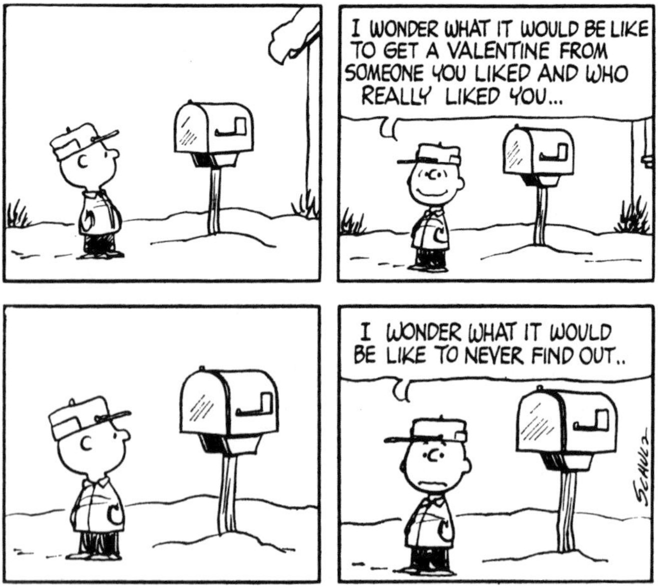
I WONDER WHAT IT WOULD BE LIKE TO GET A VALENTINE FROM SOMEONE YOU LIKED AND WHO REALLY LIKED YOU...
I WONDER WHAT IT WOULD BE LIKE TO NEVER FIND OUT..
SCHULZ

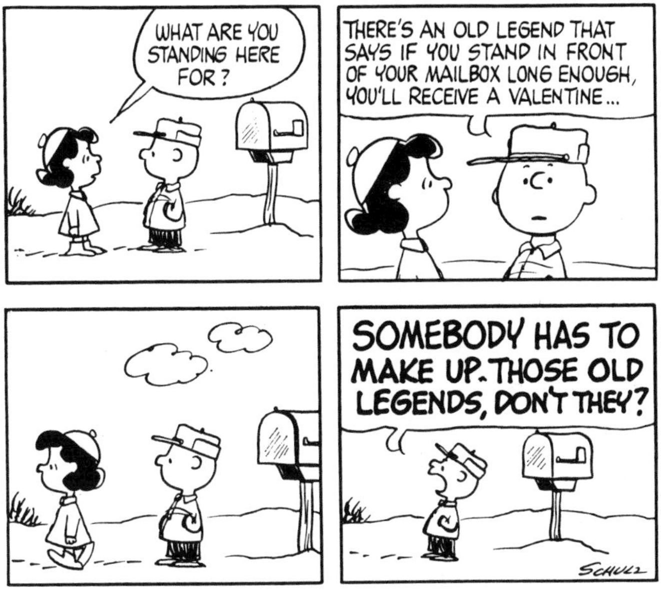
WHAT ARE YOU STANDING HERE FOR?
THERE'S AN OLD LEGEND THAT SAYS IF YOU STAND IN FRONT OF YOUR MAILBOX LONG ENOUGH, YOU'LL RECEIVE A VALENTINE...
SOMEBODY HAS TO MAKE UP THOSE OLD LEGENDS, DON'T THEY?

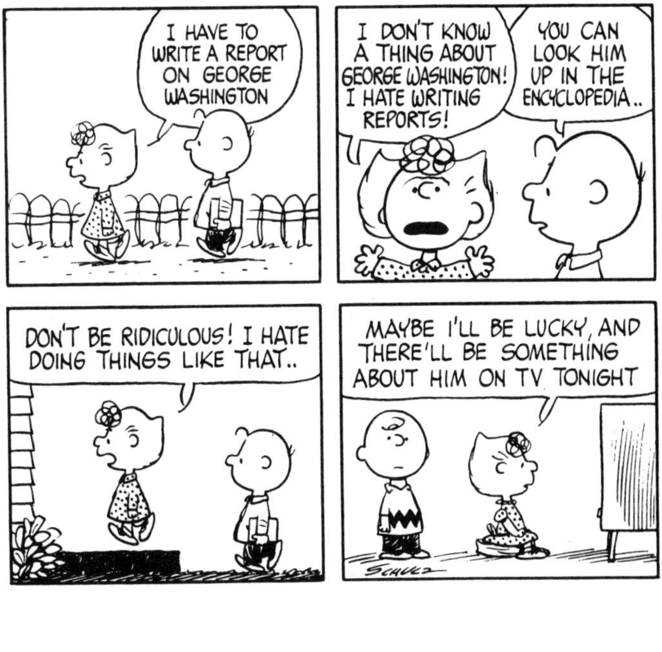
I HAVE TO WRITE A REPORT ON GEORGE WASHINGTON
I DON'T KNOW A THING ABOUT GEORGE WASHINGTON! I HATE WRITING REPORTS!
YOU CAN LOOK HIM UP IN THE ENCYCLOPEDIA..
DON'T BE RIDICULOUS! I HATE DOING THINGS LIKE THAT..
MAYBE I'LL BE LUCKY, AND THERE'LL BE SOMETHING ABOUT HIM ON TV TONIGHT

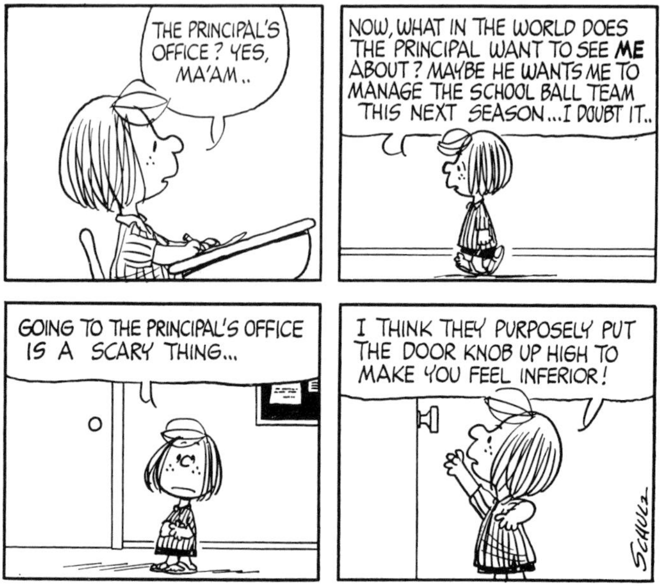
THE PRINCIPAL'S OFFICE? YES, MA'AM..
NOW, WHAT IN THE WORLD DOES THE PRINCIPAL WANT TO SEE **ME** ABOUT? MAYBE HE WANTS ME TO MANAGE THE SCHOOL BALL TEAM THIS NEXT SEASON...I DOUBT IT..
GOING TO THE PRINCIPAL'S OFFICE IS A SCARY THING...
I THINK THEY PURPOSELY PUT THE DOOR KNOB UP HIGH TO MAKE YOU FEEL INFERIOR!
SCHULZ

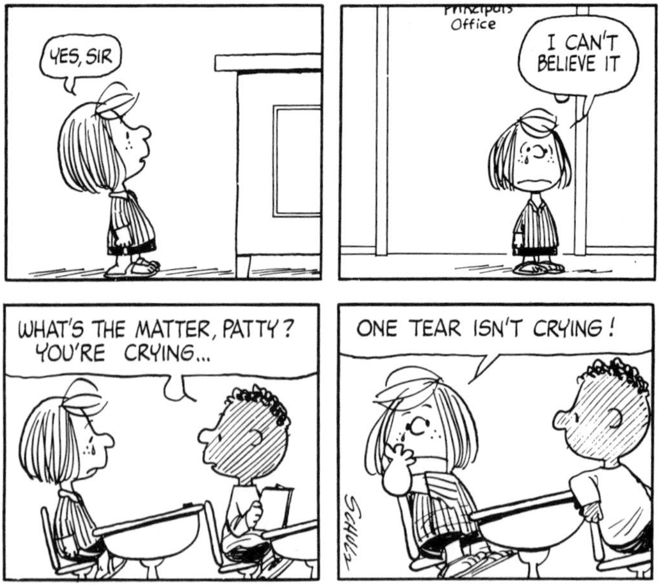
YES, SIR
Office
I CAN'T BELIEVE IT
WHAT'S THE MATTER, PATTY? YOU'RE CRYING...
ONE TEAR ISN'T CRYING!
SCHULZ

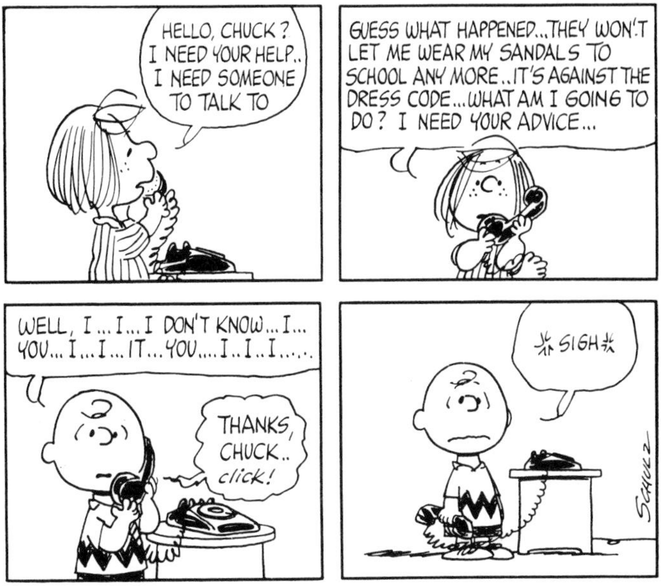
HELLO, CHUCK? I NEED YOUR HELP.. I NEED SOMEONE TO TALK TO
GUESS WHAT HAPPENED...THEY WON'T LET ME WEAR MY SANDALS TO SCHOOL ANY MORE..IT'S AGAINST THE DRESS CODE...WHAT AM I GOING TO DO? I NEED YOUR ADVICE...
WELL, I...I...I DON'T KNOW...I... YOU...I...I...IT...YOU....I..I..I.....
THANKS, CHUCK.. click!
SIGH
SCHULZ

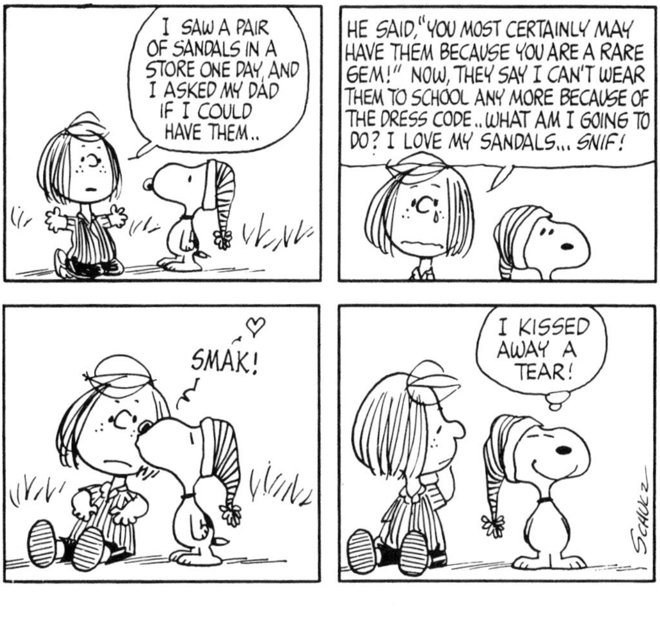
I SAW A PAIR OF SANDALS IN A STORE ONE DAY, AND I ASKED MY DAD IF I COULD HAVE THEM..
HE SAID, "YOU MOST CERTAINLY MAY HAVE THEM BECAUSE YOU ARE A RARE GEM!" NOW, THEY SAY I CAN'T WEAR THEM TO SCHOOL ANY MORE BECAUSE OF THE DRESS CODE..WHAT AM I GOING TO DO? I LOVE MY SANDALS... SNIF!
SMAK!
I KISSED AWAY A TEAR!
SCHULZ

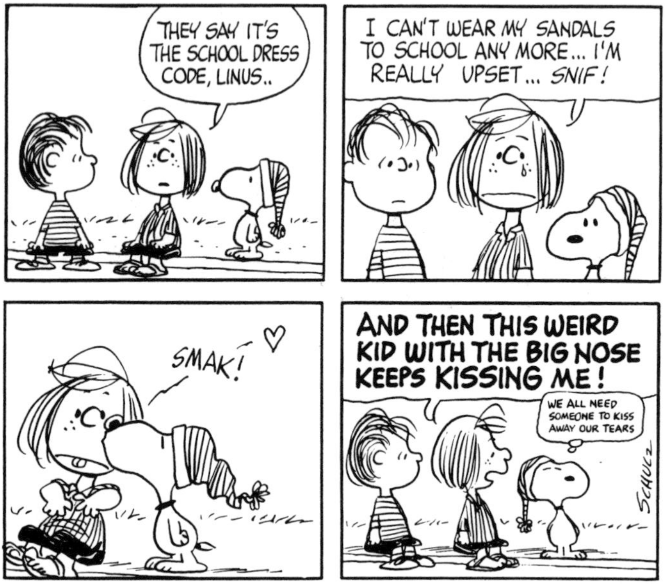
THEY SAY IT'S THE SCHOOL DRESS CODE, LINUS..
I CAN'T WEAR MY SANDALS TO SCHOOL ANY MORE... I'M REALLY UPSET... SNIF!
SMAK!
AND THEN THIS WEIRD KID WITH THE BIG NOSE KEEPS KISSING ME!
WE ALL NEED SOMEONE TO KISS AWAY OUR TEARS
SCHULZ

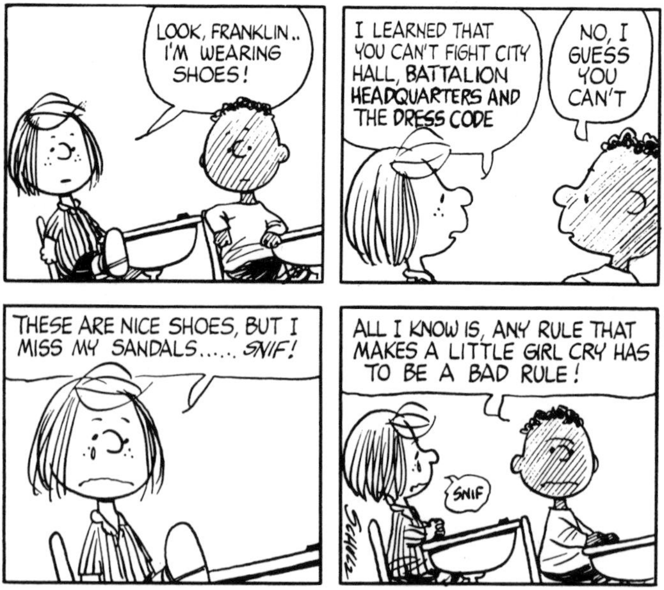
LOOK, FRANKLIN.. I'M WEARING SHOES!
I LEARNED THAT YOU CAN'T FIGHT CITY HALL, BATTALION HEADQUARTERS AND THE DRESS CODE
NO, I GUESS YOU CAN'T
THESE ARE NICE SHOES, BUT I MISS MY SANDALS..... SNIF!
ALL I KNOW IS, ANY RULE THAT MAKES A LITTLE GIRL CRY HAS TO BE A BAD RULE!
SNIF
SCHULZ

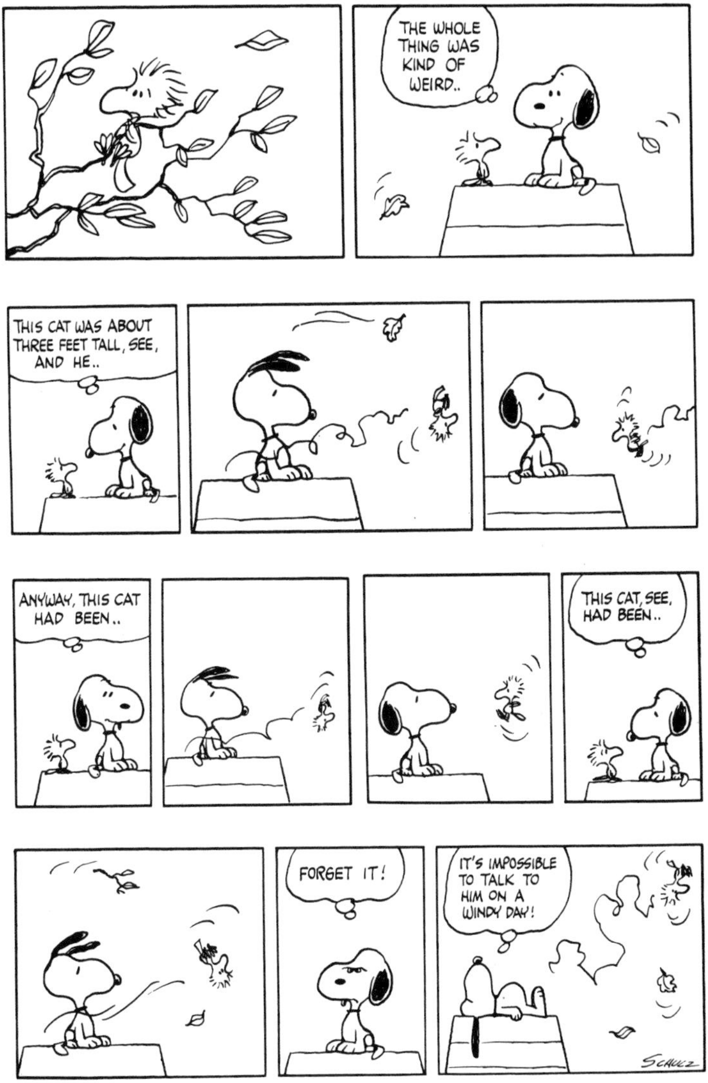
THE WHOLE THING WAS KIND OF WEIRD..
THIS CAT WAS ABOUT THREE FEET TALL, SEE, AND HE..
ANYWAY, THIS CAT HAD BEEN..
THIS CAT, SEE, HAD BEEN..
FORGET IT!
IT'S IMPOSSIBLE TO TALK TO HIM ON A WINDY DAY!
SCHULZ

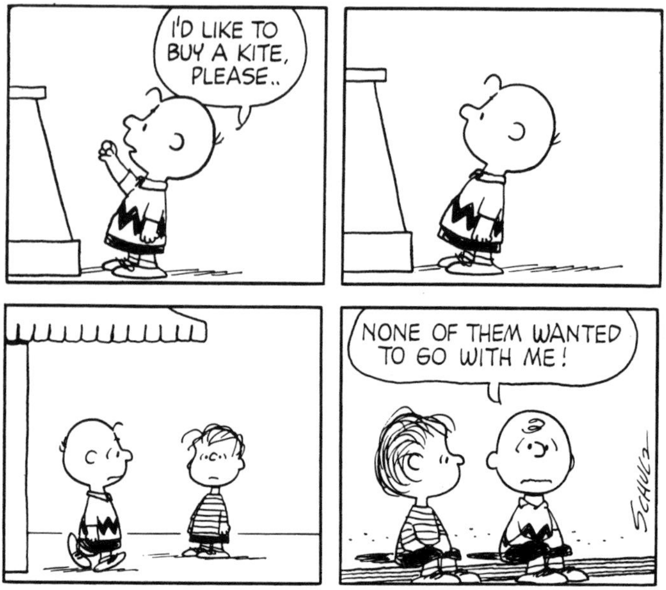
I'D LIKE TO BUY A KITE, PLEASE..
NONE OF THEM WANTED TO GO WITH ME!
SCHULZ

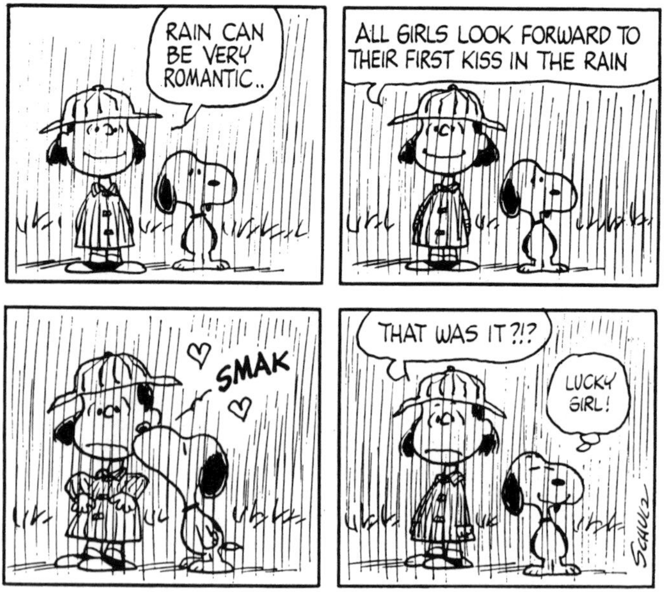
RAIN CAN BE VERY ROMANTIC..
ALL GIRLS LOOK FORWARD TO THEIR FIRST KISS IN THE RAIN
SMAK
THAT WAS IT?!?
LUCKY GIRL!
SCHULZ

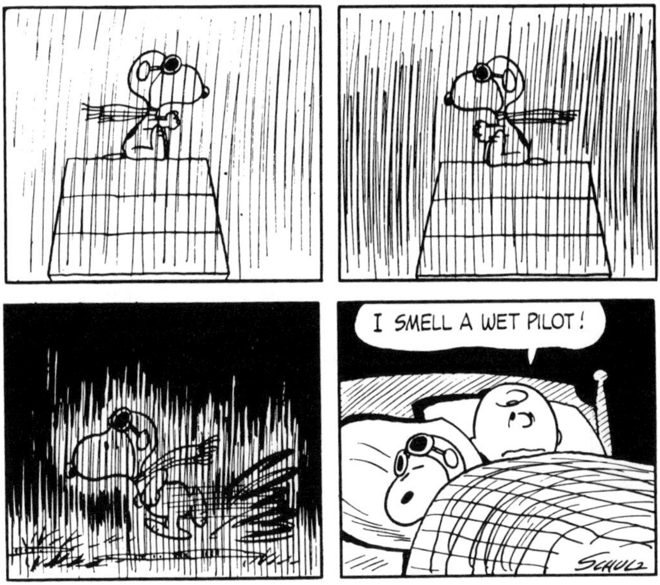
I SMELL A WET PILOT!
SCHULZ

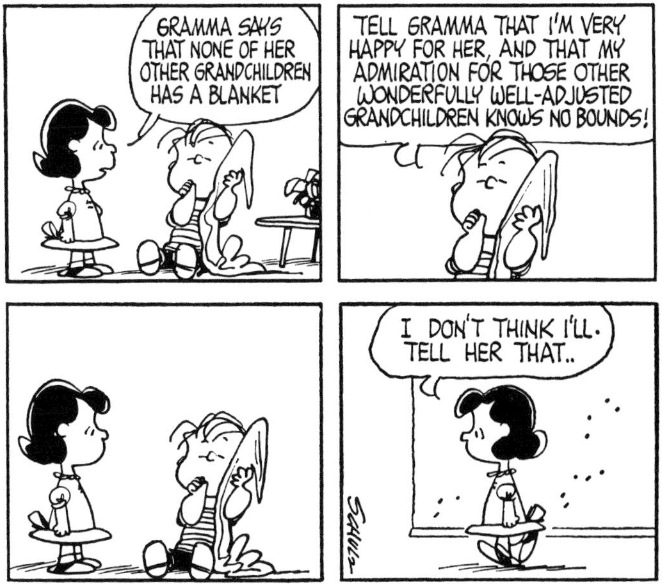
GRAMMA SAYS THAT NONE OF HER OTHER GRANDCHILDREN HAS A BLANKET
TELL GRAMMA THAT I'M VERY HAPPY FOR HER, AND THAT MY ADMIRATION FOR THOSE OTHER WONDERFULLY WELL-ADJUSTED GRANDCHILDREN KNOWS NO BOUNDS!
SCHULZ
I DON'T THINK I'LL TELL HER THAT..

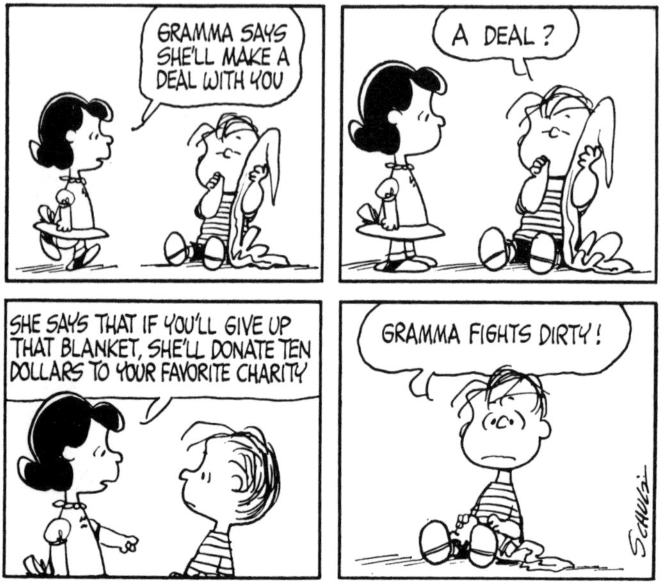
GRAMMA SAYS SHE'LL MAKE A DEAL WITH YOU
A DEAL ?
SHE SAYS THAT IF YOU'LL GIVE UP THAT BLANKET, SHE'LL DONATE TEN DOLLARS TO YOUR FAVORITE CHARITY
GRAMMA FIGHTS DIRTY !
SCHULZ

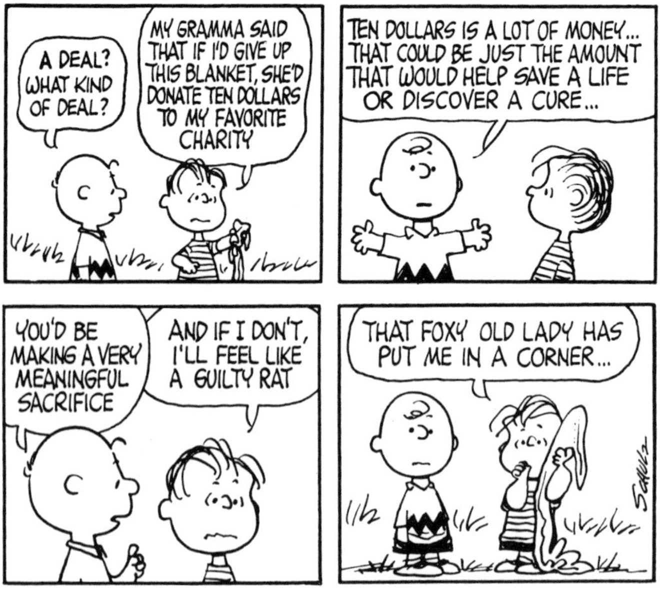
A DEAL? WHAT KIND OF DEAL?
MY GRAMMA SAID THAT IF I'D GIVE UP THIS BLANKET, SHE'D DONATE TEN DOLLARS TO MY FAVORITE CHARITY
TEN DOLLARS IS A LOT OF MONEY... THAT COULD BE JUST THE AMOUNT THAT WOULD HELP SAVE A LIFE OR DISCOVER A CURE...
YOU'D BE MAKING A VERY MEANINGFUL SACRIFICE
AND IF I DON'T, I'LL FEEL LIKE A GUILTY RAT
THAT FOXY OLD LADY HAS PUT ME IN A CORNER...
SCHULZ

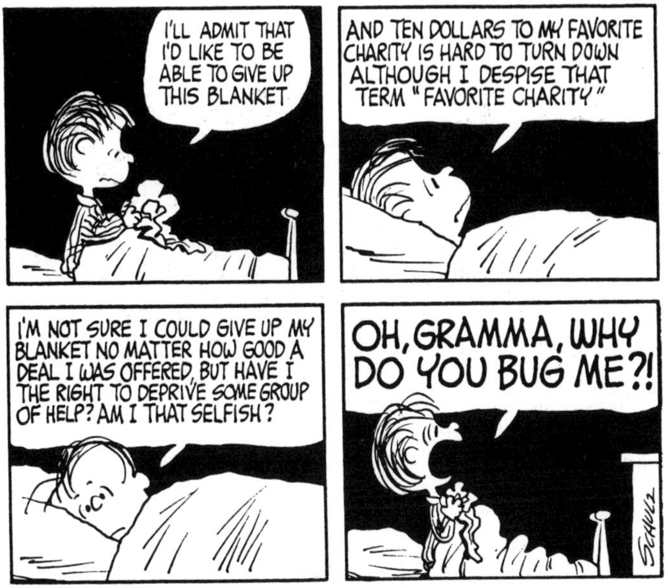
I'LL ADMIT THAT I'D LIKE TO BE ABLE TO GIVE UP THIS BLANKET
AND TEN DOLLARS TO MY FAVORITE CHARITY IS HARD TO TURN DOWN ALTHOUGH I DESPISE THAT TERM "FAVORITE CHARITY"
I'M NOT SURE I COULD GIVE UP MY BLANKET NO MATTER HOW GOOD A DEAL I WAS OFFERED, BUT HAVE I THE RIGHT TO DEPRIVE SOME GROUP OF HELP? AM I THAT SELFISH?
OH, GRAMMA, WHY DO YOU BUG ME?!
SCHULZ

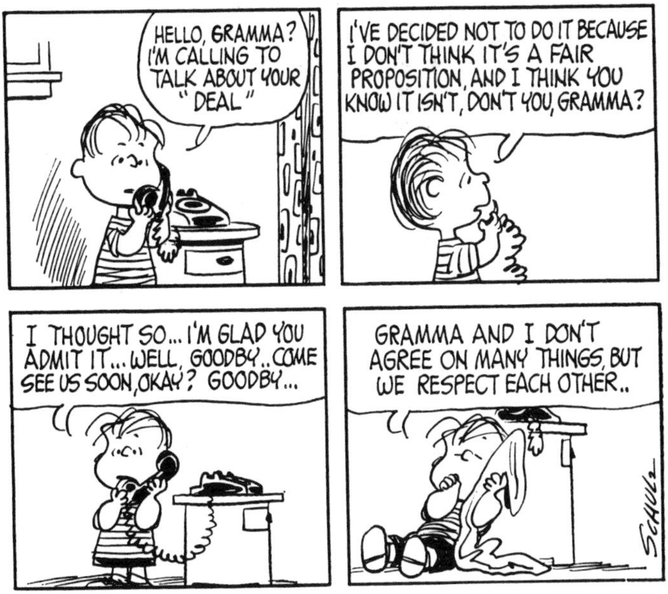
HELLO, GRAMMA? I'M CALLING TO TALK ABOUT YOUR "DEAL"
I'VE DECIDED NOT TO DO IT BECAUSE I DON'T THINK IT'S A FAIR PROPOSITION, AND I THINK YOU KNOW IT ISN'T, DON'T YOU, GRAMMA?
I THOUGHT SO... I'M GLAD YOU ADMIT IT... WELL, GOODBY.. COME SEE US SOON, OKAY? GOODBY...
GRAMMA AND I DON'T AGREE ON MANY THINGS, BUT WE RESPECT EACH OTHER..
SCHULZ

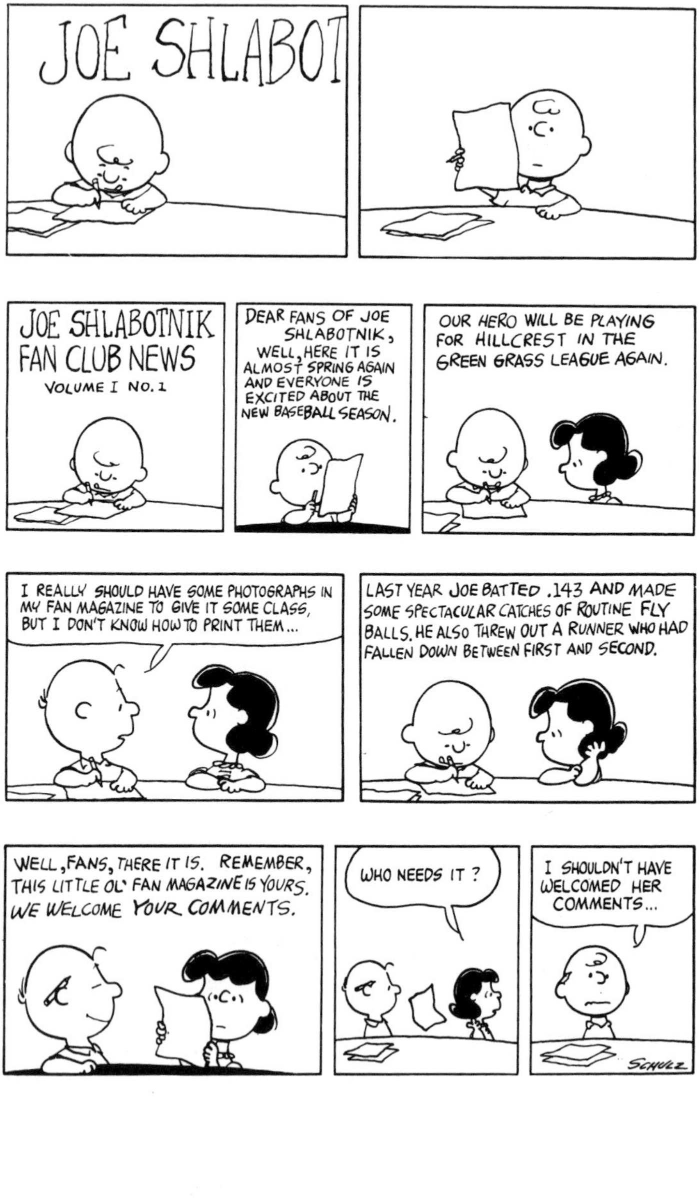
JOE SHLABOT
JOE SHLABOTNIK FAN CLUB NEWS
VOLUME I NO. 1
DEAR FANS OF JOE SHLABOTNIK,
WELL, HERE IT IS ALMOST SPRING AGAIN AND EVERYONE IS EXCITED ABOUT THE NEW BASEBALL SEASON.
OUR HERO WILL BE PLAYING FOR HILLCREST IN THE GREEN GRASS LEAGUE AGAIN.
I REALLY SHOULD HAVE SOME PHOTOGRAPHS IN MY FAN MAGAZINE TO GIVE IT SOME CLASS, BUT I DON'T KNOW HOW TO PRINT THEM...
LAST YEAR JOE BATTED .143 AND MADE SOME SPECTACULAR CATCHES OF ROUTINE FLY BALLS. HE ALSO THREW OUT A RUNNER WHO HAD FALLEN DOWN BETWEEN FIRST AND SECOND.
WELL, FANS, THERE IT IS. REMEMBER, THIS LITTLE OL' FAN MAGAZINE IS YOURS. WE WELCOME YOUR COMMENTS.
WHO NEEDS IT ?
I SHOULDN'T HAVE WELCOMED HER COMMENTS...
SCHULZ

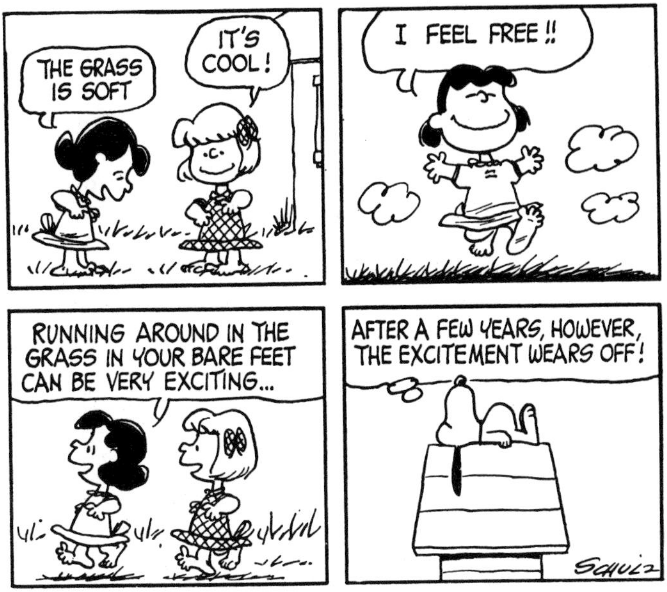
THE GRASS IS SOFT
IT'S COOL!
I FEEL FREE!!
RUNNING AROUND IN THE GRASS IN YOUR BARE FEET CAN BE VERY EXCITING...
AFTER A FEW YEARS, HOWEVER, THE EXCITEMENT WEARS OFF!
SCHULZ

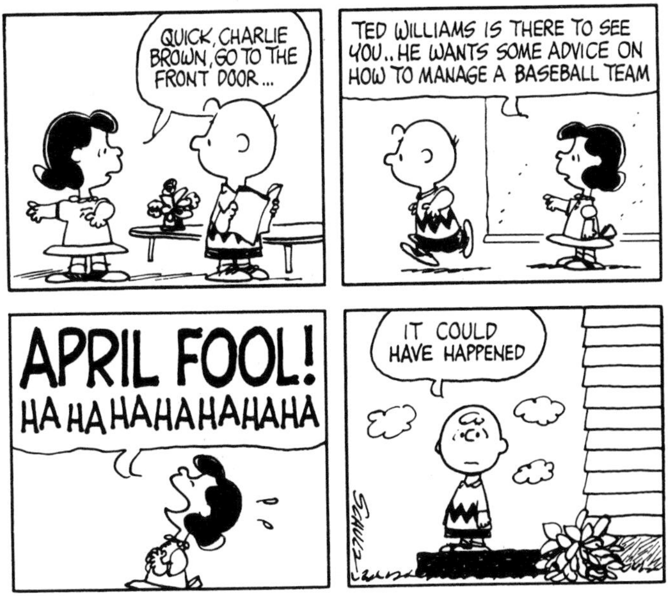
QUICK, CHARLIE BROWN, GO TO THE FRONT DOOR...
TED WILLIAMS IS THERE TO SEE YOU.. HE WANTS SOME ADVICE ON HOW TO MANAGE A BASEBALL TEAM
APRIL FOOL! HA HA HAHAHAHAHAHA
IT COULD HAVE HAPPENED
SCHULZ

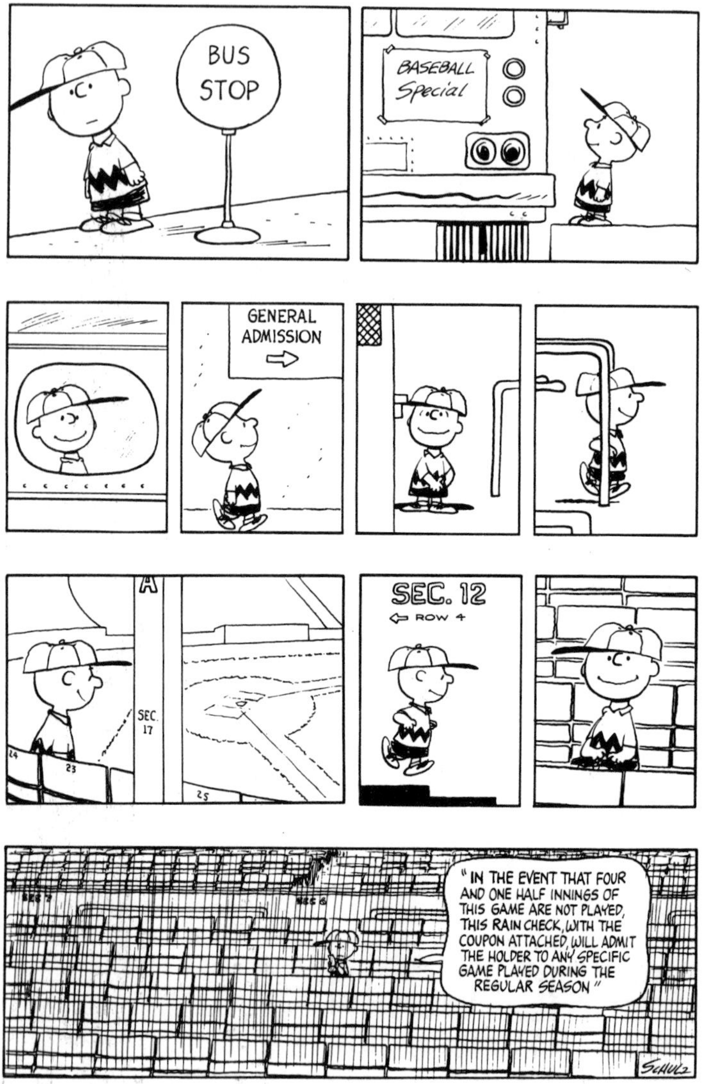
BUS STOP
BASEBALL Special
GENERAL ADMISSION
A
SEC. 17
24
23
25
SEC. 12
ROW 4
" IN THE EVENT THAT FOUR AND ONE HALF INNINGS OF THIS GAME ARE NOT PLAYED, THIS RAIN CHECK, WITH THE COUPON ATTACHED, WILL ADMIT THE HOLDER TO ANY SPECIFIC GAME PLAYED DURING THE REGULAR SEASON "
SCHULZ

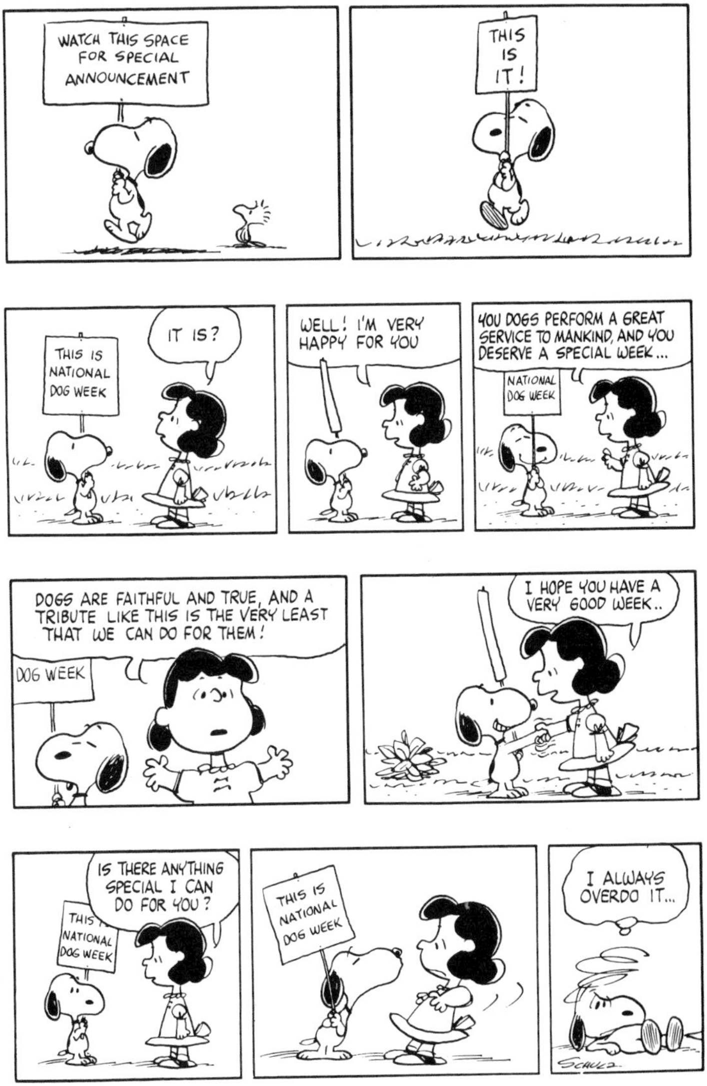

WATCH THIS SPACE FOR SPECIAL ANNOUNCEMENT
THIS IS IT!
THIS IS NATIONAL DOG WEEK
IT IS?
WELL! I'M VERY HAPPY FOR YOU
YOU DOGS PERFORM A GREAT SERVICE TO MANKIND, AND YOU DESERVE A SPECIAL WEEK...
NATIONAL DOG WEEK
DOGS ARE FAITHFUL AND TRUE, AND A TRIBUTE LIKE THIS IS THE VERY LEAST THAT WE CAN DO FOR THEM!
DOG WEEK
I HOPE YOU HAVE A VERY GOOD WEEK..
IS THERE ANYTHING SPECIAL I CAN DO FOR YOU?
NATIONAL DOG WEEK
THIS IS NATIONAL DOG WEEK
I ALWAYS OVERDO IT...
SCHULZ

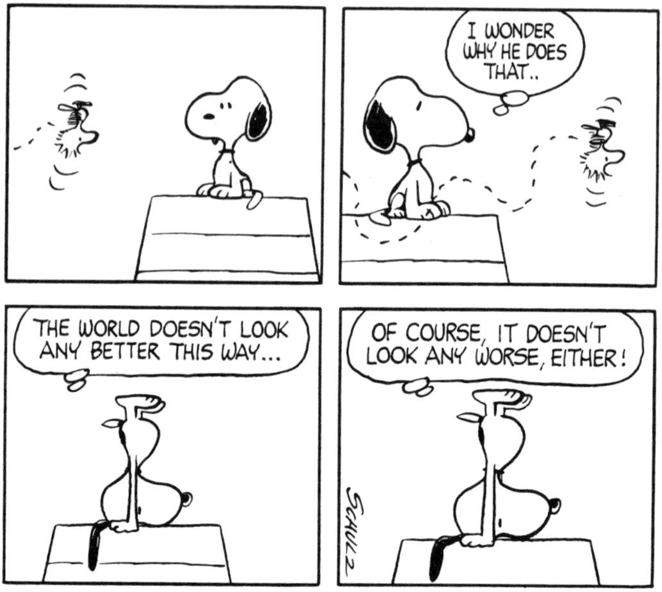
I WONDER WHY HE DOES THAT..
THE WORLD DOESN'T LOOK ANY BETTER THIS WAY...
OF COURSE, IT DOESN'T LOOK ANY WORSE, EITHER!
SCHULZ

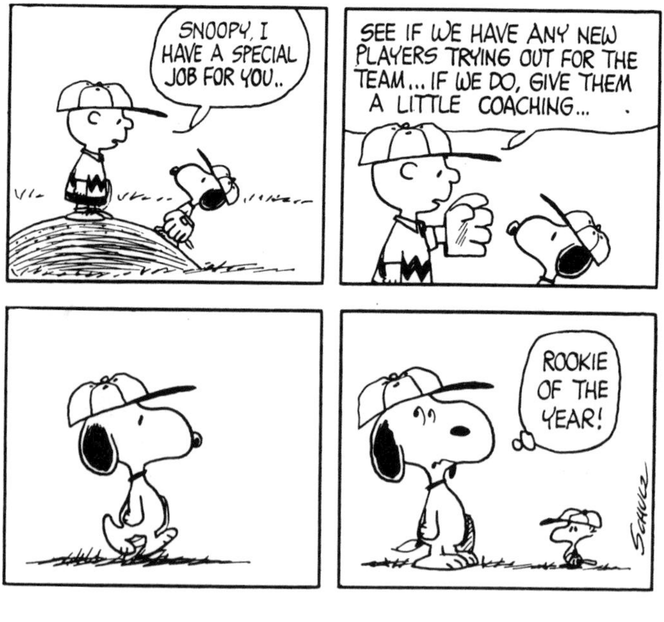
SNOOPY, I HAVE A SPECIAL JOB FOR YOU..
SEE IF WE HAVE ANY NEW PLAYERS TRYING OUT FOR THE TEAM... IF WE DO, GIVE THEM A LITTLE COACHING...
ROOKIE OF THE YEAR!
SCHULZ

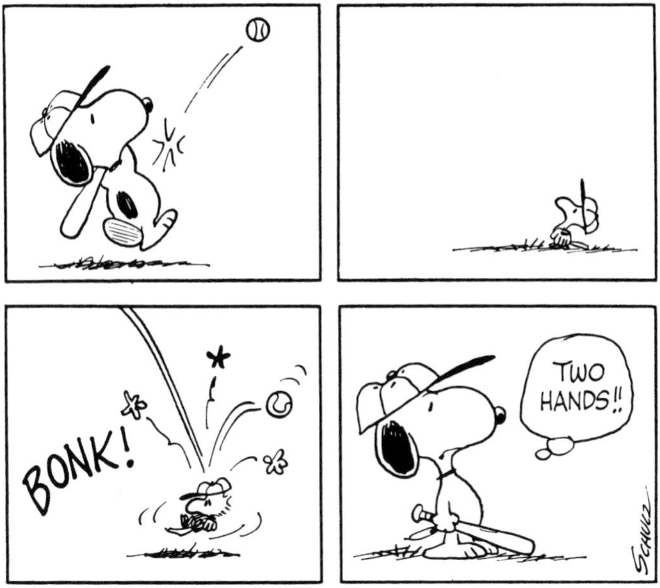
BONK!
TWO HANDS!!

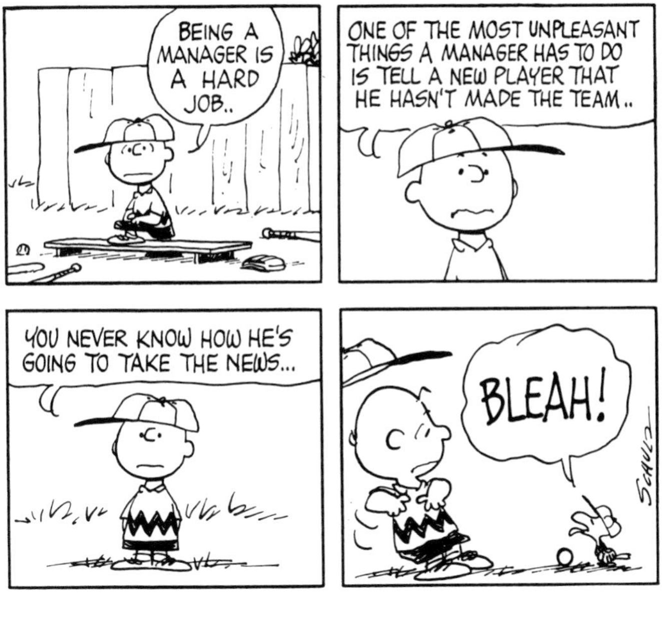
BEING A MANAGER IS A HARD JOB..
ONE OF THE MOST UNPLEASANT THINGS A MANAGER HAS TO DO IS TELL A NEW PLAYER THAT HE HASN'T MADE THE TEAM..
YOU NEVER KNOW HOW HE'S GOING TO TAKE THE NEWS...
BLEAH!

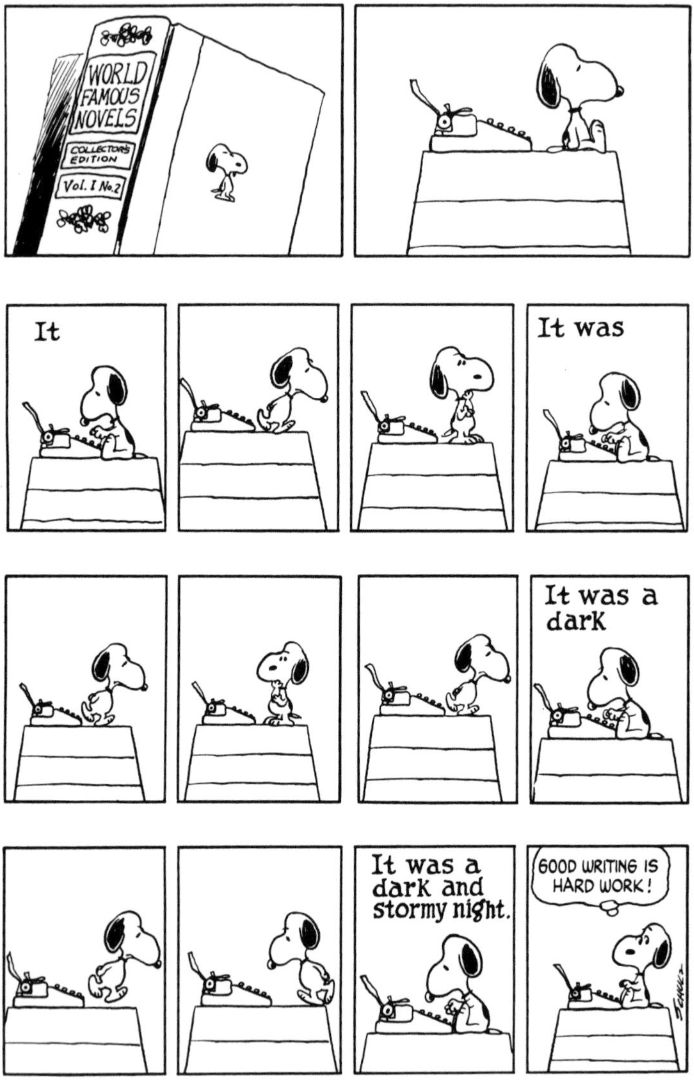

WORLD FAMOUS NOVELS
COLLECTOR'S EDITION
Vol. I No. 2
It
It was
It was a dark
It was a dark and stormy night.
GOOD WRITING IS HARD WORK!

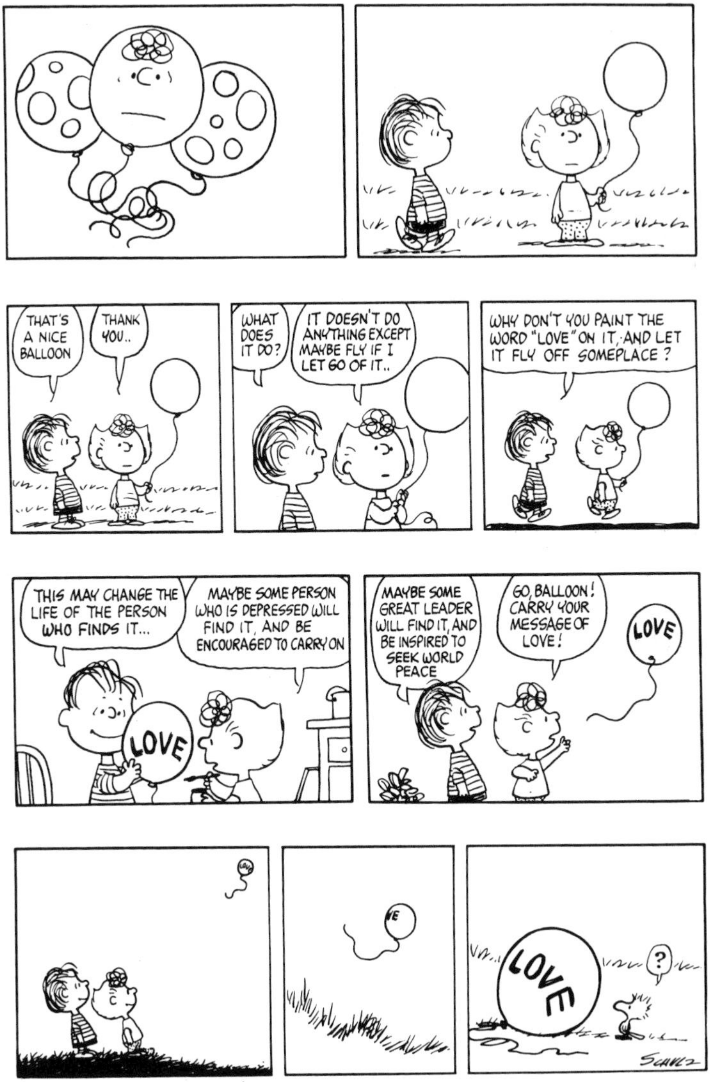
THAT'S A NICE BALLOON
THANK YOU..
WHAT DOES IT DO?
IT DOESN'T DO ANYTHING EXCEPT MAYBE FLY IF I LET GO OF IT..
WHY DON'T YOU PAINT THE WORD "LOVE" ON IT, AND LET IT FLY OFF SOMEPLACE?
THIS MAY CHANGE THE LIFE OF THE PERSON WHO FINDS IT...
MAYBE SOME PERSON WHO IS DEPRESSED WILL FIND IT, AND BE ENCOURAGED TO CARRY ON
LOVE
MAYBE SOME GREAT LEADER WILL FIND IT, AND BE INSPIRED TO SEEK WORLD PEACE
GO, BALLOON! CARRY YOUR MESSAGE OF LOVE!
LOVE
LOVE
?
SCHULZ

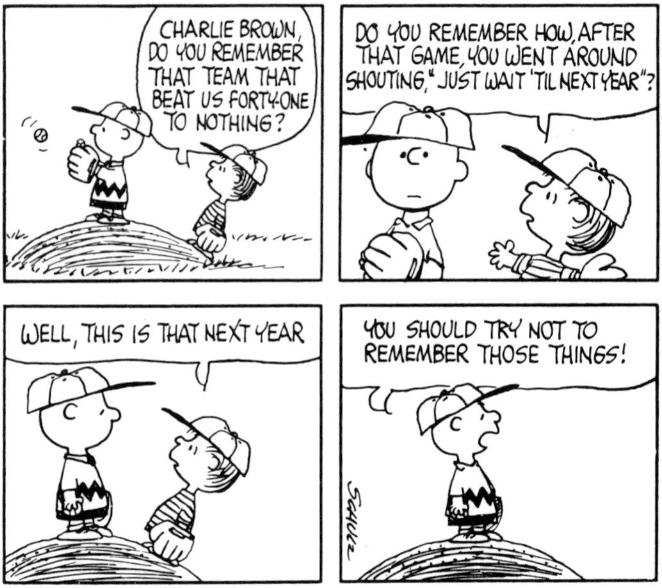
CHARLIE BROWN, DO YOU REMEMBER THAT TEAM THAT BEAT US FORTY-ONE TO NOTHING?
DO YOU REMEMBER HOW, AFTER THAT GAME, YOU WENT AROUND SHOUTING, "JUST WAIT 'TIL NEXT YEAR"?
WELL, THIS IS THAT NEXT YEAR
YOU SHOULD TRY NOT TO REMEMBER THOSE THINGS!
SCHULZ

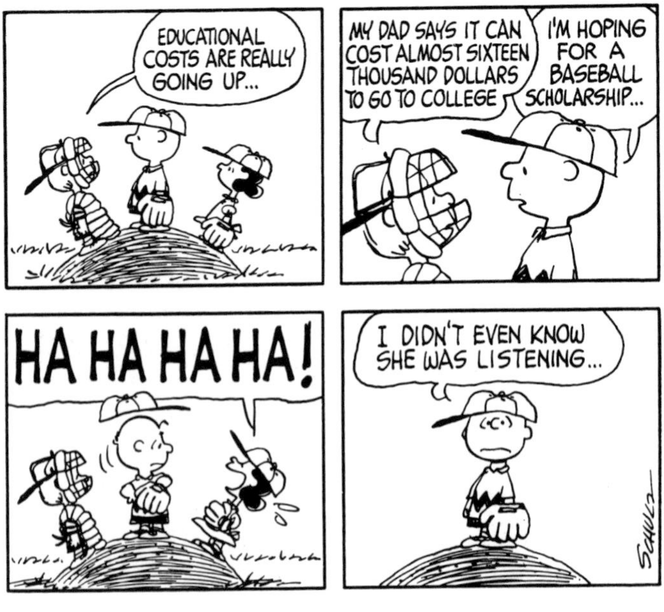
EDUCATIONAL COSTS ARE REALLY GOING UP...
MY DAD SAYS IT CAN COST ALMOST SIXTEEN THOUSAND DOLLARS TO GO TO COLLEGE
I'M HOPING FOR A BASEBALL SCHOLARSHIP...
HA HA HA HA HA!
I DIDN'T EVEN KNOW SHE WAS LISTENING...
SCHULZ

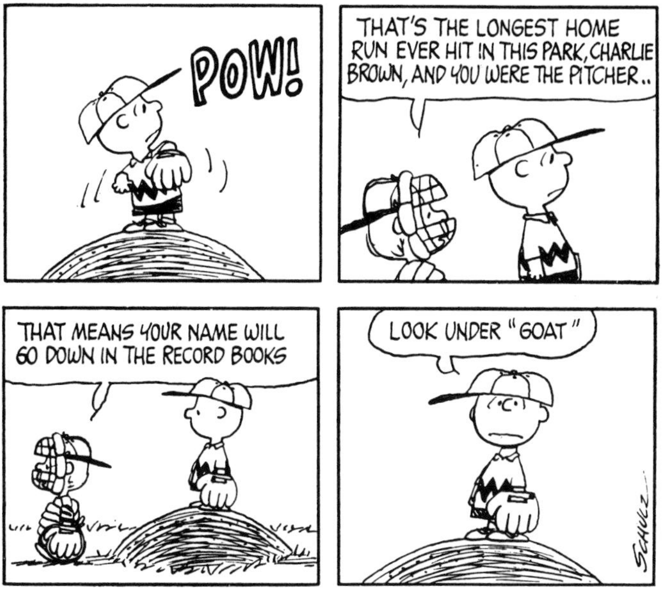
POW!
THAT'S THE LONGEST HOME RUN EVER HIT IN THIS PARK, CHARLIE BROWN, AND YOU WERE THE PITCHER..
THAT MEANS YOUR NAME WILL GO DOWN IN THE RECORD BOOKS
LOOK UNDER "GOAT"
SCHULZ

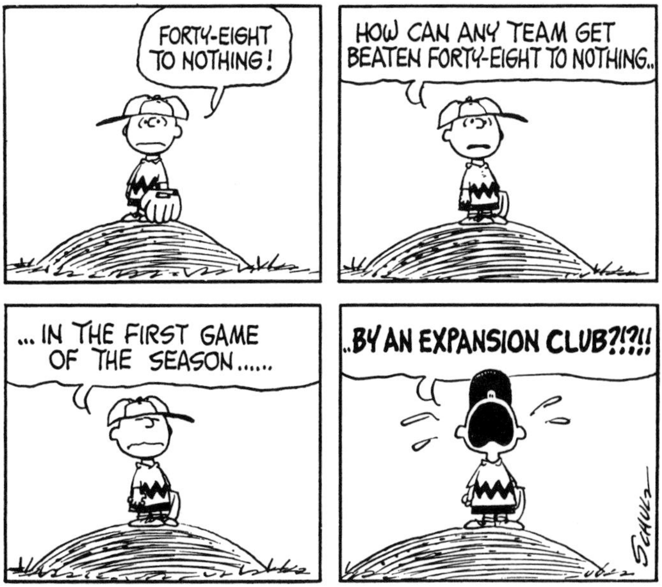
FORTY-EIGHT TO NOTHING!
HOW CAN ANY TEAM GET BEATEN FORTY-EIGHT TO NOTHING..
... IN THE FIRST GAME OF THE SEASON......
..BY AN EXPANSION CLUB?!?!!
SCHULZ

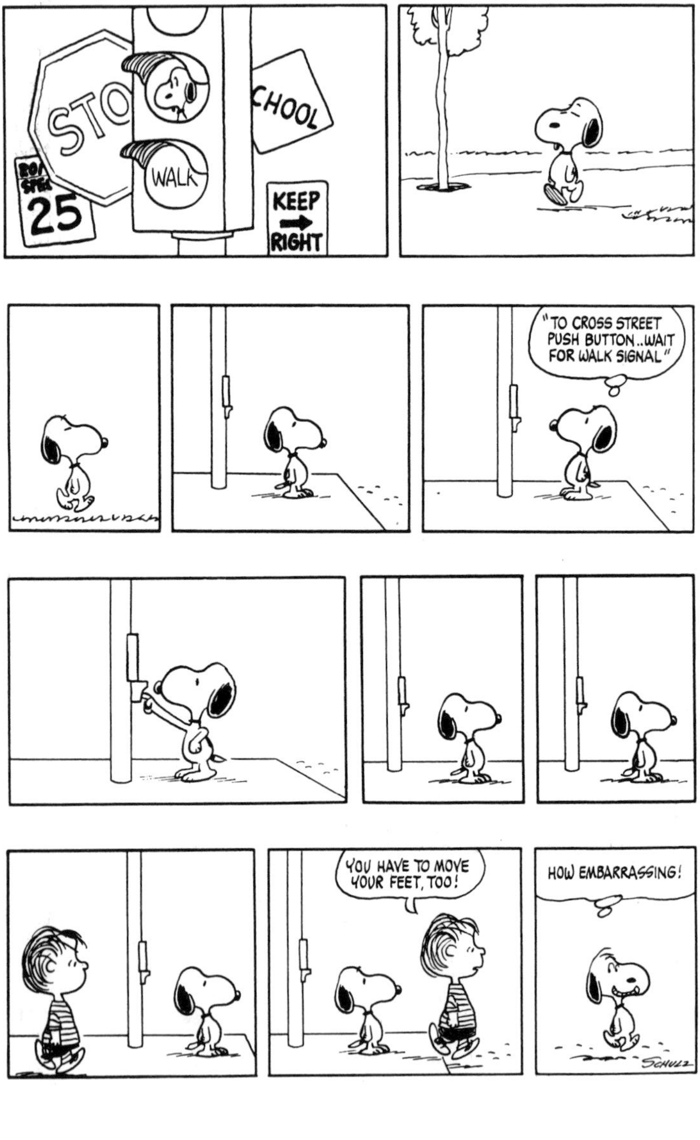
STO
WALK
CHOOL
25
KEEP RIGHT
"TO CROSS STREET PUSH BUTTON..WAIT FOR WALK SIGNAL"
YOU HAVE TO MOVE YOUR FEET, TOO!
HOW EMBARRASSING!
SCHULZ

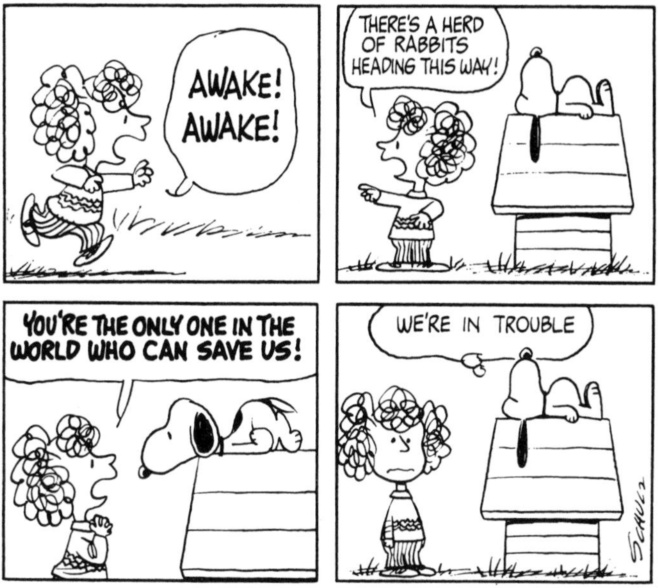
AWAKE! AWAKE!
THERE'S A HERD OF RABBITS HEADING THIS WAY!
YOU'RE THE ONLY ONE IN THE WORLD WHO CAN SAVE US!
WE'RE IN TROUBLE

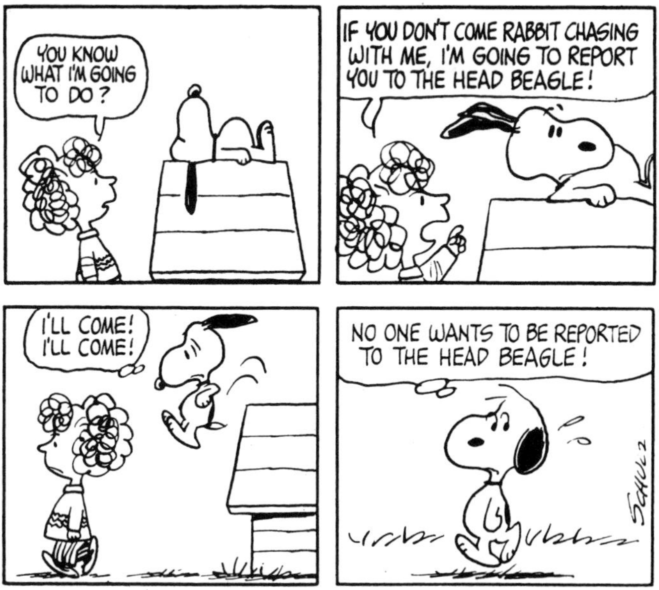
YOU KNOW WHAT I'M GOING TO DO?
IF YOU DON'T COME RABBIT CHASING WITH ME, I'M GOING TO REPORT YOU TO THE HEAD BEAGLE!
I'LL COME! I'LL COME!
NO ONE WANTS TO BE REPORTED TO THE HEAD BEAGLE!

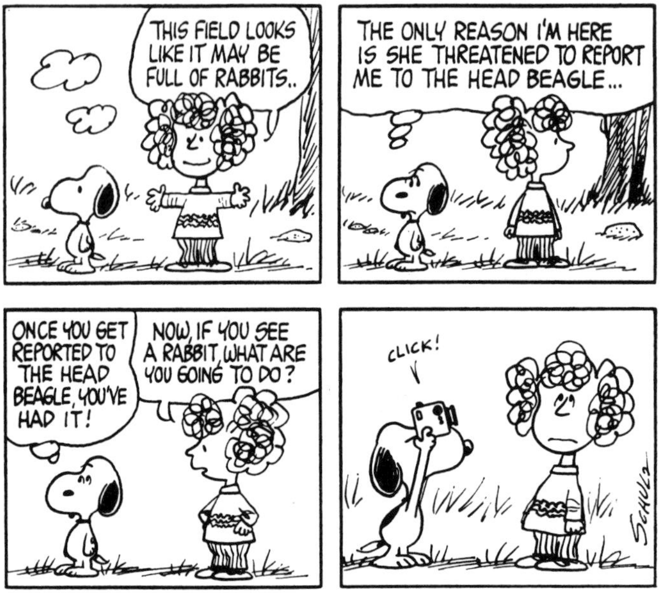
THIS FIELD LOOKS LIKE IT MAY BE FULL OF RABBITS..
THE ONLY REASON I'M HERE IS SHE THREATENED TO REPORT ME TO THE HEAD BEAGLE...
ONCE YOU GET REPORTED TO THE HEAD BEAGLE, YOU'VE HAD IT!
NOW, IF YOU SEE A RABBIT, WHAT ARE YOU GOING TO DO?
CLICK!
SCHULZ

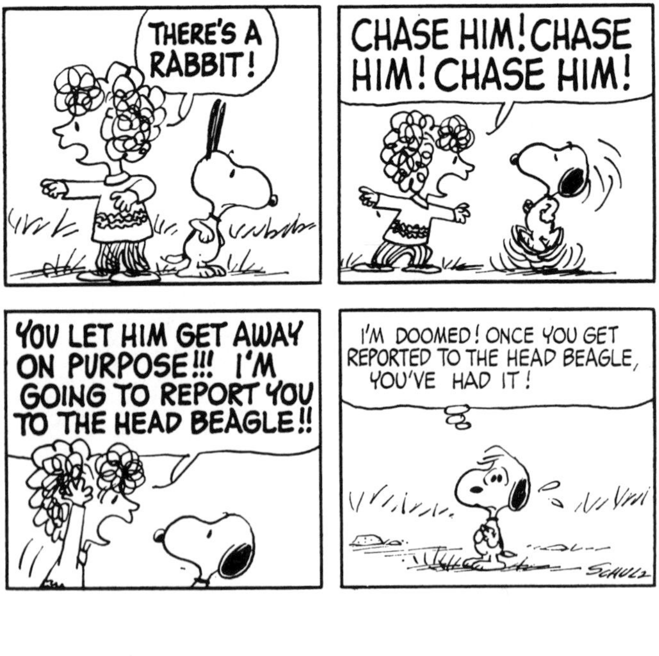
THERE'S A RABBIT!
CHASE HIM! CHASE HIM! CHASE HIM!
YOU LET HIM GET AWAY ON PURPOSE!!! I'M GOING TO REPORT YOU TO THE HEAD BEAGLE!!
I'M DOOMED! ONCE YOU GET REPORTED TO THE HEAD BEAGLE, YOU'VE HAD IT!
SCHULZ

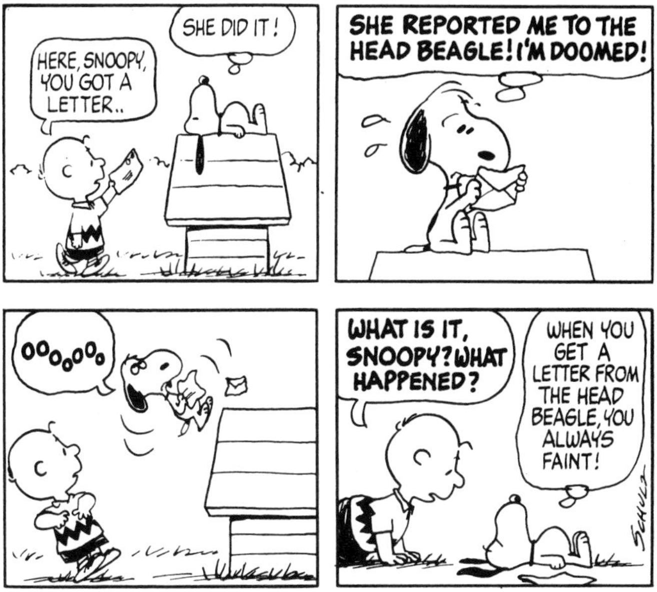
HERE, SNOOPY, YOU GOT A LETTER..
SHE DID IT!
SHE REPORTED ME TO THE HEAD BEAGLE! I'M DOOMED!
OOOOOO
WHAT IS IT, SNOOPY? WHAT HAPPENED?
WHEN YOU GET A LETTER FROM THE HEAD BEAGLE, YOU ALWAYS FAINT!
SCHULZ

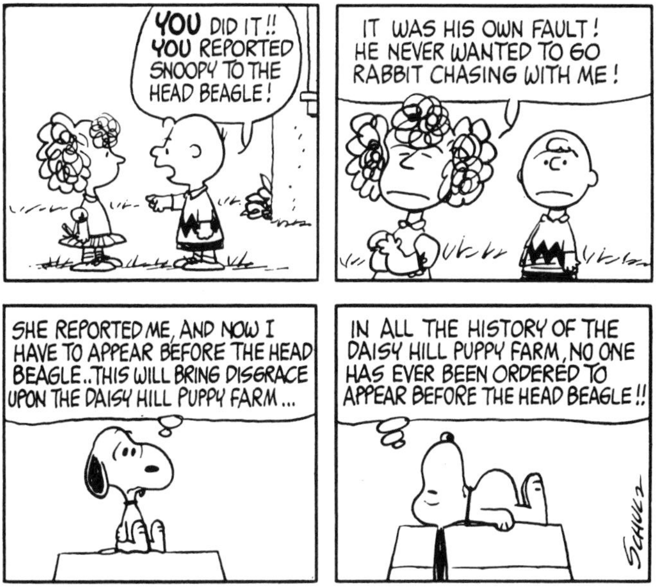
YOU DID IT!! YOU REPORTED SNOOPY TO THE HEAD BEAGLE!
IT WAS HIS OWN FAULT! HE NEVER WANTED TO GO RABBIT CHASING WITH ME!
SHE REPORTED ME, AND NOW I HAVE TO APPEAR BEFORE THE HEAD BEAGLE..THIS WILL BRING DISGRACE UPON THE DAISY HILL PUPPY FARM...
IN ALL THE HISTORY OF THE DAISY HILL PUPPY FARM, NO ONE HAS EVER BEEN ORDERED TO APPEAR BEFORE THE HEAD BEAGLE!!
SCHULZ

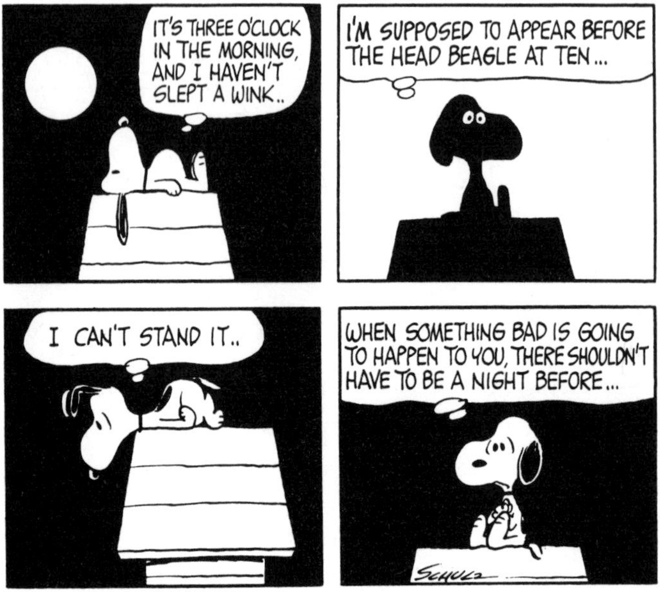
IT'S THREE O'CLOCK IN THE MORNING, AND I HAVEN'T SLEPT A WINK..
I'M SUPPOSED TO APPEAR BEFORE THE HEAD BEAGLE AT TEN...
I CAN'T STAND IT..
WHEN SOMETHING BAD IS GOING TO HAPPEN TO YOU, THERE SHOULDN'T HAVE TO BE A NIGHT BEFORE...

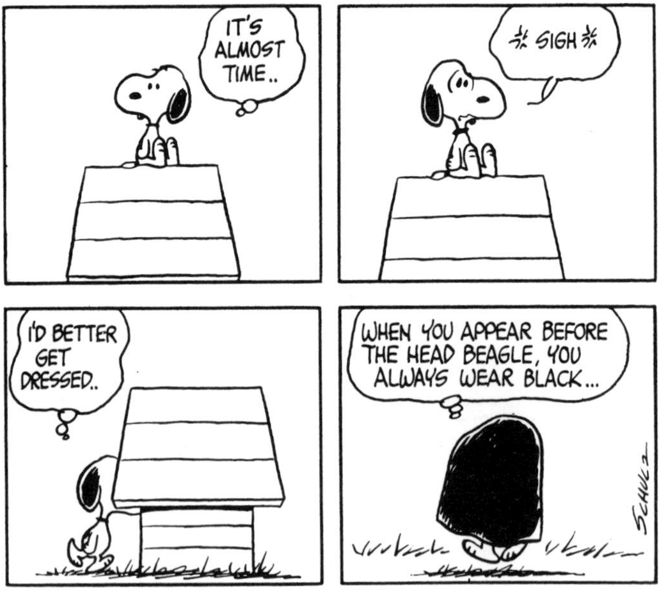
IT'S ALMOST TIME..
SIGH
I'D BETTER GET DRESSED..
WHEN YOU APPEAR BEFORE THE HEAD BEAGLE, YOU ALWAYS WEAR BLACK...

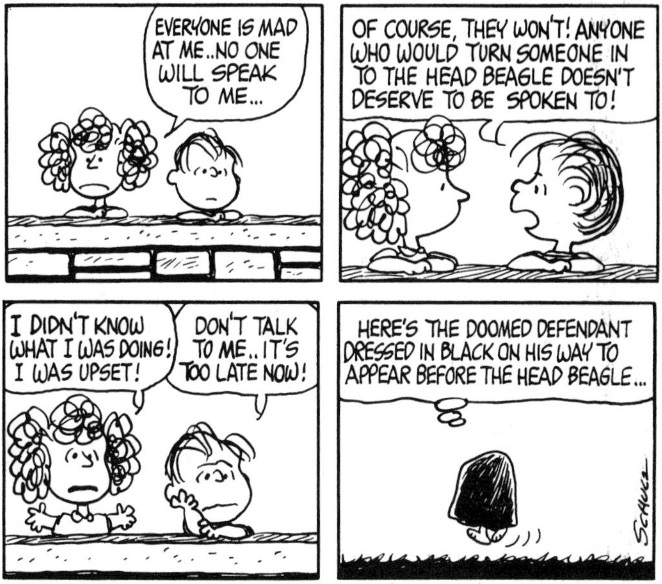
EVERYONE IS MAD AT ME..NO ONE WILL SPEAK TO ME...
OF COURSE, THEY WON'T! ANYONE WHO WOULD TURN SOMEONE IN TO THE HEAD BEAGLE DOESN'T DESERVE TO BE SPOKEN TO!
I DIDN'T KNOW WHAT I WAS DOING! I WAS UPSET!
DON'T TALK TO ME..IT'S TOO LATE NOW!
HERE'S THE DOOMED DEFENDANT DRESSED IN BLACK ON HIS WAY TO APPEAR BEFORE THE HEAD BEAGLE...
SCHULZ

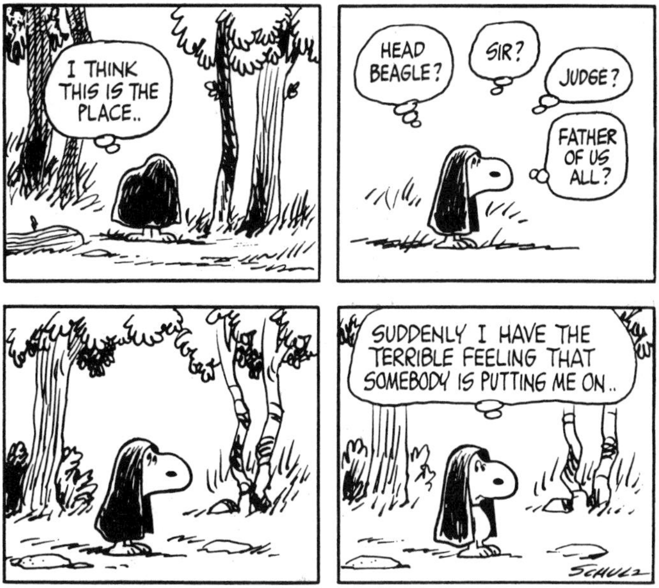
I THINK THIS IS THE PLACE..
HEAD BEAGLE?
SIR?
JUDGE?
FATHER OF US ALL?
SUDDENLY I HAVE THE TERRIBLE FEELING THAT SOMEBODY IS PUTTING ME ON..
SCHULZ

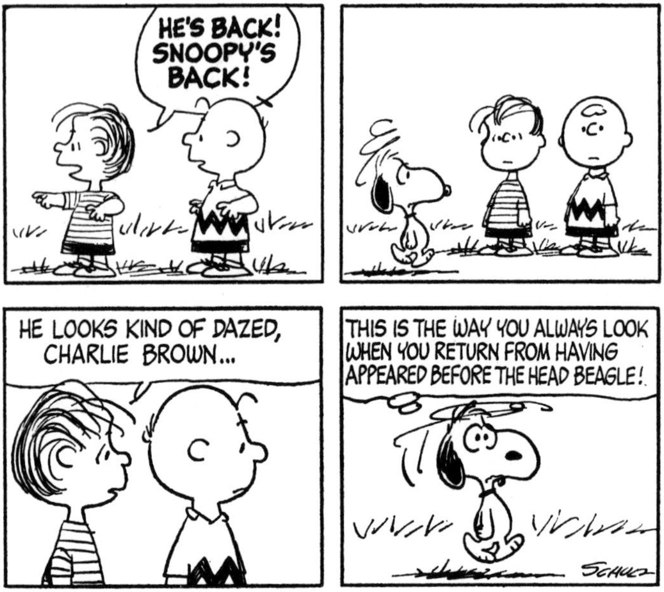
HE'S BACK! SNOOPY'S BACK!
HE LOOKS KIND OF DAZED, CHARLIE BROWN...
THIS IS THE WAY YOU ALWAYS LOOK WHEN YOU RETURN FROM HAVING APPEARED BEFORE THE HEAD BEAGLE!
SCHULZ

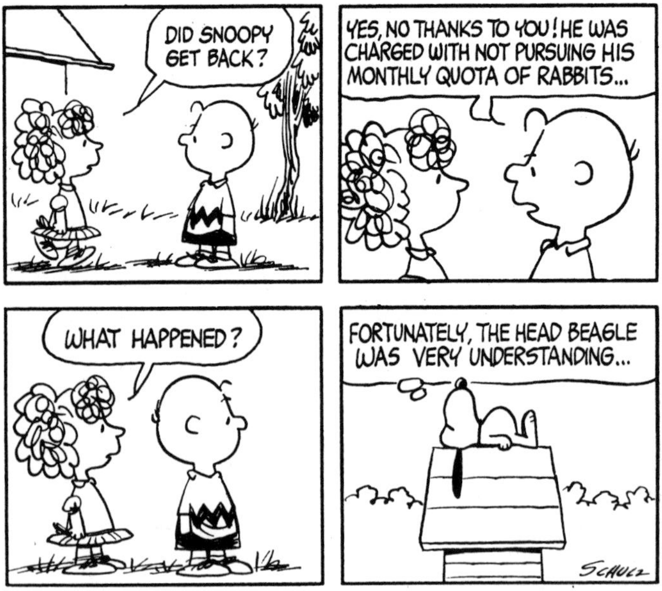
DID SNOOPY GET BACK?
YES, NO THANKS TO YOU! HE WAS CHARGED WITH NOT PURSUING HIS MONTHLY QUOTA OF RABBITS...
WHAT HAPPENED?
FORTUNATELY, THE HEAD BEAGLE WAS VERY UNDERSTANDING...
SCHULZ

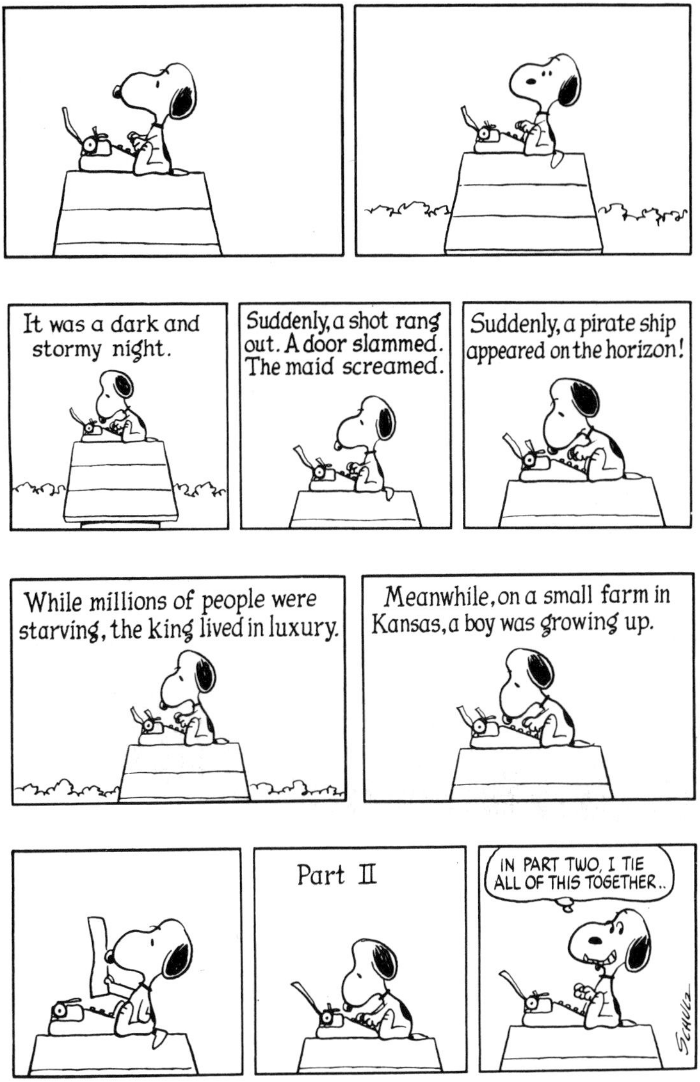
It was a dark and stormy night.
Suddenly, a shot rang out. A door slammed. The maid screamed.
Suddenly, a pirate ship appeared on the horizon!
While millions of people were starving, the king lived in luxury.
Meanwhile, on a small farm in Kansas, a boy was growing up.
Part II
IN PART TWO, I TIE ALL OF THIS TOGETHER..
SCHULZ

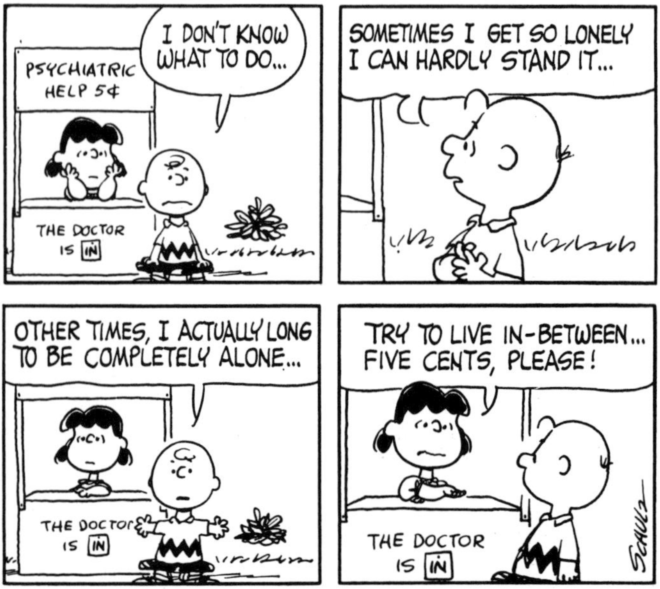
PSYCHIATRIC HELP 5¢
I DON'T KNOW WHAT TO DO...
THE DOCTOR IS IN
SOMETIMES I GET SO LONELY I CAN HARDLY STAND IT...
OTHER TIMES, I ACTUALLY LONG TO BE COMPLETELY ALONE...
THE DOCTOR IS IN
TRY TO LIVE IN-BETWEEN... FIVE CENTS, PLEASE!
THE DOCTOR IS IN
SCHULZ

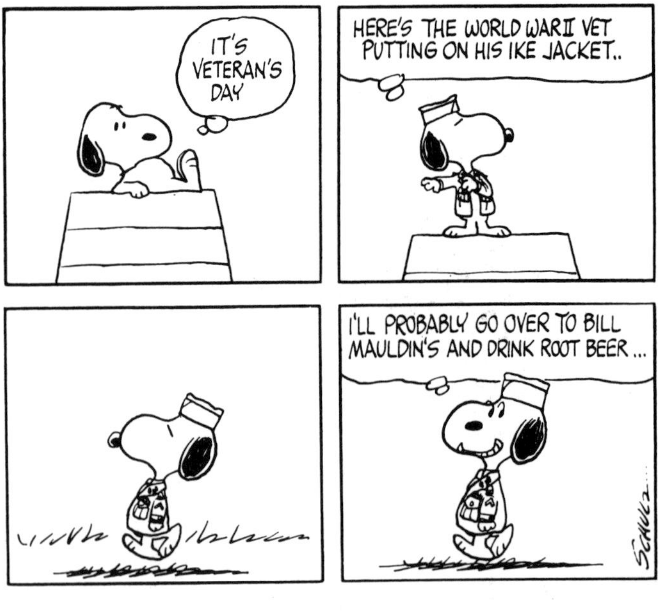
IT'S VETERAN'S DAY
HERE'S THE WORLD WAR II VET PUTTING ON HIS IKE JACKET..
I'LL PROBABLY GO OVER TO BILL MAULDIN'S AND DRINK ROOT BEER ...
SCHULZ

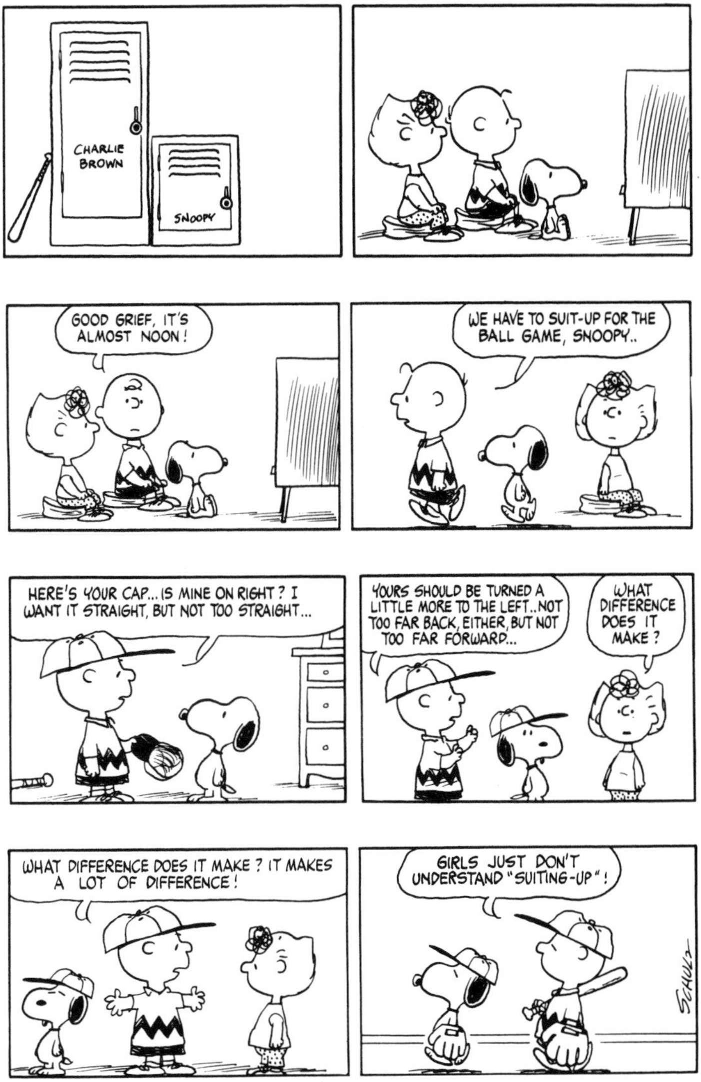
CHARLIE BROWN
SNOOPY
GOOD GRIEF, IT'S ALMOST NOON!
WE HAVE TO SUIT-UP FOR THE BALL GAME, SNOOPY..
HERE'S YOUR CAP... IS MINE ON RIGHT? I WANT IT STRAIGHT, BUT NOT TOO STRAIGHT...
YOURS SHOULD BE TURNED A LITTLE MORE TO THE LEFT..NOT TOO FAR BACK, EITHER, BUT NOT TOO FAR FORWARD...
WHAT DIFFERENCE DOES IT MAKE?
WHAT DIFFERENCE DOES IT MAKE? IT MAKES A LOT OF DIFFERENCE!
GIRLS JUST DON'T UNDERSTAND "SUITING-UP"!
SCHULZ

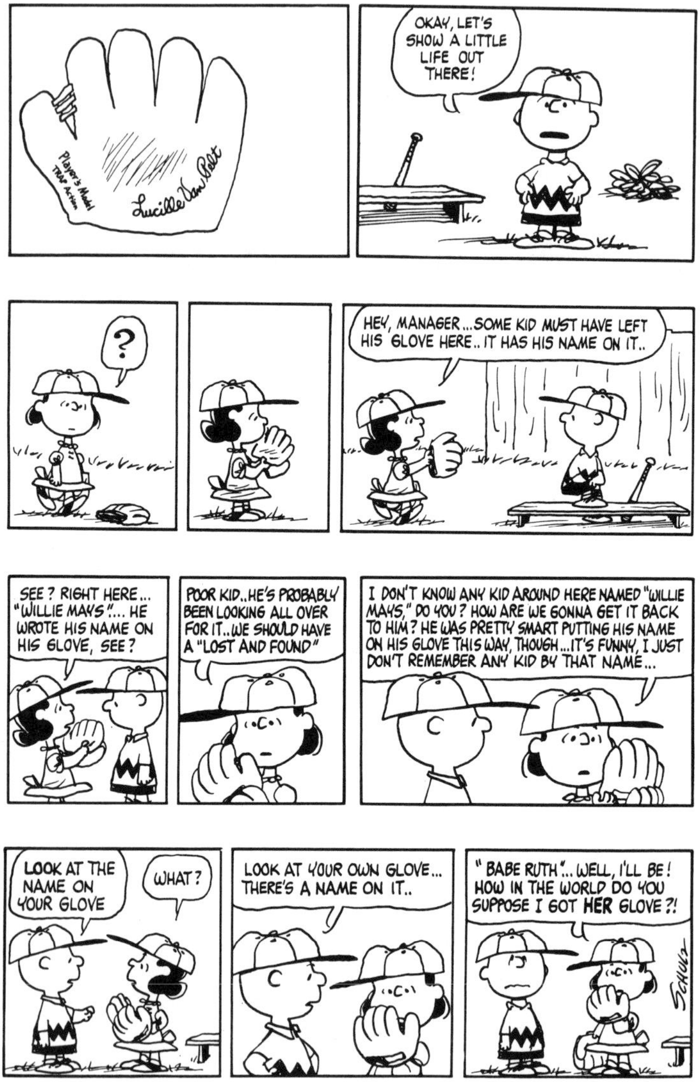
Player's Model
TRAP Action
Lucille Van Pelt
OKAY, LET'S SHOW A LITTLE LIFE OUT THERE!
?
HEY, MANAGER...SOME KID MUST HAVE LEFT HIS GLOVE HERE.. IT HAS HIS NAME ON IT..
SEE? RIGHT HERE... "WILLIE MAYS"... HE WROTE HIS NAME ON HIS GLOVE, SEE?
POOR KID..HE'S PROBABLY BEEN LOOKING ALL OVER FOR IT..WE SHOULD HAVE A "LOST AND FOUND"
I DON'T KNOW ANY KID AROUND HERE NAMED "WILLIE MAYS," DO YOU? HOW ARE WE GONNA GET IT BACK TO HIM? HE WAS PRETTY SMART PUTTING HIS NAME ON HIS GLOVE THIS WAY, THOUGH...IT'S FUNNY, I JUST DON'T REMEMBER ANY KID BY THAT NAME...
LOOK AT THE NAME ON YOUR GLOVE
WHAT?
LOOK AT YOUR OWN GLOVE... THERE'S A NAME ON IT..
"BABE RUTH"... WELL, I'LL BE! HOW IN THE WORLD DO YOU SUPPOSE I GOT HER GLOVE?!
SCHULZ

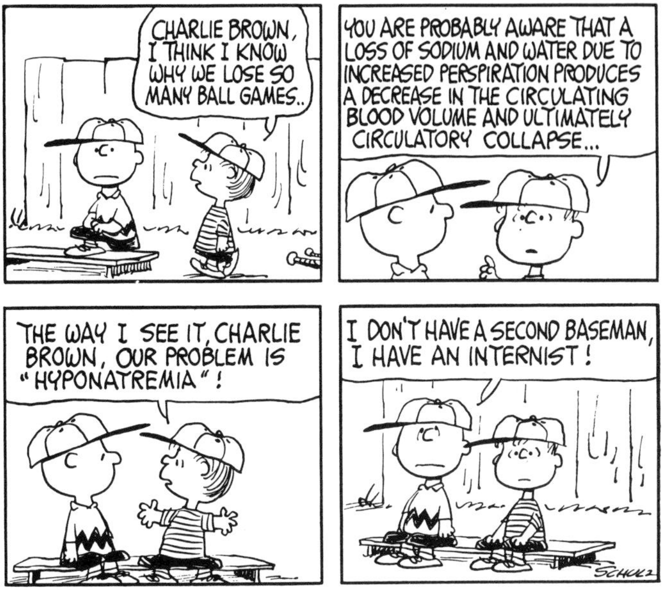
CHARLIE BROWN, I THINK I KNOW WHY WE LOSE SO MANY BALL GAMES..
YOU ARE PROBABLY AWARE THAT A LOSS OF SODIUM AND WATER DUE TO INCREASED PERSPIRATION PRODUCES A DECREASE IN THE CIRCULATING BLOOD VOLUME AND ULTIMATELY CIRCULATORY COLLAPSE...
THE WAY I SEE IT, CHARLIE BROWN, OUR PROBLEM IS "HYPONATREMIA"!
I DON'T HAVE A SECOND BASEMAN, I HAVE AN INTERNIST!
SCHULZ

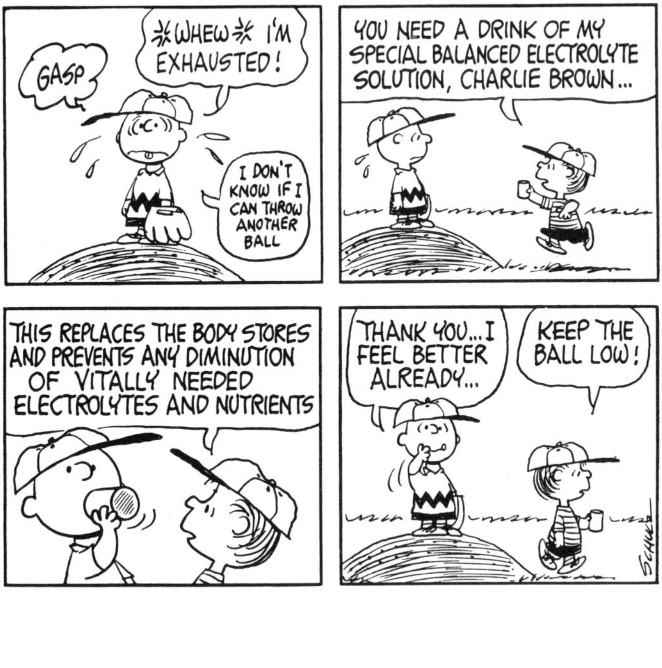
GASP
WHEW I'M EXHAUSTED!
I DON'T KNOW IF I CAN THROW ANOTHER BALL
YOU NEED A DRINK OF MY SPECIAL BALANCED ELECTROLYTE SOLUTION, CHARLIE BROWN...
THIS REPLACES THE BODY STORES AND PREVENTS ANY DIMINUTION OF VITALLY NEEDED ELECTROLYTES AND NUTRIENTS
THANK YOU...I FEEL BETTER ALREADY...
KEEP THE BALL LOW!
SCHULZ

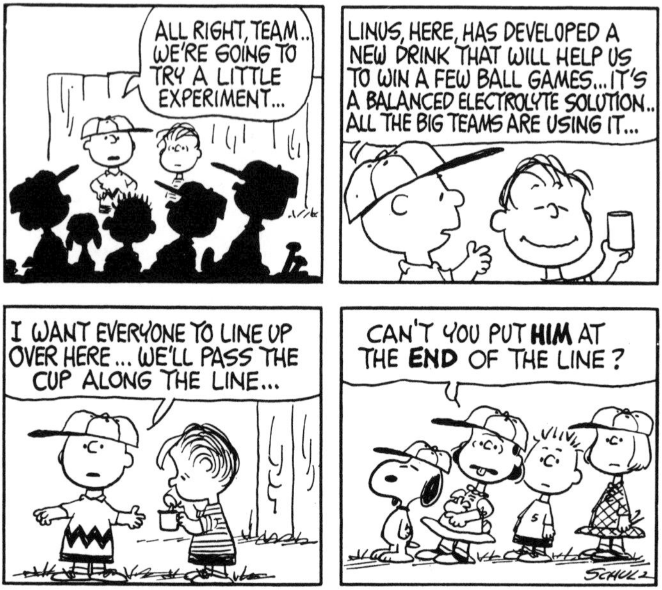
ALL RIGHT, TEAM.. WE'RE GOING TO TRY A LITTLE EXPERIMENT...
LINUS, HERE, HAS DEVELOPED A NEW DRINK THAT WILL HELP US TO WIN A FEW BALL GAMES...IT'S A BALANCED ELECTROLYTE SOLUTION.. ALL THE BIG TEAMS ARE USING IT...
I WANT EVERYONE TO LINE UP OVER HERE... WE'LL PASS THE CUP ALONG THE LINE...
CAN'T YOU PUT **HIM** AT THE **END** OF THE LINE?
SCHULZ

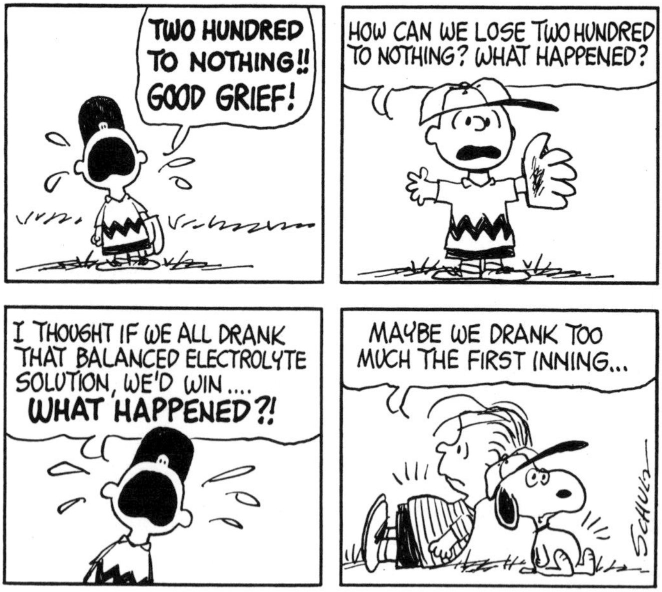
TWO HUNDRED TO NOTHING!! GOOD GRIEF!
HOW CAN WE LOSE TWO HUNDRED TO NOTHING? WHAT HAPPENED?
I THOUGHT IF WE ALL DRANK THAT BALANCED ELECTROLYTE SOLUTION, WE'D WIN.... **WHAT HAPPENED?!**
MAYBE WE DRANK TOO MUCH THE FIRST INNING...
SCHULZ

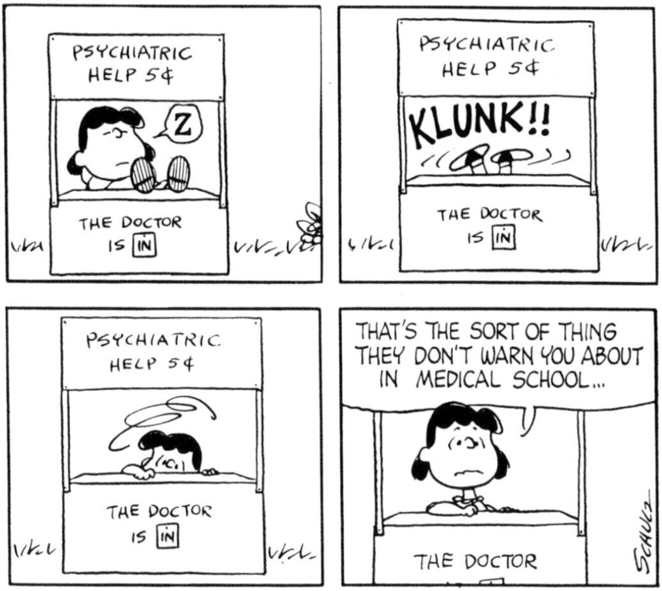
PSYCHIATRIC HELP 5¢
Z
THE DOCTOR IS IN
PSYCHIATRIC HELP 5¢
KLUNK!!
THE DOCTOR IS IN
PSYCHIATRIC HELP 5¢
THE DOCTOR IS IN
THAT'S THE SORT OF THING THEY DON'T WARN YOU ABOUT IN MEDICAL SCHOOL...
THE DOCTOR
SCHULZ

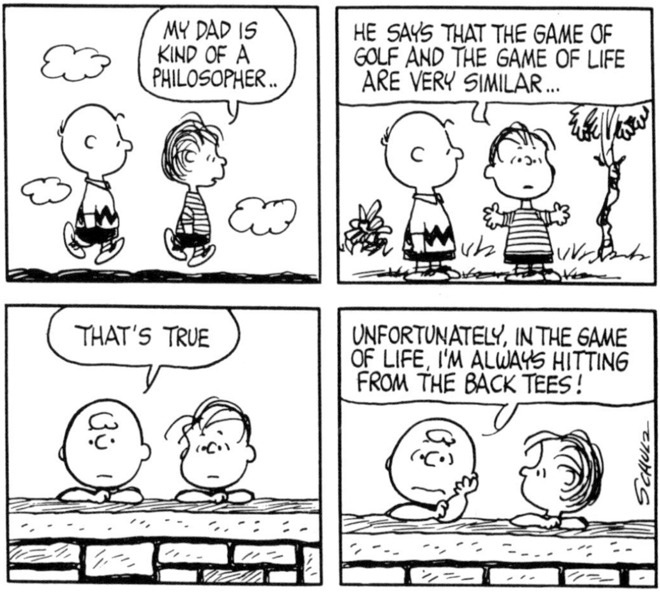
MY DAD IS KIND OF A PHILOSOPHER..
HE SAYS THAT THE GAME OF GOLF AND THE GAME OF LIFE ARE VERY SIMILAR...
THAT'S TRUE
UNFORTUNATELY, IN THE GAME OF LIFE, I'M ALWAYS HITTING FROM THE BACK TEES!
SCHULZ

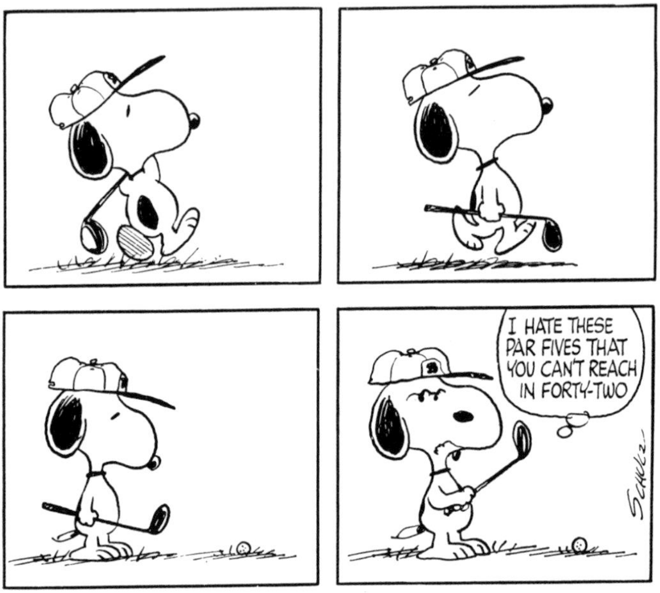
I HATE THESE PAR FIVES THAT YOU CAN'T REACH IN FORTY-TWO
SCHULZ

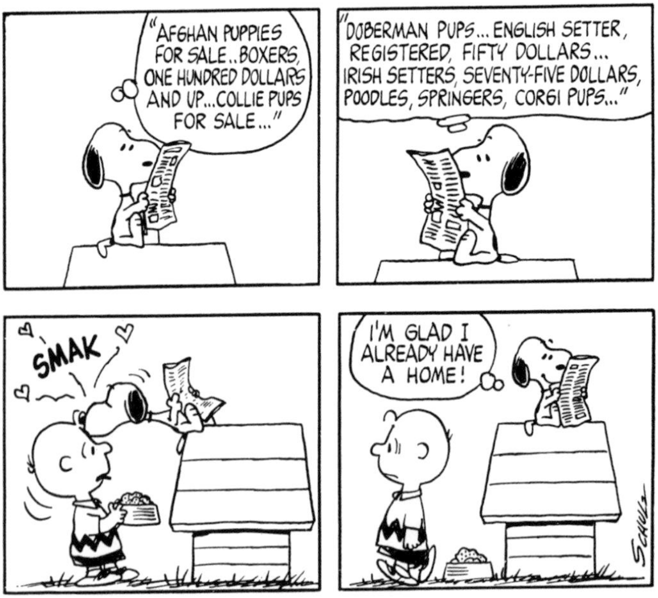
"AFGHAN PUPPIES FOR SALE..BOXERS, ONE HUNDRED DOLLARS AND UP...COLLIE PUPS FOR SALE..."
"DOBERMAN PUPS... ENGLISH SETTER, REGISTERED, FIFTY DOLLARS... IRISH SETTERS, SEVENTY-FIVE DOLLARS, POODLES, SPRINGERS, CORGI PUPS..."
SMAK
I'M GLAD I ALREADY HAVE A HOME!
SCHULZ

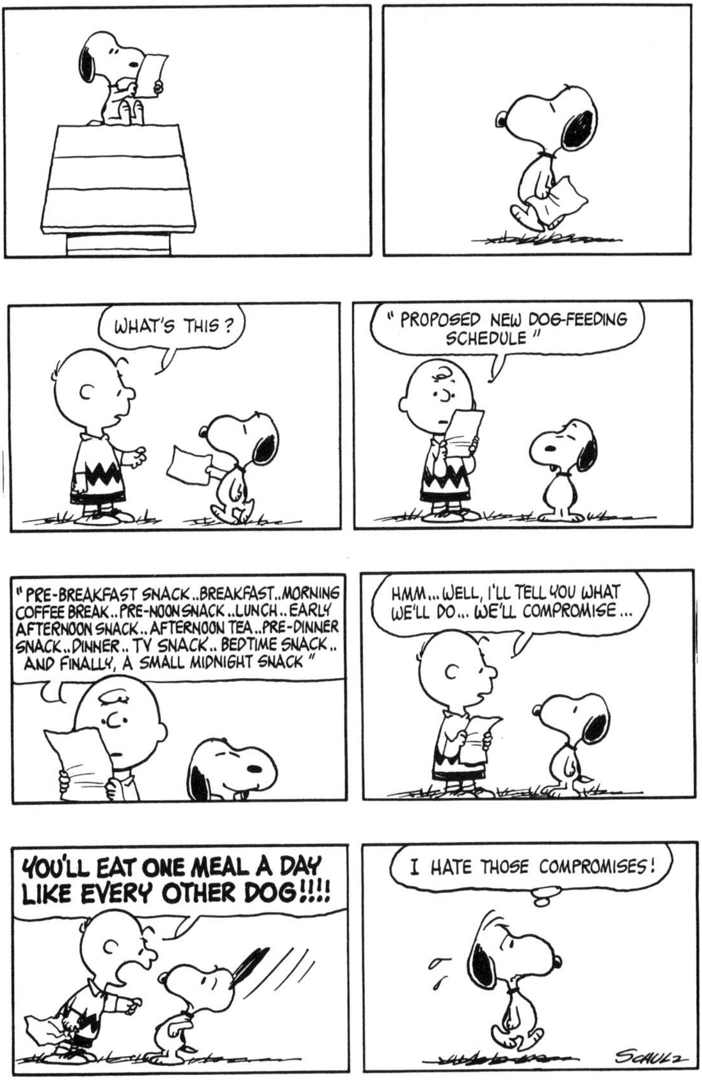
WHAT'S THIS?
" PROPOSED NEW DOG-FEEDING SCHEDULE "
" PRE-BREAKFAST SNACK..BREAKFAST..MORNING COFFEE BREAK..PRE-NOON SNACK..LUNCH..EARLY AFTERNOON SNACK..AFTERNOON TEA..PRE-DINNER SNACK..DINNER.. TV SNACK.. BEDTIME SNACK.. AND FINALLY, A SMALL MIDNIGHT SNACK "
HMM... WELL, I'LL TELL YOU WHAT WE'LL DO... WE'LL COMPROMISE...
YOU'LL EAT ONE MEAL A DAY LIKE EVERY OTHER DOG!!!!
I HATE THOSE COMPROMISES!
SCHULZ

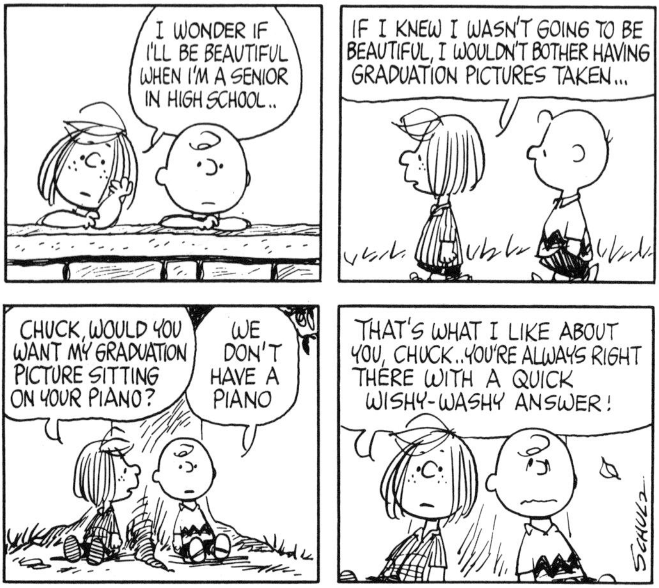
I WONDER IF I'LL BE BEAUTIFUL WHEN I'M A SENIOR IN HIGH SCHOOL..
IF I KNEW I WASN'T GOING TO BE BEAUTIFUL, I WOULDN'T BOTHER HAVING GRADUATION PICTURES TAKEN...
CHUCK, WOULD YOU WANT MY GRADUATION PICTURE SITTING ON YOUR PIANO?
WE DON'T HAVE A PIANO
THAT'S WHAT I LIKE ABOUT YOU, CHUCK..YOU'RE ALWAYS RIGHT THERE WITH A QUICK WISHY-WASHY ANSWER!

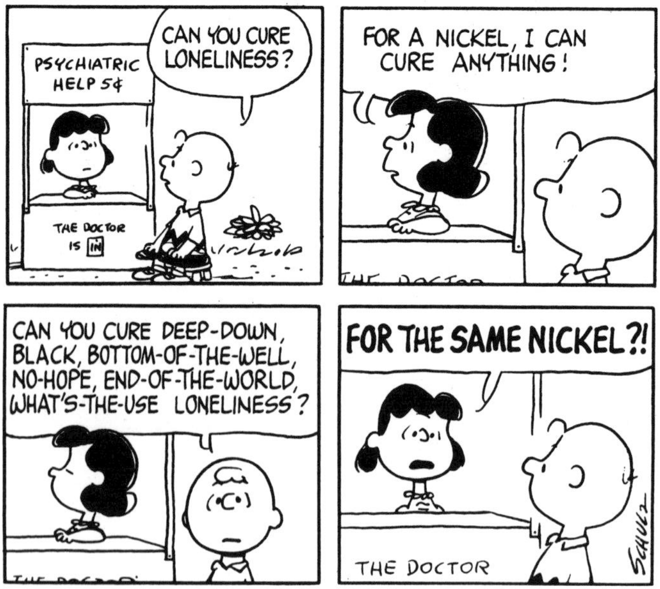
PSYCHIATRIC HELP 5¢
THE DOCTOR IS IN
CAN YOU CURE LONELINESS?
FOR A NICKEL, I CAN CURE ANYTHING!
CAN YOU CURE DEEP-DOWN, BLACK, BOTTOM-OF-THE-WELL, NO-HOPE, END-OF-THE-WORLD, WHAT'S-THE-USE LONELINESS?
FOR THE SAME NICKEL?!
THE DOCTOR

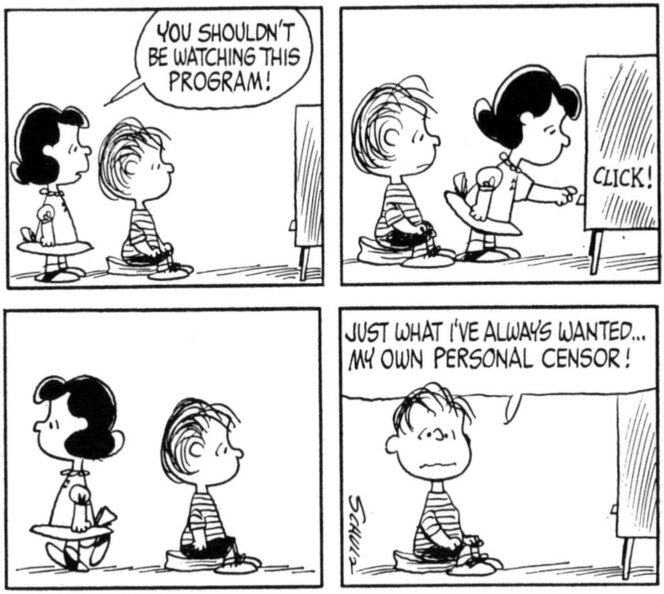
YOU SHOULDN'T BE WATCHING THIS PROGRAM!
CLICK!
JUST WHAT I'VE ALWAYS WANTED... MY OWN PERSONAL CENSOR!
SCHULZ

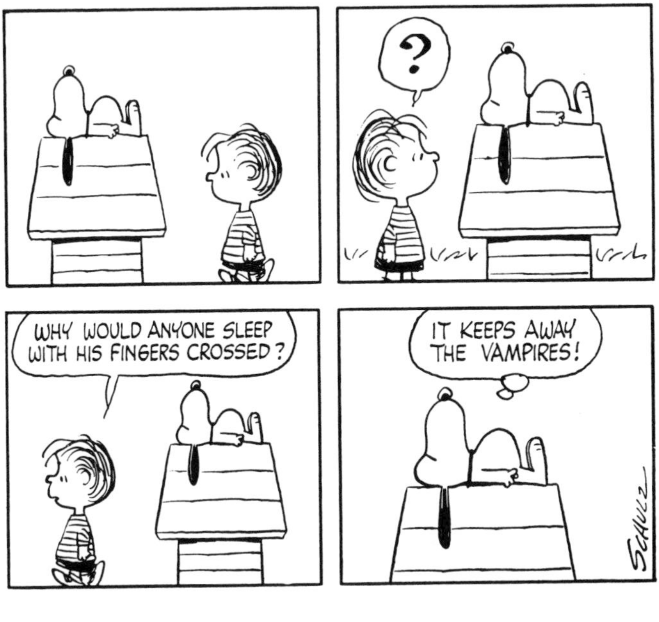
?
WHY WOULD ANYONE SLEEP WITH HIS FINGERS CROSSED?
IT KEEPS AWAY THE VAMPIRES!
SCHULZ

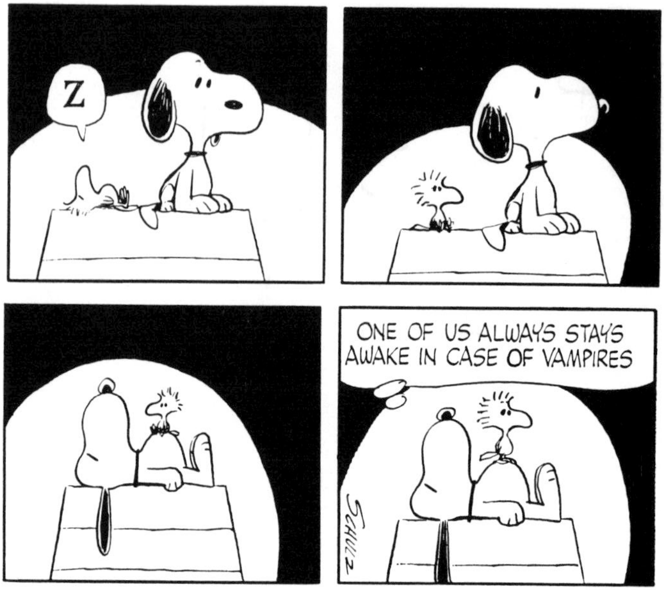
Z
ONE OF US ALWAYS STAYS AWAKE IN CASE OF VAMPIRES
SCHULZ

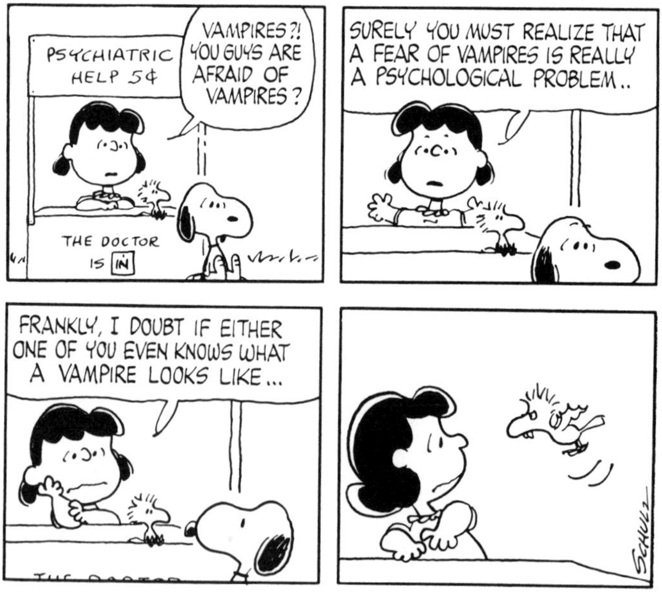
PSYCHIATRIC HELP 5¢
VAMPIRES?! YOU GUYS ARE AFRAID OF VAMPIRES?
THE DOCTOR IS IN
SURELY YOU MUST REALIZE THAT A FEAR OF VAMPIRES IS REALLY A PSYCHOLOGICAL PROBLEM..
FRANKLY, I DOUBT IF EITHER ONE OF YOU EVEN KNOWS WHAT A VAMPIRE LOOKS LIKE...
SCHULZ

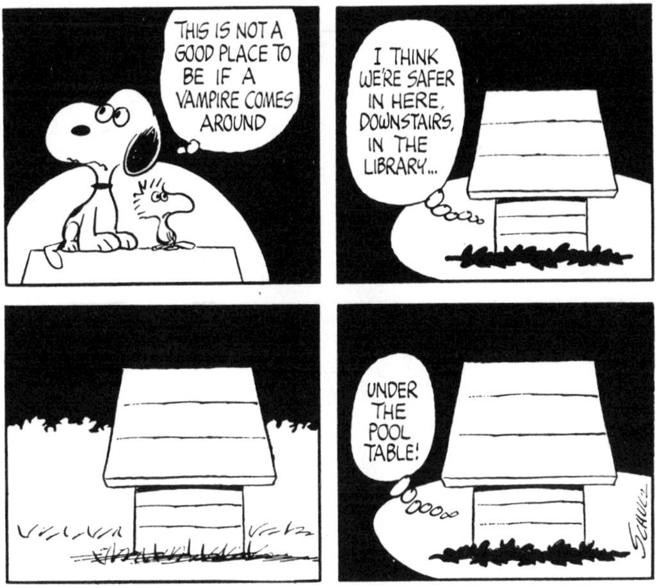
THIS IS NOT A GOOD PLACE TO BE IF A VAMPIRE COMES AROUND
I THINK WE'RE SAFER IN HERE, DOWNSTAIRS, IN THE LIBRARY...
UNDER THE POOL TABLE!
SCHULZ

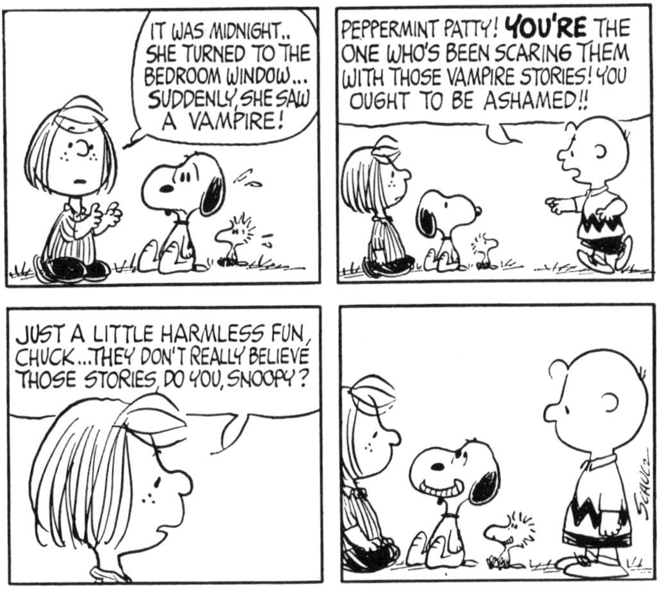
IT WAS MIDNIGHT.. SHE TURNED TO THE BEDROOM WINDOW... SUDDENLY, SHE SAW A VAMPIRE!
PEPPERMINT PATTY! YOU'RE THE ONE WHO'S BEEN SCARING THEM WITH THOSE VAMPIRE STORIES! YOU OUGHT TO BE ASHAMED!!
JUST A LITTLE HARMLESS FUN, CHUCK...THEY DON'T REALLY BELIEVE THOSE STORIES, DO YOU, SNOOPY?
SCHULZ

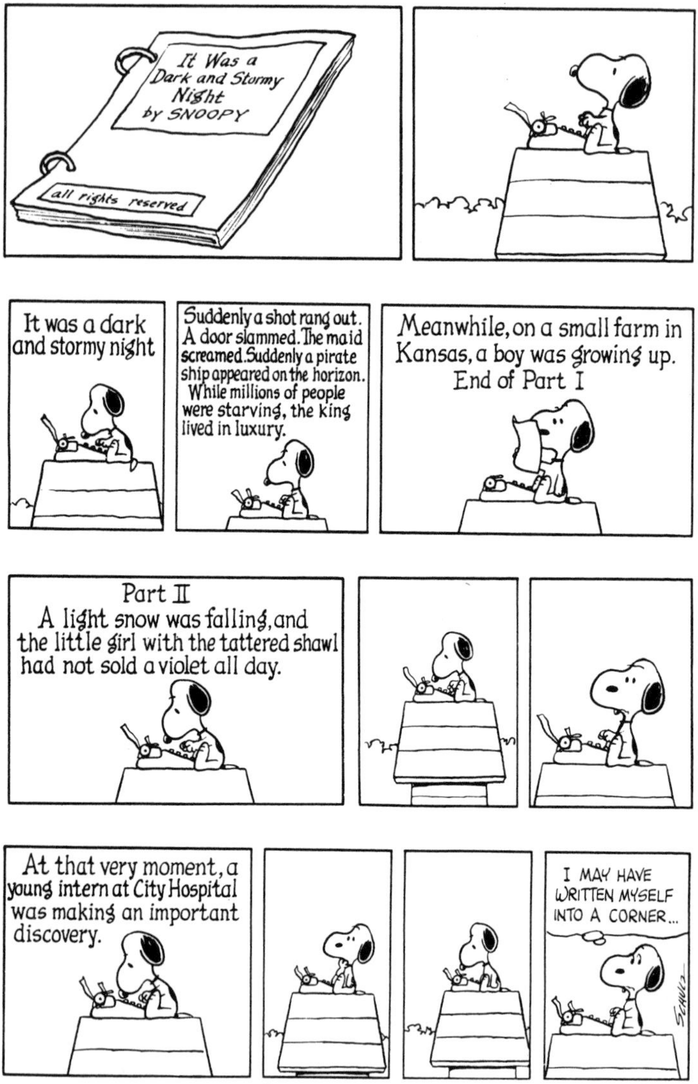
It Was a Dark and Stormy Night
by SNOOPY
all rights reserved
It was a dark and stormy night
Suddenly a shot rang out. A door slammed. The maid screamed. Suddenly a pirate ship appeared on the horizon. While millions of people were starving, the king lived in luxury.
Meanwhile, on a small farm in Kansas, a boy was growing up.
End of Part I
Part II
A light snow was falling, and the little girl with the tattered shawl had not sold a violet all day.
At that very moment, a young intern at City Hospital was making an important discovery.
I MAY HAVE WRITTEN MYSELF INTO A CORNER...
SCHULZ

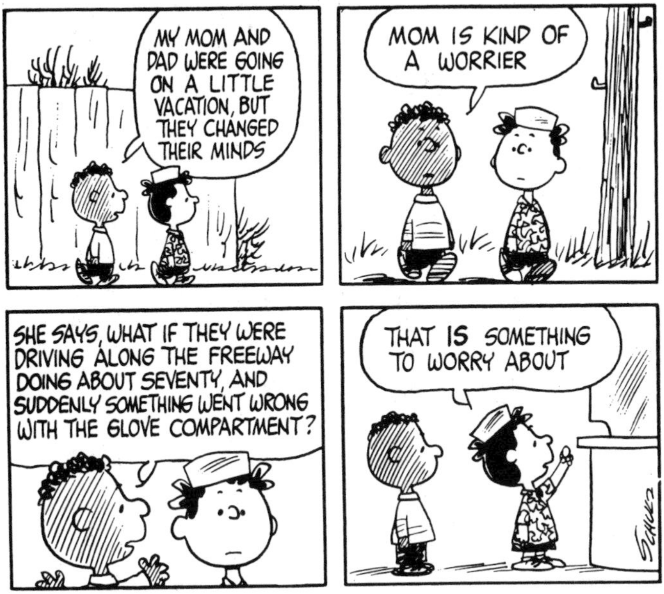
MY MOM AND DAD WERE GOING ON A LITTLE VACATION, BUT THEY CHANGED THEIR MINDS
MOM IS KIND OF A WORRIER
SHE SAYS, WHAT IF THEY WERE DRIVING ALONG THE FREEWAY DOING ABOUT SEVENTY, AND SUDDENLY SOMETHING WENT WRONG WITH THE GLOVE COMPARTMENT?
THAT IS SOMETHING TO WORRY ABOUT
SCHULZ

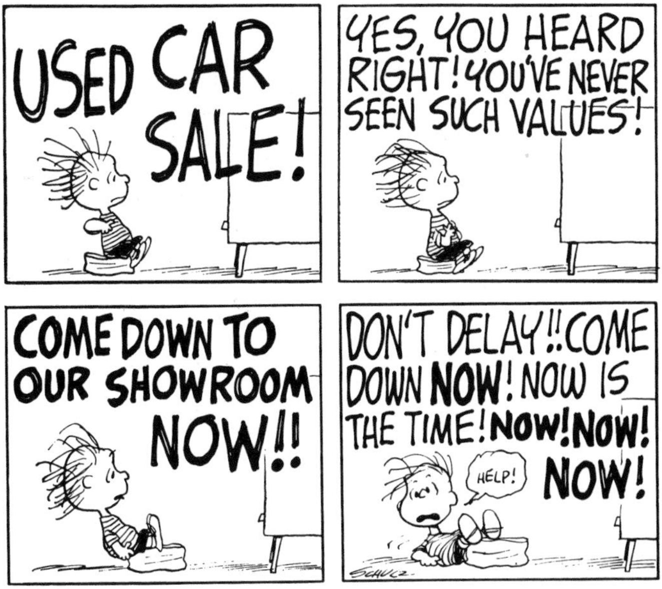
USED CAR SALE!
YES, YOU HEARD RIGHT! YOU'VE NEVER SEEN SUCH VALUES!
COME DOWN TO OUR SHOWROOM NOW!!
DON'T DELAY!! COME DOWN NOW! NOW IS THE TIME! NOW! NOW! NOW!
HELP!
SCHULZ

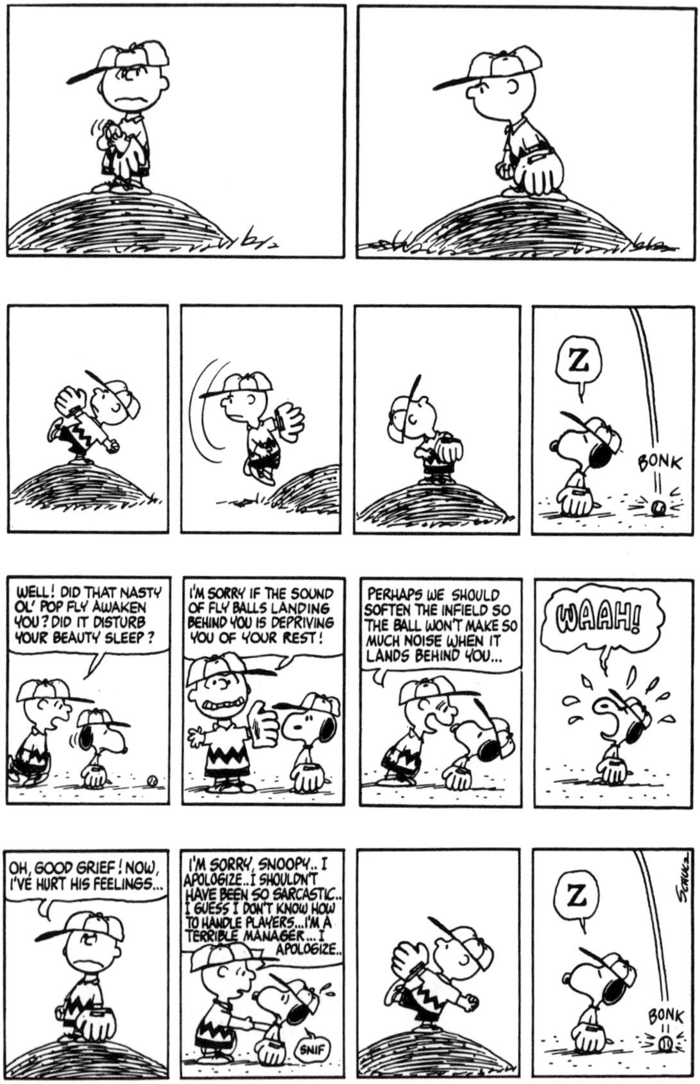
Z
BONK
WELL! DID THAT NASTY OL' POP FLY AWAKEN YOU? DID IT DISTURB YOUR BEAUTY SLEEP?
I'M SORRY IF THE SOUND OF FLY BALLS LANDING BEHIND YOU IS DEPRIVING YOU OF YOUR REST!
PERHAPS WE SHOULD SOFTEN THE INFIELD SO THE BALL WON'T MAKE SO MUCH NOISE WHEN IT LANDS BEHIND YOU...
WAAH!
OH, GOOD GRIEF! NOW, I'VE HURT HIS FEELINGS...
I'M SORRY, SNOOPY.. I APOLOGIZE..I SHOULDN'T HAVE BEEN SO SARCASTIC.. I GUESS I DON'T KNOW HOW TO HANDLE PLAYERS...I'M A TERRIBLE MANAGER... I APOLOGIZE..
SNIF
Z
BONK
SCHULZ

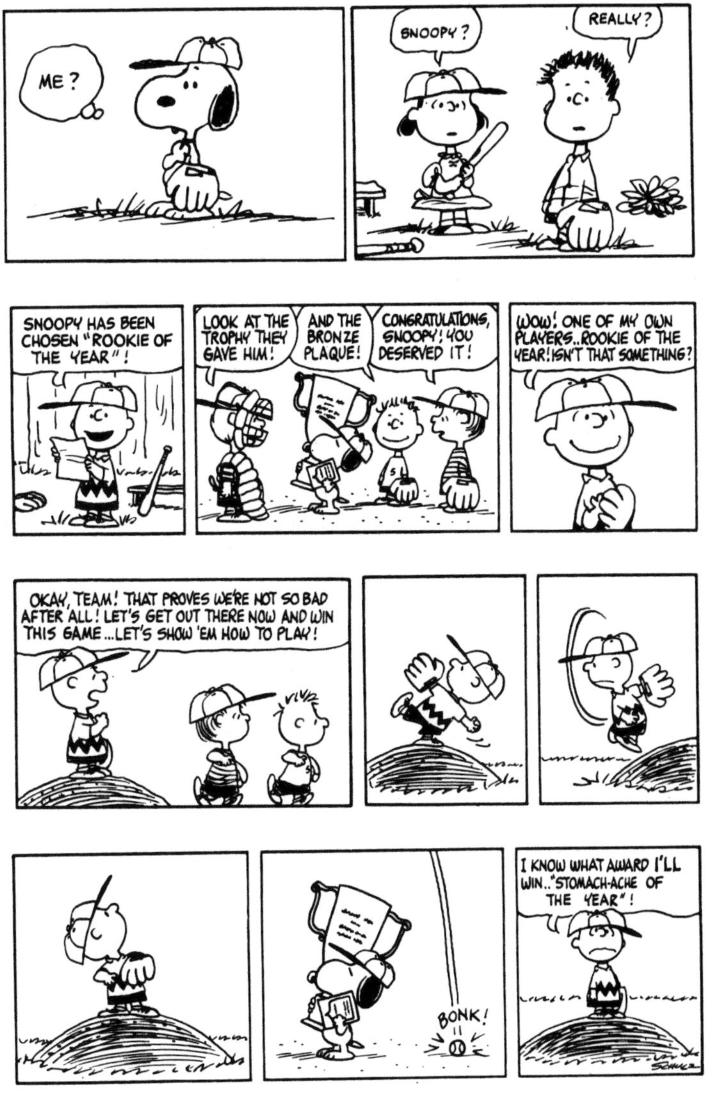

ME?
SNOOPY?
REALLY?
SNOOPY HAS BEEN CHOSEN "ROOKIE OF THE YEAR"!
LOOK AT THE TROPHY THEY GAVE HIM!
AND THE BRONZE PLAQUE!
CONGRATULATIONS, SNOOPY! YOU DESERVED IT!
WOW! ONE OF MY OWN PLAYERS..ROOKIE OF THE YEAR! ISN'T THAT SOMETHING?
OKAY, TEAM! THAT PROVES WE'RE NOT SO BAD AFTER ALL! LET'S GET OUT THERE NOW AND WIN THIS GAME...LET'S SHOW 'EM HOW TO PLAY!
BONK!
I KNOW WHAT AWARD I'LL WIN.."STOMACH-ACHE OF THE YEAR"!
SCHULZ

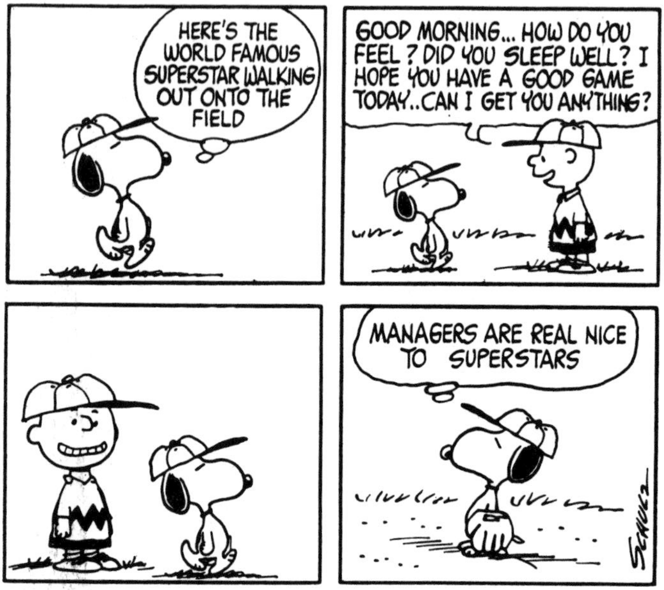
HERE'S THE WORLD FAMOUS SUPERSTAR WALKING OUT ONTO THE FIELD
GOOD MORNING... HOW DO YOU FEEL ? DID YOU SLEEP WELL ? I HOPE YOU HAVE A GOOD GAME TODAY..CAN I GET YOU ANYTHING ?
MANAGERS ARE REAL NICE TO SUPERSTARS
SCHULZ

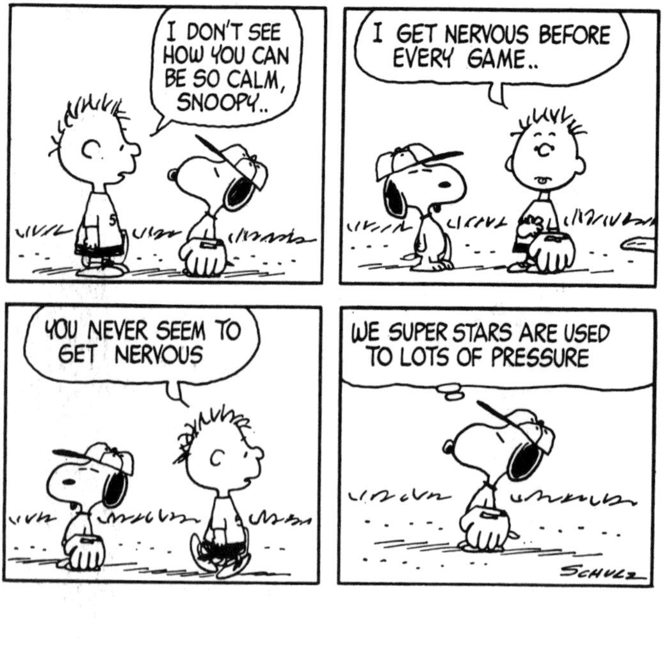
I DON'T SEE HOW YOU CAN BE SO CALM, SNOOPY..
I GET NERVOUS BEFORE EVERY GAME..
YOU NEVER SEEM TO GET NERVOUS
WE SUPER STARS ARE USED TO LOTS OF PRESSURE
SCHULZ

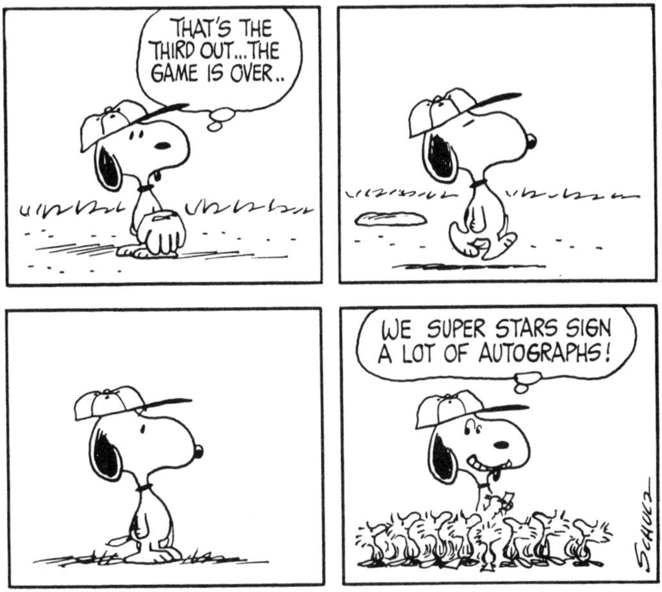

THAT'S THE THIRD OUT...THE GAME IS OVER..
WE SUPER STARS SIGN A LOT OF AUTOGRAPHS!
SCHULZ

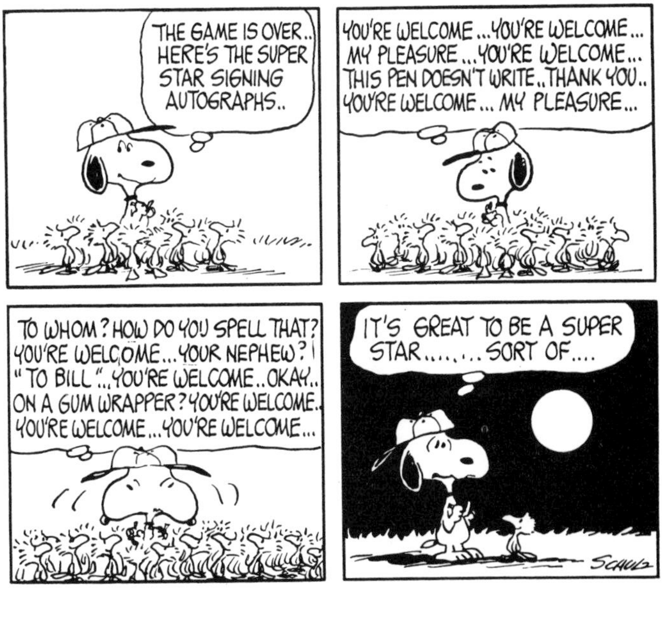

THE GAME IS OVER.. HERE'S THE SUPER STAR SIGNING AUTOGRAPHS..
YOU'RE WELCOME...YOU'RE WELCOME... MY PLEASURE...YOU'RE WELCOME... THIS PEN DOESN'T WRITE..THANK YOU.. YOU'RE WELCOME... MY PLEASURE...
TO WHOM? HOW DO YOU SPELL THAT? YOU'RE WELCOME...YOUR NEPHEW? "TO BILL"...YOU'RE WELCOME..OKAY.. ON A GUM WRAPPER? YOU'RE WELCOME.. YOU'RE WELCOME...YOU'RE WELCOME...
IT'S GREAT TO BE A SUPER STAR.......SORT OF....
SCHULZ

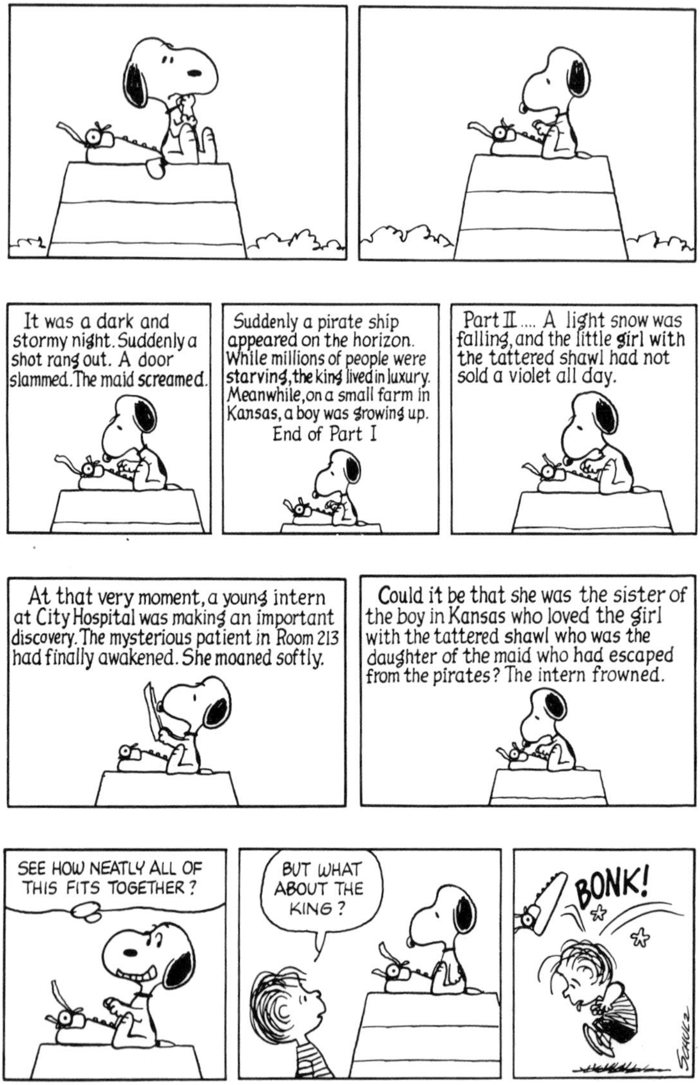
It was a dark and stormy night. Suddenly a shot rang out. A door slammed. The maid screamed.
Suddenly a pirate ship appeared on the horizon. While millions of people were starving, the king lived in luxury. Meanwhile, on a small farm in Kansas, a boy was growing up.
End of Part I
Part II .... A light snow was falling, and the little girl with the tattered shawl had not sold a violet all day.
At that very moment, a young intern at City Hospital was making an important discovery. The mysterious patient in Room 213 had finally awakened. She moaned softly.
Could it be that she was the sister of the boy in Kansas who loved the girl with the tattered shawl who was the daughter of the maid who had escaped from the pirates? The intern frowned.
SEE HOW NEATLY ALL OF THIS FITS TOGETHER?
BUT WHAT ABOUT THE KING?
BONK!
SCHULZ

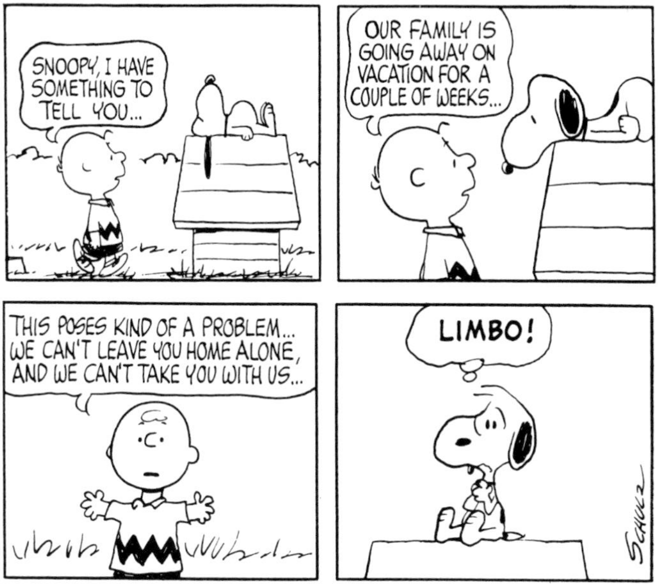
SNOOPY, I HAVE SOMETHING TO TELL YOU...
OUR FAMILY IS GOING AWAY ON VACATION FOR A COUPLE OF WEEKS...
THIS POSES KIND OF A PROBLEM... WE CAN'T LEAVE YOU HOME ALONE, AND WE CAN'T TAKE YOU WITH US...
LIMBO!

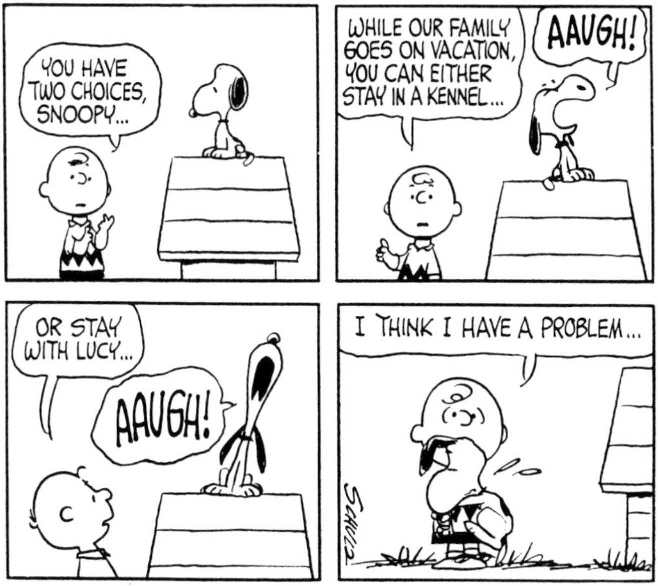
YOU HAVE TWO CHOICES, SNOOPY...
WHILE OUR FAMILY GOES ON VACATION, YOU CAN EITHER STAY IN A KENNEL...
AAUGH!
OR STAY WITH LUCY...
AAUGH!
I THINK I HAVE A PROBLEM...

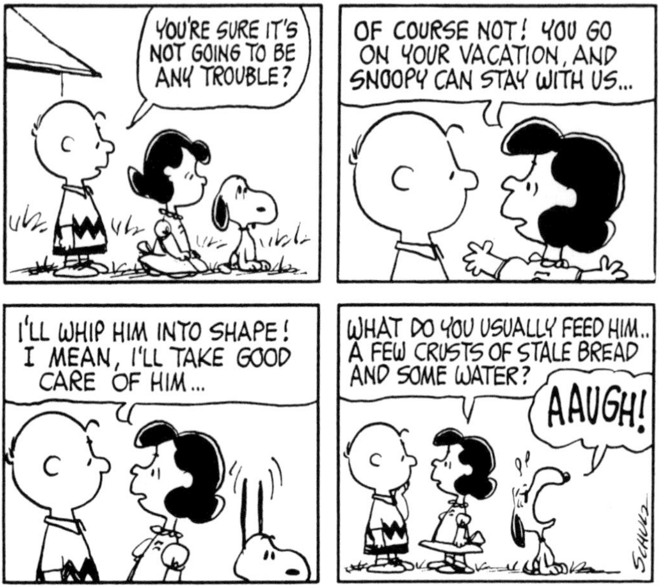
YOU'RE SURE IT'S NOT GOING TO BE ANY TROUBLE?
OF COURSE NOT! YOU GO ON YOUR VACATION, AND SNOOPY CAN STAY WITH US...
I'LL WHIP HIM INTO SHAPE! I MEAN, I'LL TAKE GOOD CARE OF HIM...
WHAT DO YOU USUALLY FEED HIM.. A FEW CRUSTS OF STALE BREAD AND SOME WATER?
AAUGH!

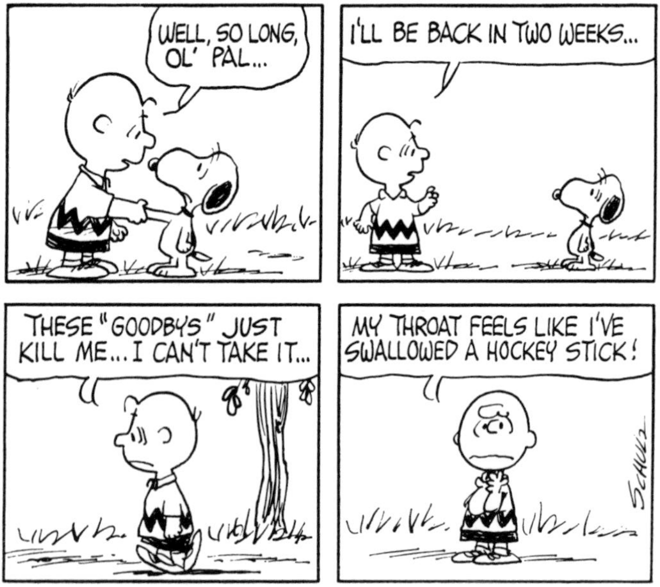
WELL, SO LONG, OL' PAL...
I'LL BE BACK IN TWO WEEKS...
THESE "GOODBYS" JUST KILL ME... I CAN'T TAKE IT...
MY THROAT FEELS LIKE I'VE SWALLOWED A HOCKEY STICK!

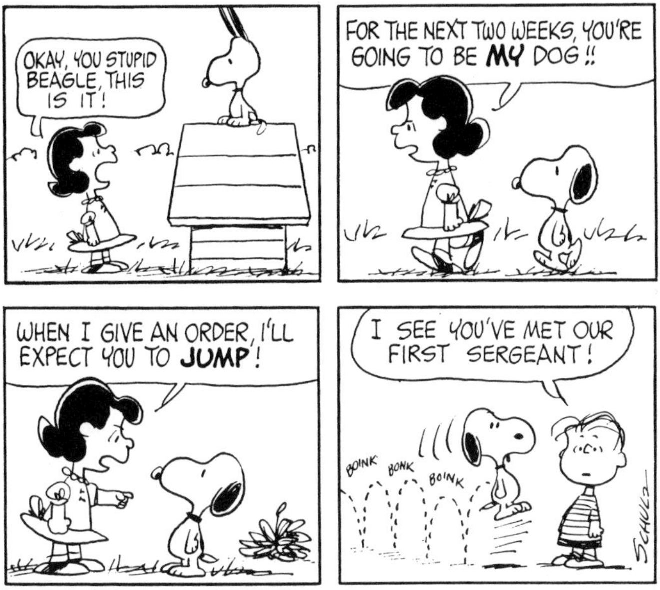
OKAY, YOU STUPID BEAGLE, THIS IS IT!
FOR THE NEXT TWO WEEKS, YOU'RE GOING TO BE MY DOG!!
WHEN I GIVE AN ORDER, I'LL EXPECT YOU TO JUMP!
I SEE YOU'VE MET OUR FIRST SERGEANT!
BOINK
BONK
BOINK
SCHULZ

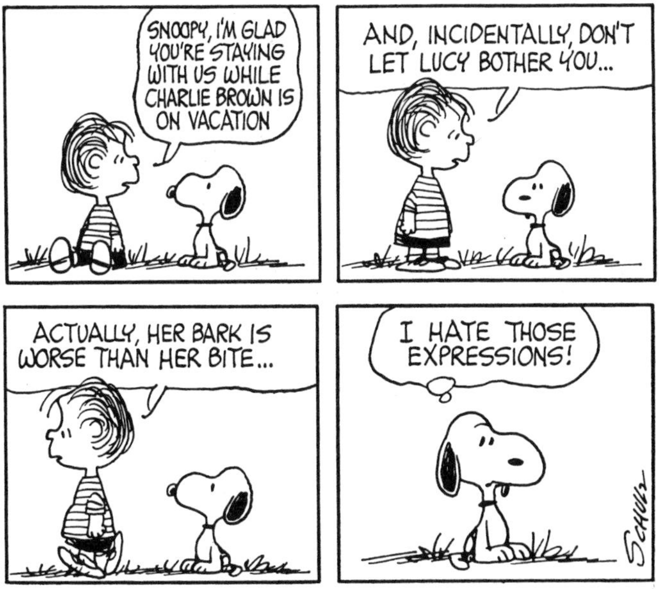
SNOOPY, I'M GLAD YOU'RE STAYING WITH US WHILE CHARLIE BROWN IS ON VACATION
AND, INCIDENTALLY, DON'T LET LUCY BOTHER YOU...
ACTUALLY, HER BARK IS WORSE THAN HER BITE...
I HATE THOSE EXPRESSIONS!
SCHULZ

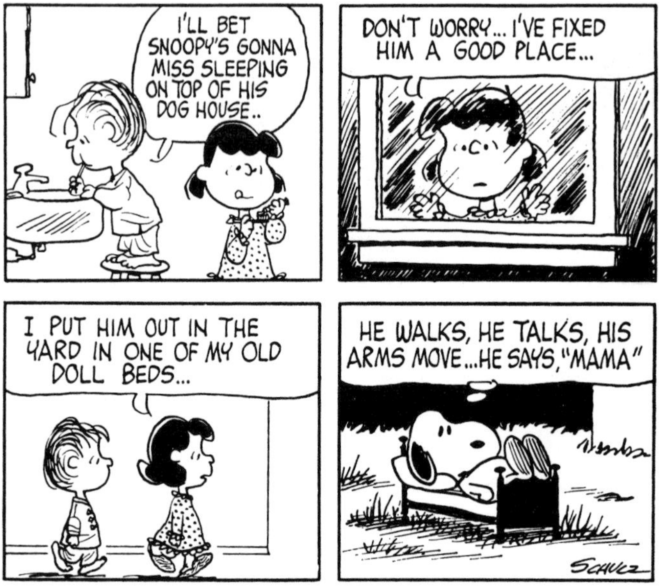
I'LL BET SNOOPY'S GONNA MISS SLEEPING ON TOP OF HIS DOG HOUSE..
DON'T WORRY... I'VE FIXED HIM A GOOD PLACE...
I PUT HIM OUT IN THE YARD IN ONE OF MY OLD DOLL BEDS...
HE WALKS, HE TALKS, HIS ARMS MOVE...HE SAYS, "MAMA"
SCHULZ

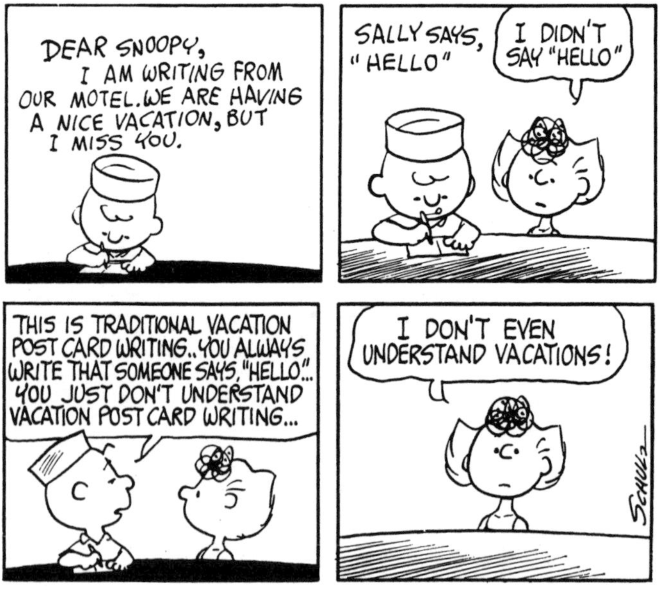
DEAR SNOOPY, I AM WRITING FROM OUR MOTEL. WE ARE HAVING A NICE VACATION, BUT I MISS YOU.
SALLY SAYS, "HELLO"
I DIDN'T SAY "HELLO"
THIS IS TRADITIONAL VACATION POST CARD WRITING..YOU ALWAYS WRITE THAT SOMEONE SAYS, "HELLO"... YOU JUST DON'T UNDERSTAND VACATION POST CARD WRITING...
I DON'T EVEN UNDERSTAND VACATIONS!
SCHULZ

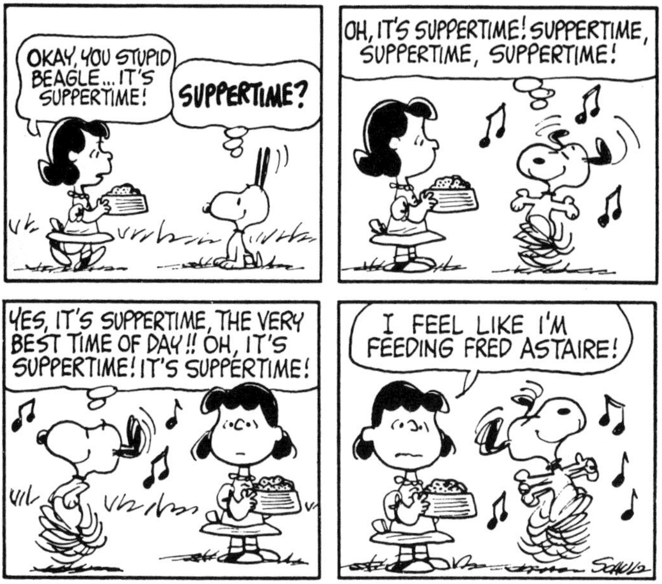
OKAY, YOU STUPID BEAGLE... IT'S SUPPERTIME!
SUPPERTIME?
OH, IT'S SUPPERTIME! SUPPERTIME, SUPPERTIME, SUPPERTIME!
YES, IT'S SUPPERTIME, THE VERY BEST TIME OF DAY!! OH, IT'S SUPPERTIME! IT'S SUPPERTIME!
I FEEL LIKE I'M FEEDING FRED ASTAIRE!

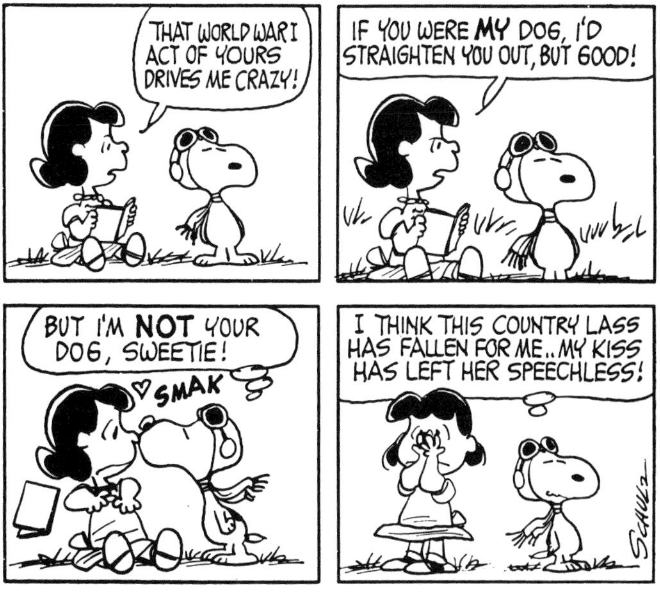
THAT WORLD WAR I ACT OF YOURS DRIVES ME CRAZY!
IF YOU WERE **MY** DOG, I'D STRAIGHTEN YOU OUT, BUT GOOD!
BUT I'M **NOT** YOUR DOG, SWEETIE!
SMAK
I THINK THIS COUNTRY LASS HAS FALLEN FOR ME.. MY KISS HAS LEFT HER SPEECHLESS!

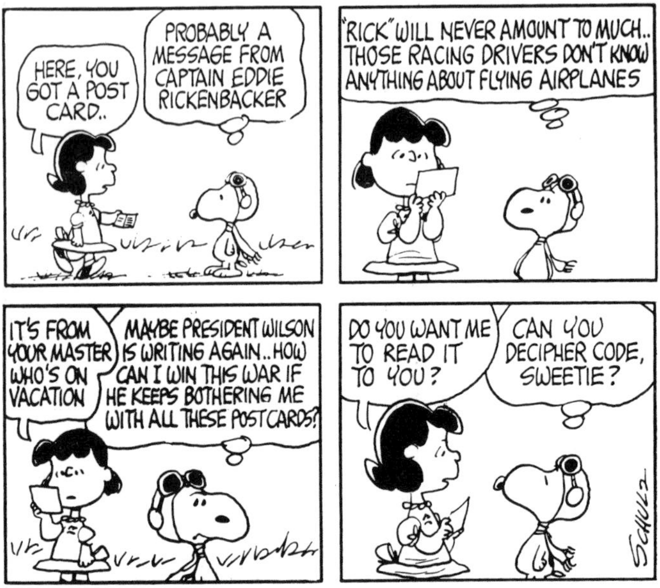
HERE, YOU GOT A POST CARD..
PROBABLY A MESSAGE FROM CAPTAIN EDDIE RICKENBACKER
"RICK" WILL NEVER AMOUNT TO MUCH.. THOSE RACING DRIVERS DON'T KNOW ANYTHING ABOUT FLYING AIRPLANES
IT'S FROM YOUR MASTER WHO'S ON VACATION
MAYBE PRESIDENT WILSON IS WRITING AGAIN..HOW CAN I WIN THIS WAR IF HE KEEPS BOTHERING ME WITH ALL THESE POSTCARDS?
DO YOU WANT ME TO READ IT TO YOU?
CAN YOU DECIPHER CODE, SWEETIE?
SCHULZ

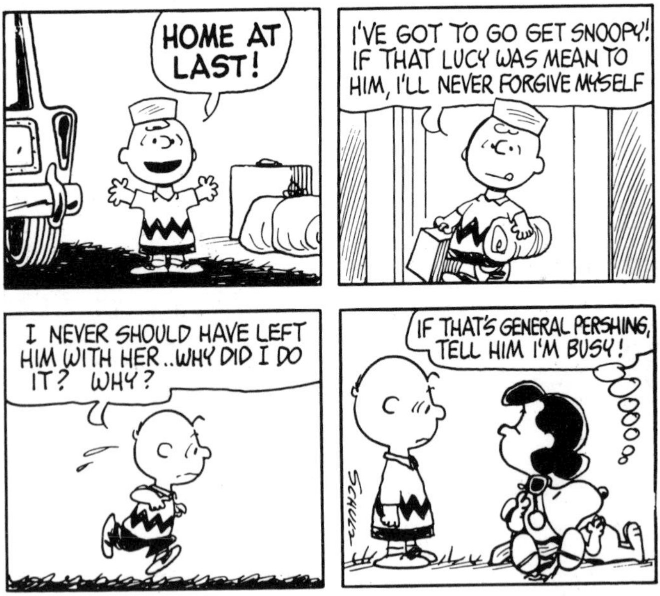
HOME AT LAST!
I'VE GOT TO GO GET SNOOPY! IF THAT LUCY WAS MEAN TO HIM, I'LL NEVER FORGIVE MYSELF
I NEVER SHOULD HAVE LEFT HIM WITH HER..WHY DID I DO IT? WHY?
IF THAT'S GENERAL PERSHING, TELL HIM I'M BUSY!
SCHULZ

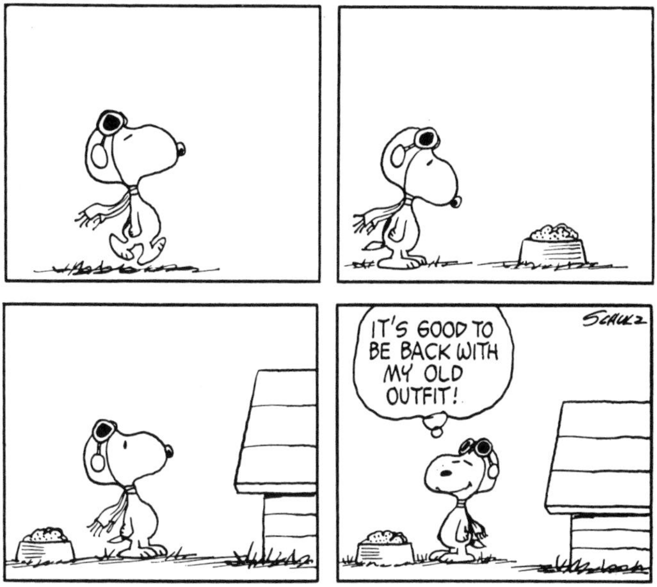
IT'S GOOD TO BE BACK WITH MY OLD OUTFIT!
SCHULZ

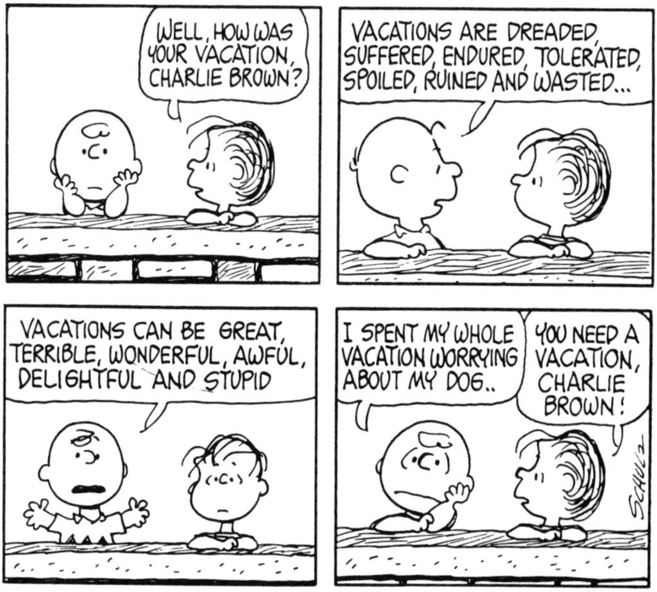
WELL, HOW WAS YOUR VACATION, CHARLIE BROWN?
VACATIONS ARE DREADED, SUFFERED, ENDURED, TOLERATED, SPOILED, RUINED AND WASTED...
VACATIONS CAN BE GREAT, TERRIBLE, WONDERFUL, AWFUL, DELIGHTFUL AND STUPID
I SPENT MY WHOLE VACATION WORRYING ABOUT MY DOG..
YOU NEED A VACATION, CHARLIE BROWN!
SCHULZ

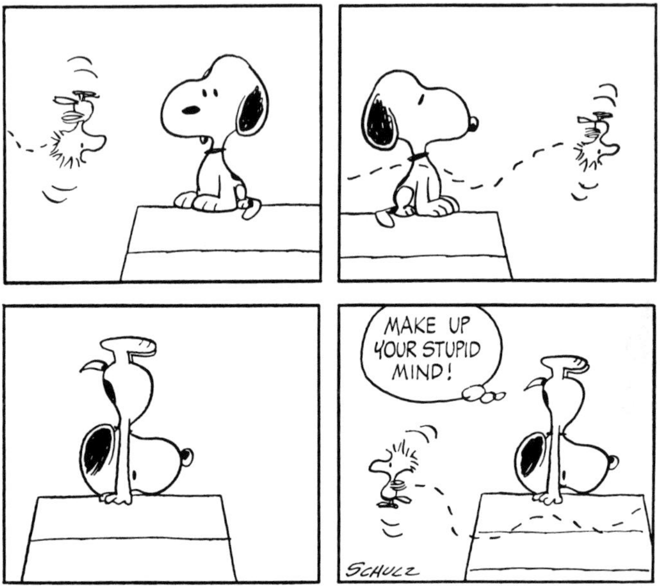
MAKE UP YOUR STUPID MIND!
SCHULZ

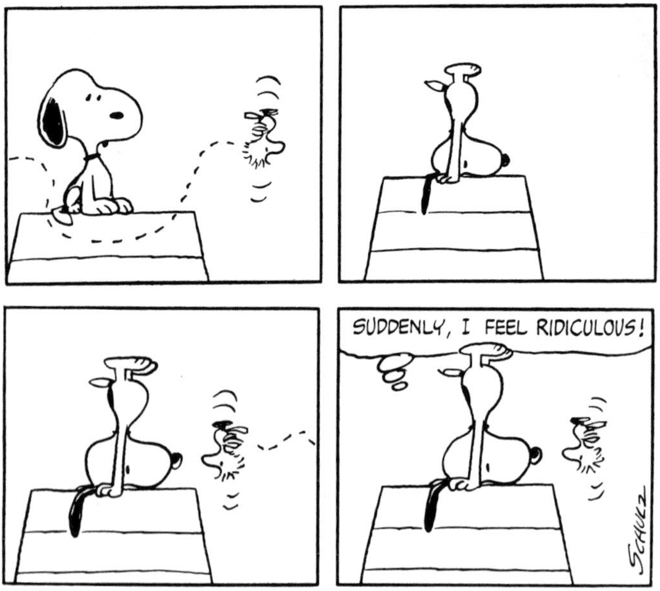
SUDDENLY, I FEEL RIDICULOUS!
SCHULZ

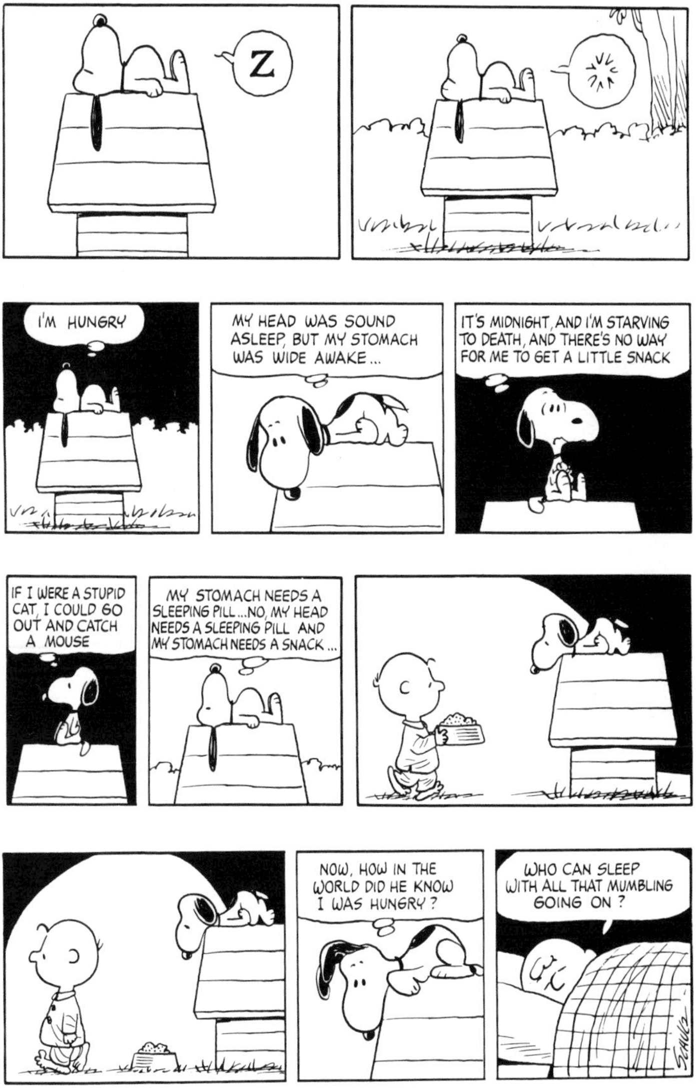
Z
I'M HUNGRY
MY HEAD WAS SOUND ASLEEP, BUT MY STOMACH WAS WIDE AWAKE...
IT'S MIDNIGHT, AND I'M STARVING TO DEATH, AND THERE'S NO WAY FOR ME TO GET A LITTLE SNACK
IF I WERE A STUPID CAT, I COULD GO OUT AND CATCH A MOUSE
MY STOMACH NEEDS A SLEEPING PILL...NO, MY HEAD NEEDS A SLEEPING PILL AND MY STOMACH NEEDS A SNACK...
NOW, HOW IN THE WORLD DID HE KNOW I WAS HUNGRY?
WHO CAN SLEEP WITH ALL THAT MUMBLING GOING ON?
SCHULZ

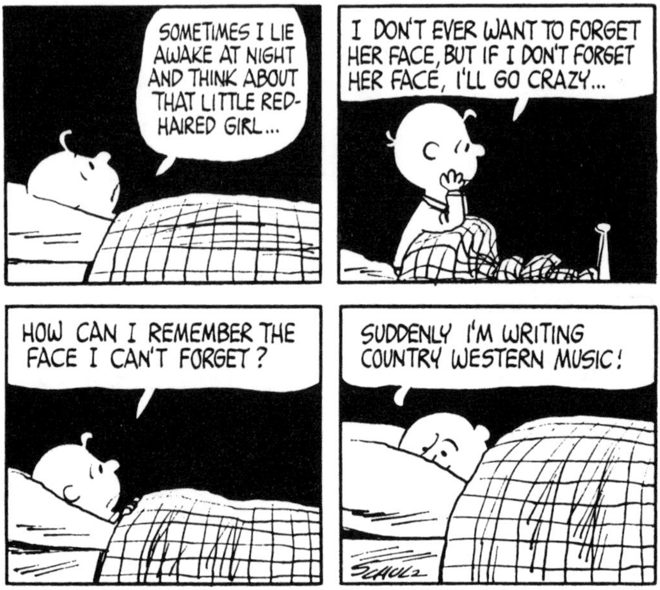
SOMETIMES I LIE AWAKE AT NIGHT AND THINK ABOUT THAT LITTLE RED-HAIRED GIRL...
I DON'T EVER WANT TO FORGET HER FACE, BUT IF I DON'T FORGET HER FACE, I'LL GO CRAZY...
HOW CAN I REMEMBER THE FACE I CAN'T FORGET?
SUDDENLY I'M WRITING COUNTRY WESTERN MUSIC!

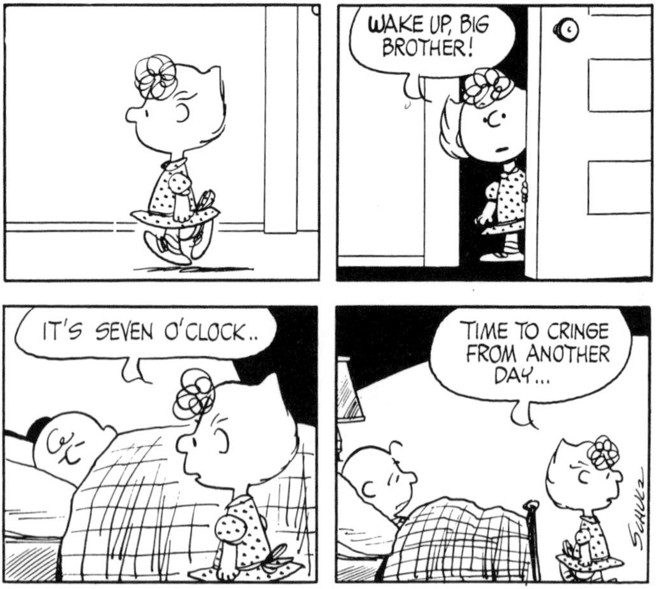
WAKE UP, BIG BROTHER!
IT'S SEVEN O'CLOCK..
TIME TO CRINGE FROM ANOTHER DAY...

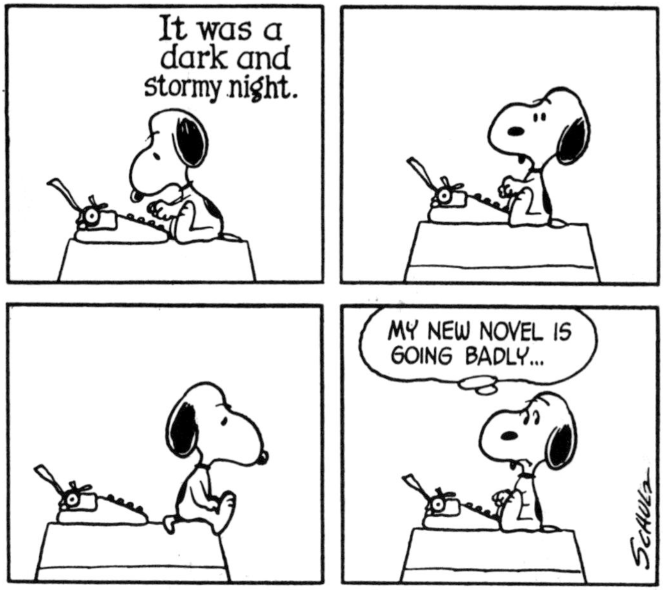
It was a dark and stormy night.
MY NEW NOVEL IS GOING BADLY...
SCHULZ

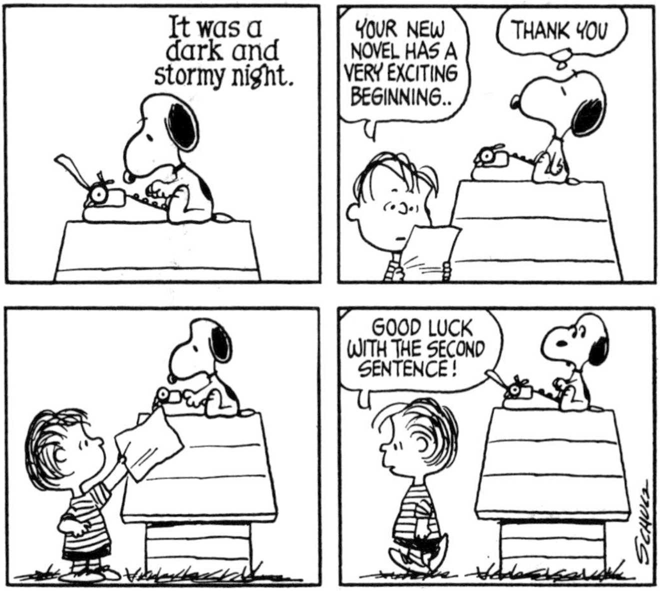
It was a dark and stormy night.
YOUR NEW NOVEL HAS A VERY EXCITING BEGINNING..
THANK YOU
GOOD LUCK WITH THE SECOND SENTENCE!
SCHULZ

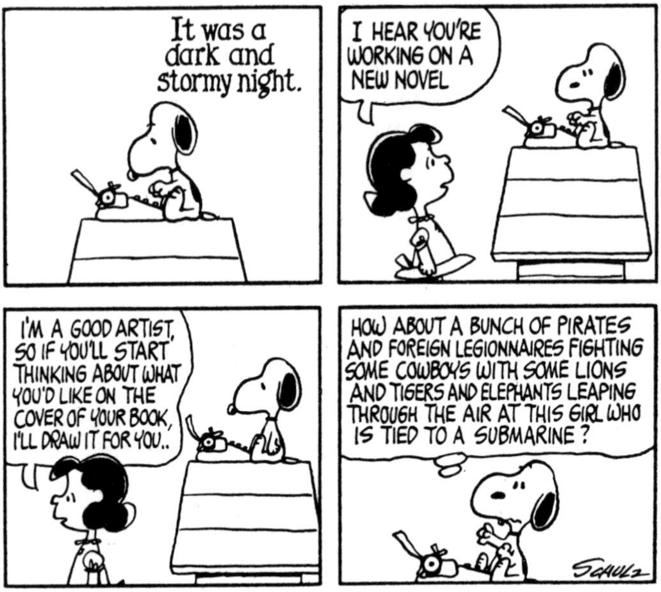
It was a dark and stormy night.
I HEAR YOU'RE WORKING ON A NEW NOVEL
I'M A GOOD ARTIST, SO IF YOU'LL START THINKING ABOUT WHAT YOU'D LIKE ON THE COVER OF YOUR BOOK, I'LL DRAW IT FOR YOU..
HOW ABOUT A BUNCH OF PIRATES AND FOREIGN LEGIONNAIRES FIGHTING SOME COWBOYS WITH SOME LIONS AND TIGERS AND ELEPHANTS LEAPING THROUGH THE AIR AT THIS GIRL WHO IS TIED TO A SUBMARINE?
SCHULZ

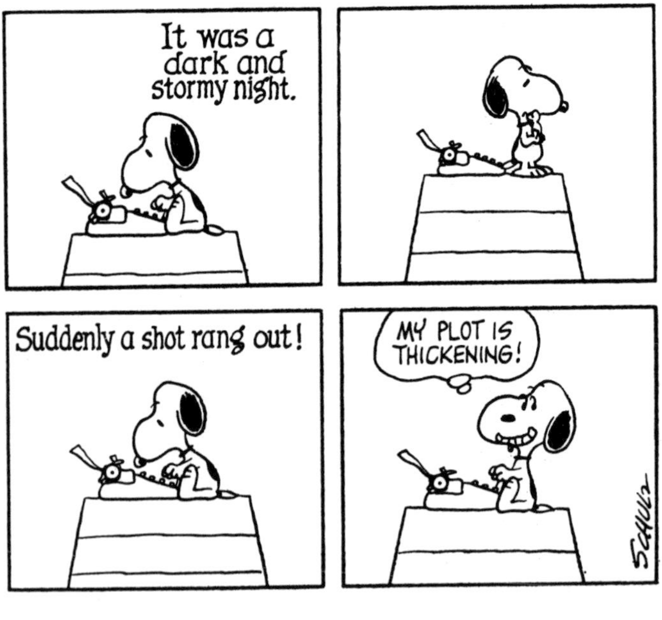
It was a dark and stormy night.
Suddenly a shot rang out!
MY PLOT IS THICKENING!
SCHULZ

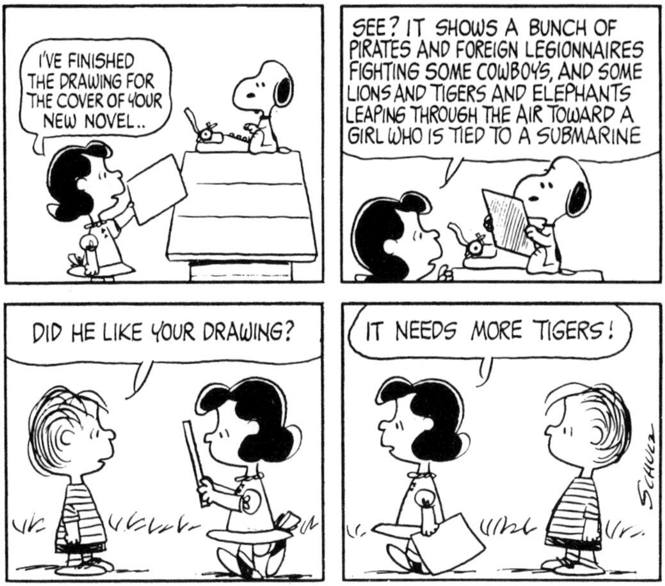
I'VE FINISHED THE DRAWING FOR THE COVER OF YOUR NEW NOVEL..
SEE? IT SHOWS A BUNCH OF PIRATES AND FOREIGN LEGIONNAIRES FIGHTING SOME COWBOYS, AND SOME LIONS AND TIGERS AND ELEPHANTS LEAPING THROUGH THE AIR TOWARD A GIRL WHO IS TIED TO A SUBMARINE
DID HE LIKE YOUR DRAWING?
IT NEEDS MORE TIGERS!
SCHULZ

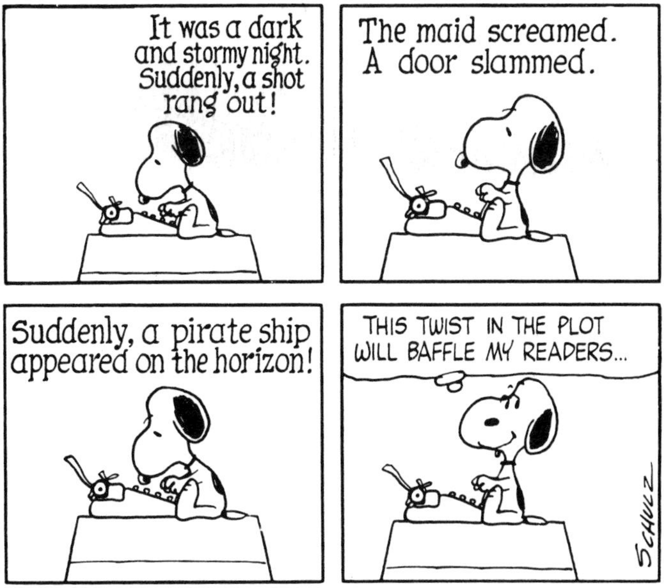
It was a dark and stormy night. Suddenly, a shot rang out!
The maid screamed. A door slammed.
Suddenly, a pirate ship appeared on the horizon!
THIS TWIST IN THE PLOT WILL BAFFLE MY READERS...
SCHULZ

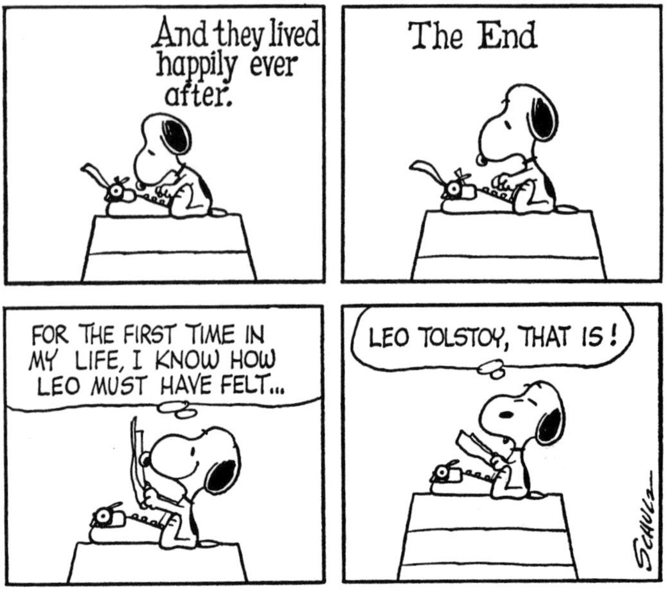
And they lived happily ever after.
The End
FOR THE FIRST TIME IN MY LIFE, I KNOW HOW LEO MUST HAVE FELT...
LEO TOLSTOY, THAT IS!

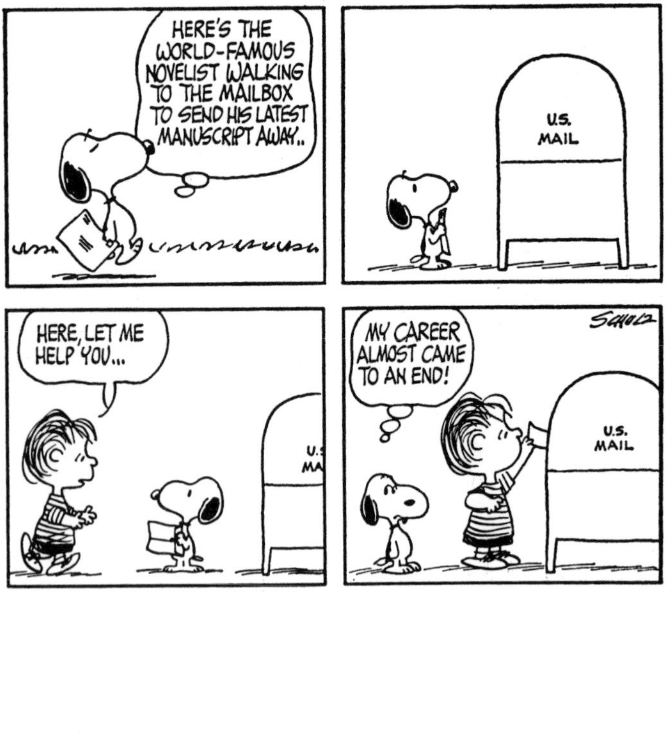
HERE'S THE WORLD-FAMOUS NOVELIST WALKING TO THE MAILBOX TO SEND HIS LATEST MANUSCRIPT AWAY..
U.S. MAIL
HERE, LET ME HELP YOU...
MY CAREER ALMOST CAME TO AN END!
U.S. MAIL

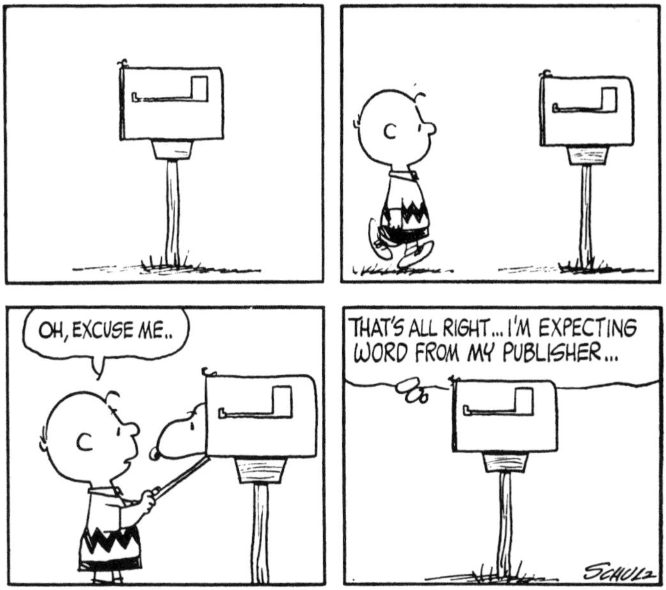
OH, EXCUSE ME..
THAT'S ALL RIGHT... I'M EXPECTING WORD FROM MY PUBLISHER...
SCHULZ

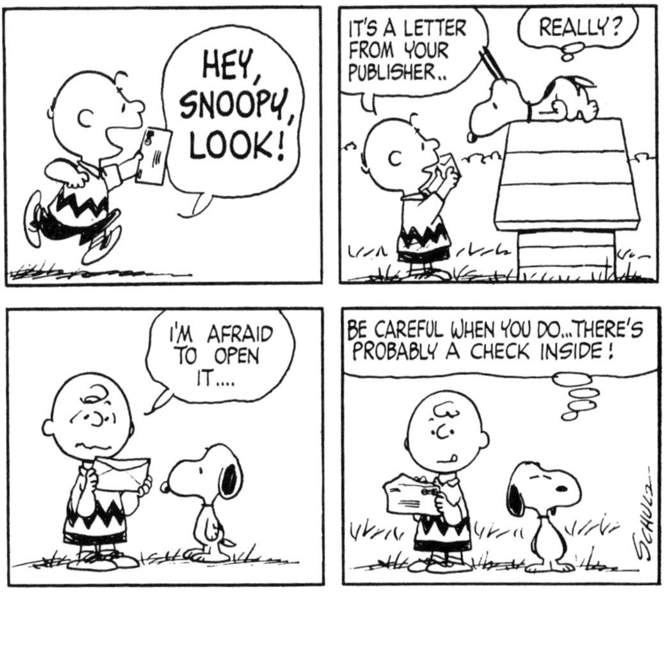
HEY, SNOOPY, LOOK!
IT'S A LETTER FROM YOUR PUBLISHER..
REALLY?
I'M AFRAID TO OPEN IT....
BE CAREFUL WHEN YOU DO...THERE'S PROBABLY A CHECK INSIDE!
SCHULZ

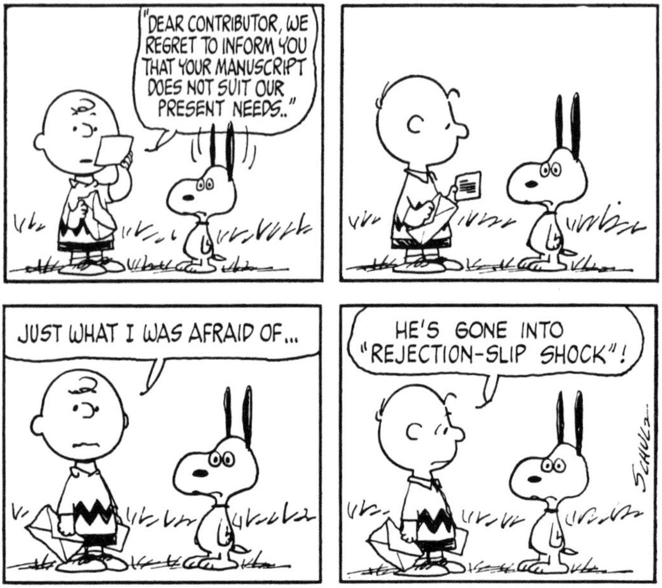
"DEAR CONTRIBUTOR, WE REGRET TO INFORM YOU THAT YOUR MANUSCRIPT DOES NOT SUIT OUR PRESENT NEEDS.."
JUST WHAT I WAS AFRAID OF...
HE'S GONE INTO "REJECTION-SLIP SHOCK"!
SCHULZ

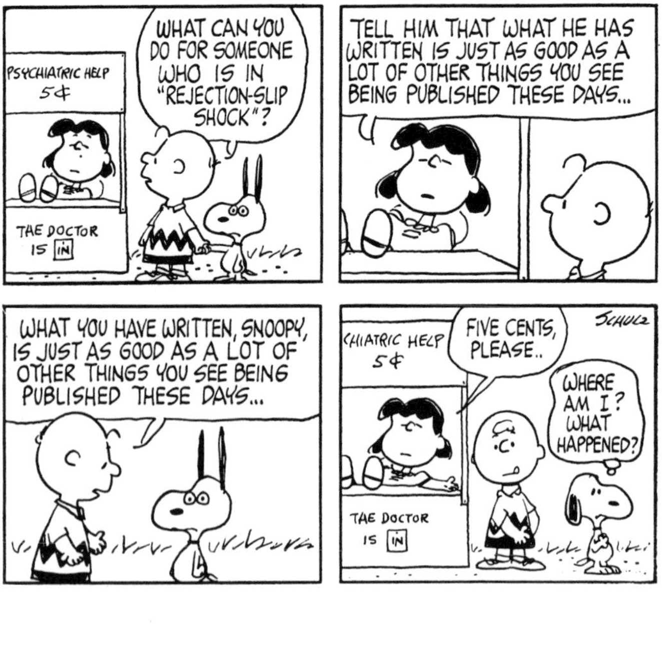
PSYCHIATRIC HELP 5¢
THE DOCTOR IS IN
WHAT CAN YOU DO FOR SOMEONE WHO IS IN "REJECTION-SLIP SHOCK"?
TELL HIM THAT WHAT HE HAS WRITTEN IS JUST AS GOOD AS A LOT OF OTHER THINGS YOU SEE BEING PUBLISHED THESE DAYS...
WHAT YOU HAVE WRITTEN, SNOOPY, IS JUST AS GOOD AS A LOT OF OTHER THINGS YOU SEE BEING PUBLISHED THESE DAYS...
SCHULZ
CHIATRIC HELP 5¢
FIVE CENTS, PLEASE..
WHERE AM I? WHAT HAPPENED?
THE DOCTOR IS IN

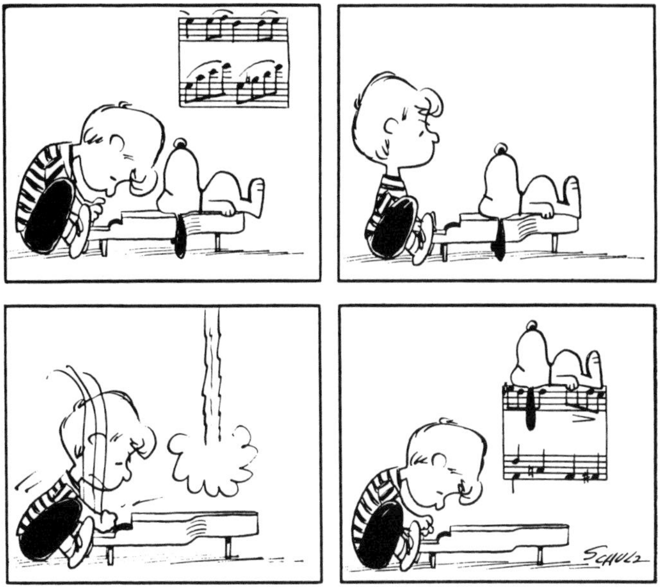
SCHULZ

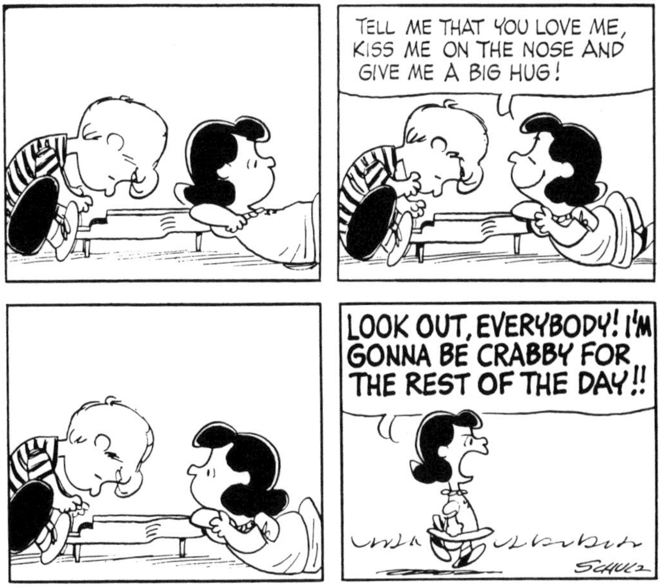
TELL ME THAT YOU LOVE ME, KISS ME ON THE NOSE AND GIVE ME A BIG HUG!
LOOK OUT, EVERYBODY! I'M GONNA BE CRABBY FOR THE REST OF THE DAY!!
SCHULZ

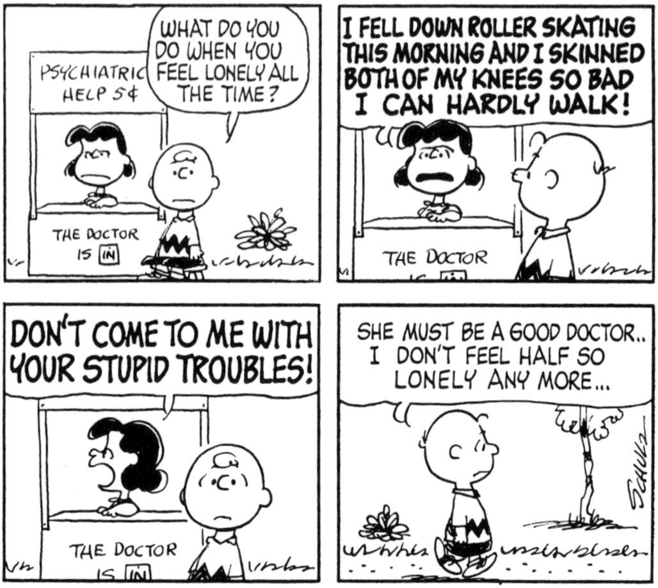
PSYCHIATRIC HELP 5¢
WHAT DO YOU DO WHEN YOU FEEL LONELY ALL THE TIME?
THE DOCTOR IS IN
I FELL DOWN ROLLER SKATING THIS MORNING AND I SKINNED BOTH OF MY KNEES SO BAD I CAN HARDLY WALK!
THE DOCTOR
DON'T COME TO ME WITH YOUR STUPID TROUBLES!
THE DOCTOR
SHE MUST BE A GOOD DOCTOR.. I DON'T FEEL HALF SO LONELY ANY MORE...
SCHULZ

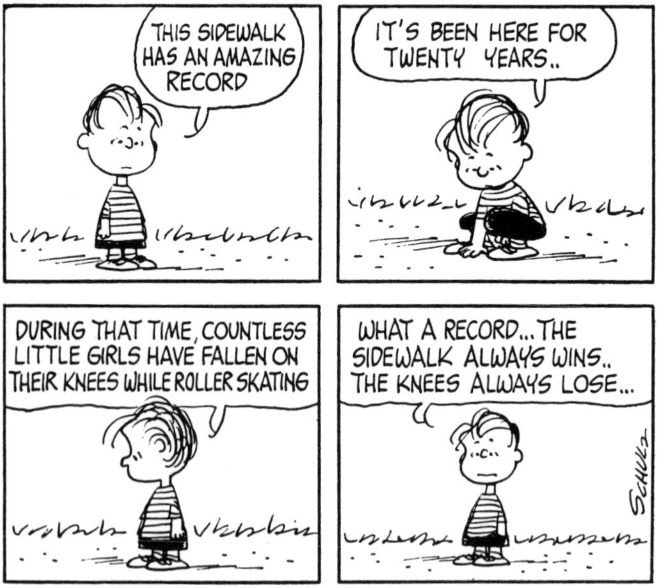
THIS SIDEWALK HAS AN AMAZING RECORD
IT'S BEEN HERE FOR TWENTY YEARS..
DURING THAT TIME, COUNTLESS LITTLE GIRLS HAVE FALLEN ON THEIR KNEES WHILE ROLLER SKATING
WHAT A RECORD... THE SIDEWALK ALWAYS WINS.. THE KNEES ALWAYS LOSE...
SCHULZ

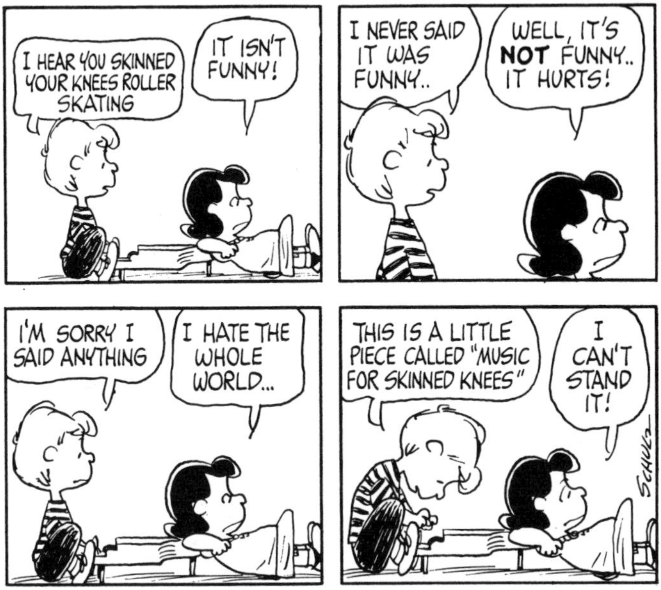
I HEAR YOU SKINNED YOUR KNEES ROLLER SKATING
IT ISN'T FUNNY!
I NEVER SAID IT WAS FUNNY..
WELL, IT'S **NOT** FUNNY.. IT HURTS!
I'M SORRY I SAID ANYTHING
I HATE THE WHOLE WORLD...
THIS IS A LITTLE PIECE CALLED "MUSIC FOR SKINNED KNEES"
I CAN'T STAND IT!
SCHULZ

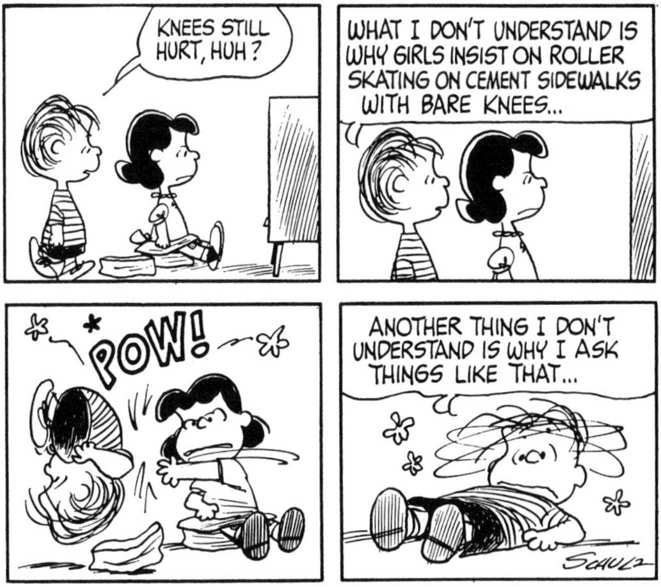
KNEES STILL HURT, HUH?
WHAT I DON'T UNDERSTAND IS WHY GIRLS INSIST ON ROLLER SKATING ON CEMENT SIDEWALKS WITH BARE KNEES...
POW!
ANOTHER THING I DON'T UNDERSTAND IS WHY I ASK THINGS LIKE THAT...
SCHULZ

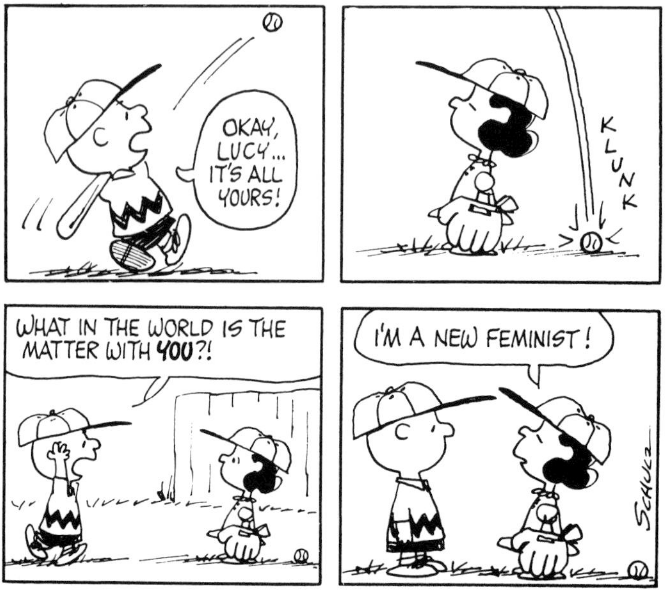
OKAY, LUCY... IT'S ALL YOURS!
KLUNK
WHAT IN THE WORLD IS THE MATTER WITH YOU?!
I'M A NEW FEMINIST!
SCHULZ

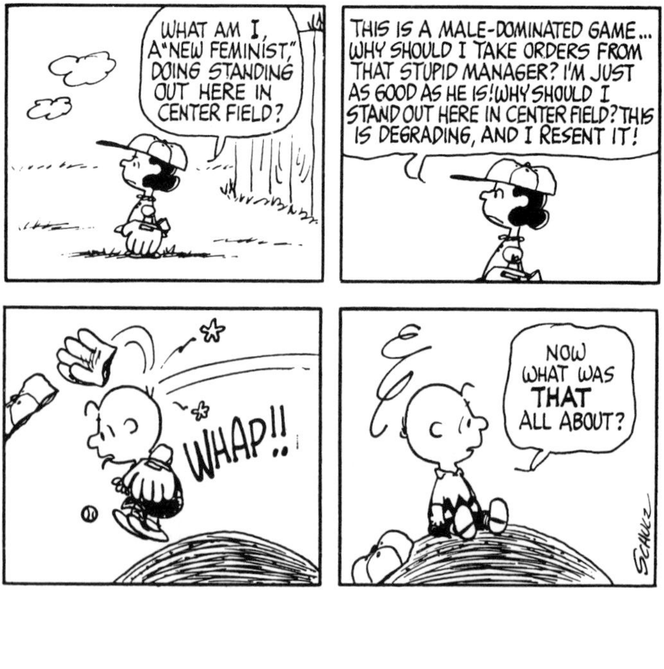
WHAT AM I, A "NEW FEMINIST," DOING STANDING OUT HERE IN CENTER FIELD?
THIS IS A MALE-DOMINATED GAME... WHY SHOULD I TAKE ORDERS FROM THAT STUPID MANAGER? I'M JUST AS GOOD AS HE IS! WHY SHOULD I STAND OUT HERE IN CENTER FIELD? THIS IS DEGRADING, AND I RESENT IT!
WHAP!!
NOW WHAT WAS THAT ALL ABOUT?
SCHULZ

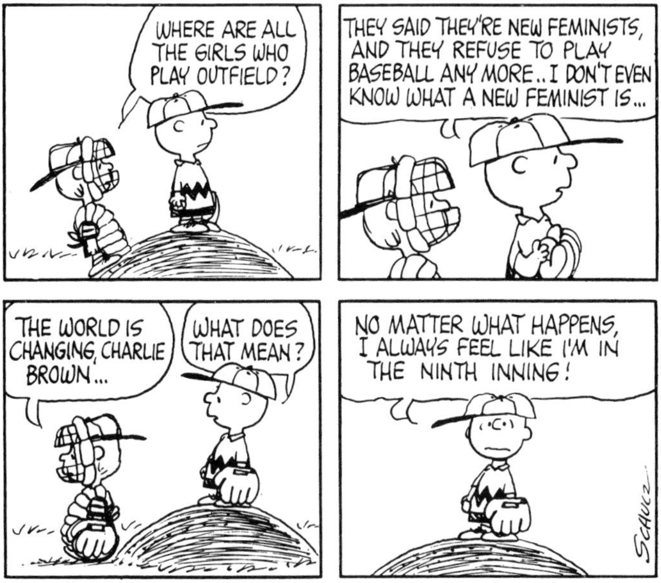
WHERE ARE ALL THE GIRLS WHO PLAY OUTFIELD?
THEY SAID THEY'RE NEW FEMINISTS, AND THEY REFUSE TO PLAY BASEBALL ANY MORE.. I DON'T EVEN KNOW WHAT A NEW FEMINIST IS...
THE WORLD IS CHANGING, CHARLIE BROWN...
WHAT DOES THAT MEAN?
NO MATTER WHAT HAPPENS, I ALWAYS FEEL LIKE I'M IN THE NINTH INNING!
SCHULZ

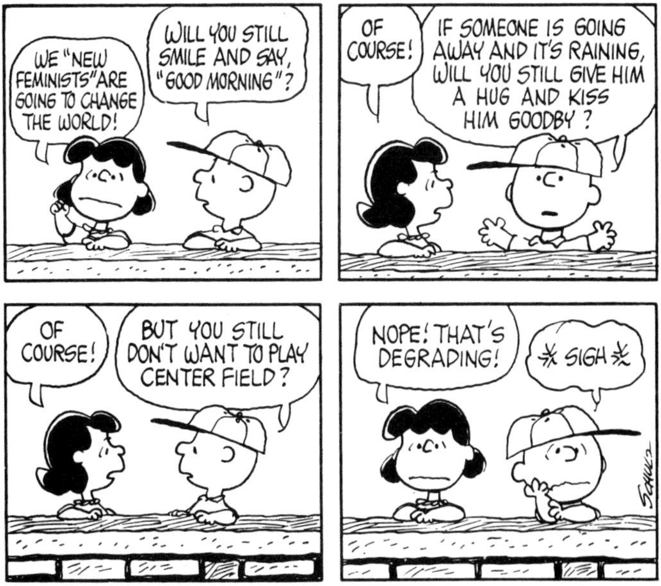
WE "NEW FEMINISTS" ARE GOING TO CHANGE THE WORLD!
WILL YOU STILL SMILE AND SAY, "GOOD MORNING"?
OF COURSE!
IF SOMEONE IS GOING AWAY AND IT'S RAINING, WILL YOU STILL GIVE HIM A HUG AND KISS HIM GOODBY?
OF COURSE!
BUT YOU STILL DON'T WANT TO PLAY CENTER FIELD?
NOPE! THAT'S DEGRADING!
SIGH
SCHULZ

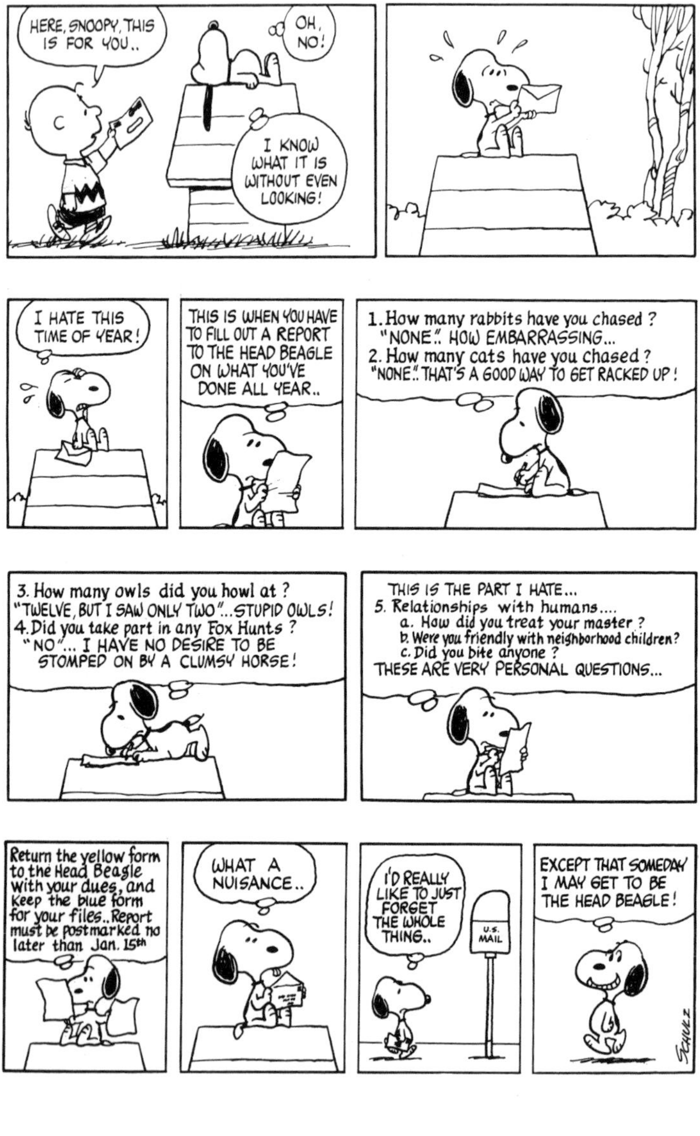
HERE, SNOOPY, THIS IS FOR YOU..
OH, NO!
I KNOW WHAT IT IS WITHOUT EVEN LOOKING!
I HATE THIS TIME OF YEAR!
THIS IS WHEN YOU HAVE TO FILL OUT A REPORT TO THE HEAD BEAGLE ON WHAT YOU'VE DONE ALL YEAR..
1. How many rabbits have you chased? "NONE".. HOW EMBARRASSING...
2. How many cats have you chased? "NONE".. THAT'S A GOOD WAY TO GET RACKED UP!
3. How many owls did you howl at? "TWELVE, BUT I SAW ONLY TWO"... STUPID OWLS!
4. Did you take part in any Fox Hunts? "NO"... I HAVE NO DESIRE TO BE STOMPED ON BY A CLUMSY HORSE!
THIS IS THE PART I HATE...
5. Relationships with humans....
a. How did you treat your master?
b. Were you friendly with neighborhood children?
c. Did you bite anyone?
THESE ARE VERY PERSONAL QUESTIONS...
Return the yellow form to the Head Beagle with your dues, and keep the blue form for your files.. Report must be postmarked no later than Jan. 15th
WHAT A NUISANCE..
I'D REALLY LIKE TO JUST FORGET THE WHOLE THING..
U.S. MAIL
EXCEPT THAT SOMEDAY I MAY GET TO BE THE HEAD BEAGLE!
SCHULZ

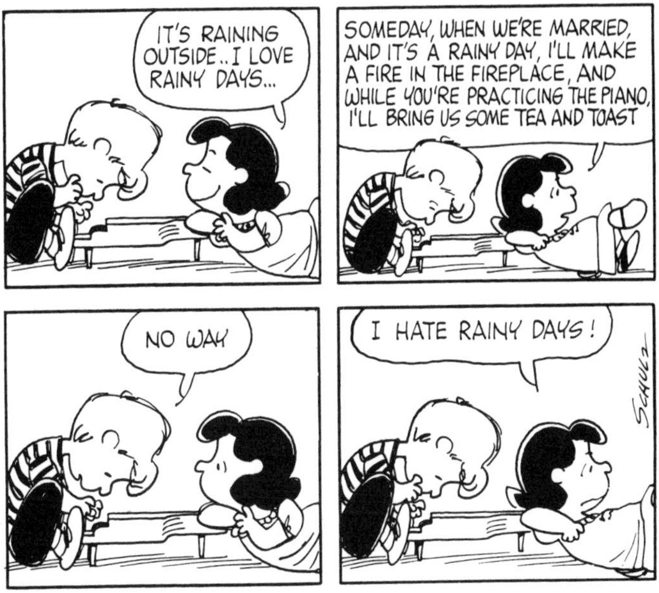
IT'S RAINING OUTSIDE.. I LOVE RAINY DAYS...
SOMEDAY, WHEN WE'RE MARRIED, AND IT'S A RAINY DAY, I'LL MAKE A FIRE IN THE FIREPLACE, AND WHILE YOU'RE PRACTICING THE PIANO, I'LL BRING US SOME TEA AND TOAST
NO WAY
I HATE RAINY DAYS!
SCHULZ

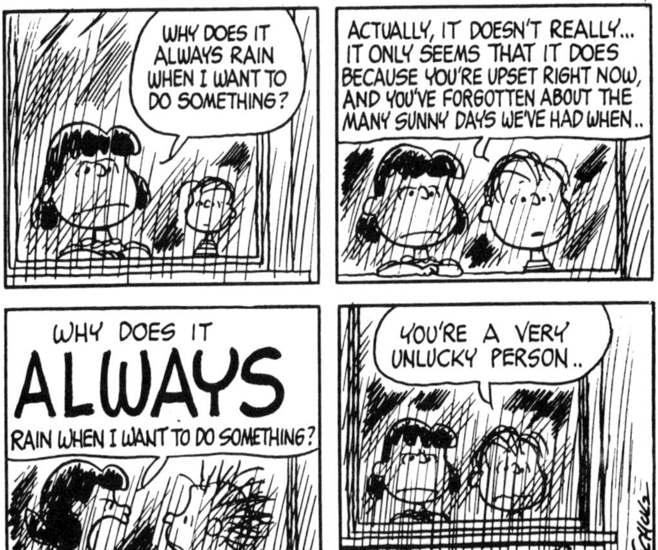
WHY DOES IT ALWAYS RAIN WHEN I WANT TO DO SOMETHING?
ACTUALLY, IT DOESN'T REALLY... IT ONLY SEEMS THAT IT DOES BECAUSE YOU'RE UPSET RIGHT NOW, AND YOU'VE FORGOTTEN ABOUT THE MANY SUNNY DAYS WE'VE HAD WHEN..
WHY DOES IT ALWAYS RAIN WHEN I WANT TO DO SOMETHING?
YOU'RE A VERY UNLUCKY PERSON..
SCHULZ

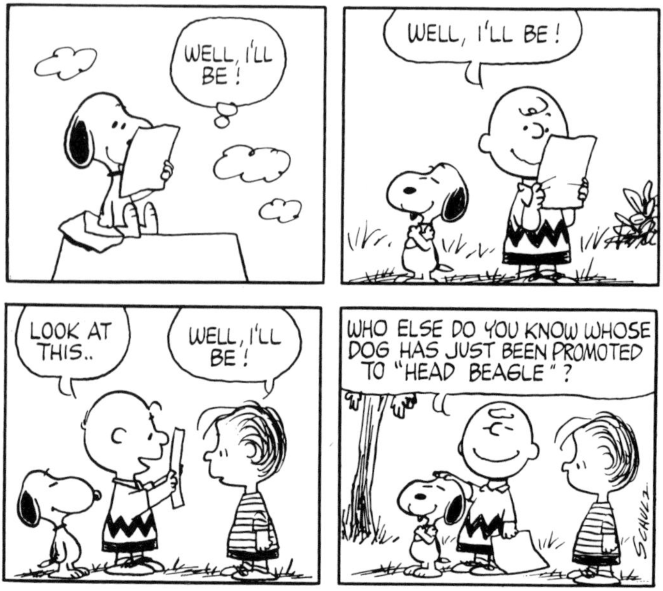
WELL, I'LL BE!
WELL, I'LL BE!
LOOK AT THIS..
WELL, I'LL BE!
WHO ELSE DO YOU KNOW WHOSE DOG HAS JUST BEEN PROMOTED TO "HEAD BEAGLE"?
SCHULZ

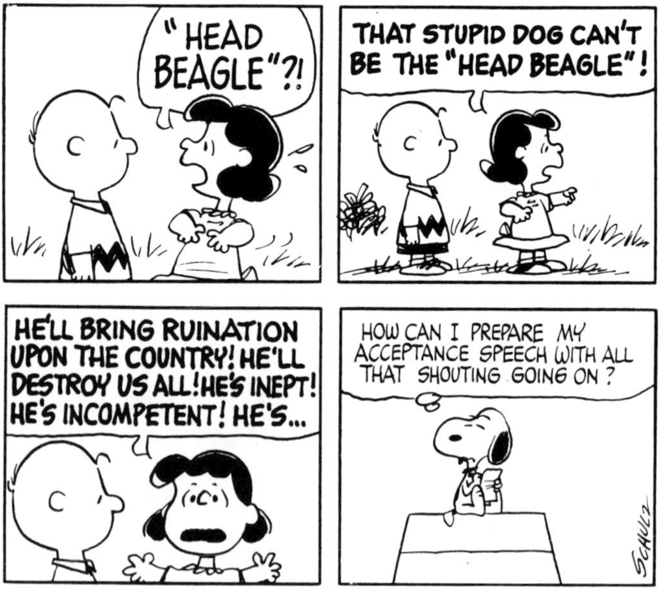
"HEAD BEAGLE"?!
THAT STUPID DOG CAN'T BE THE "HEAD BEAGLE"!
HE'LL BRING RUINATION UPON THE COUNTRY! HE'LL DESTROY US ALL! HE'S INEPT! HE'S INCOMPETENT! HE'S...
HOW CAN I PREPARE MY ACCEPTANCE SPEECH WITH ALL THAT SHOUTING GOING ON?
SCHULZ

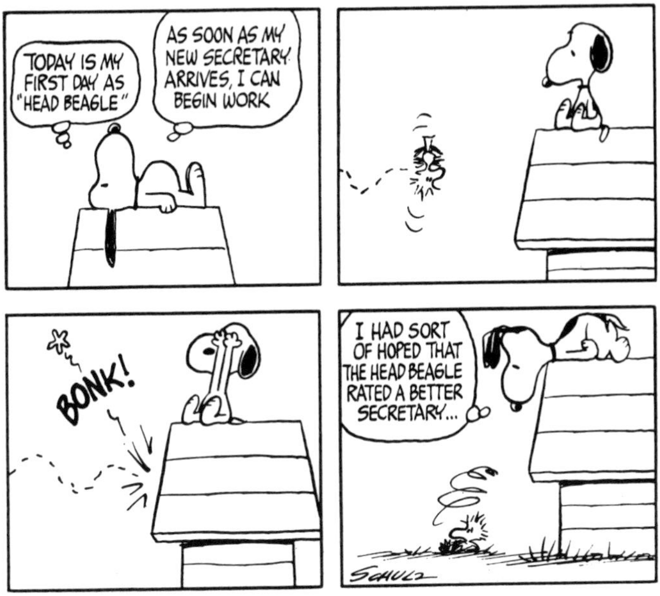
TODAY IS MY FIRST DAY AS "HEAD BEAGLE"
AS SOON AS MY NEW SECRETARY ARRIVES, I CAN BEGIN WORK
BONK!
I HAD SORT OF HOPED THAT THE HEAD BEAGLE RATED A BETTER SECRETARY...
SCHULZ

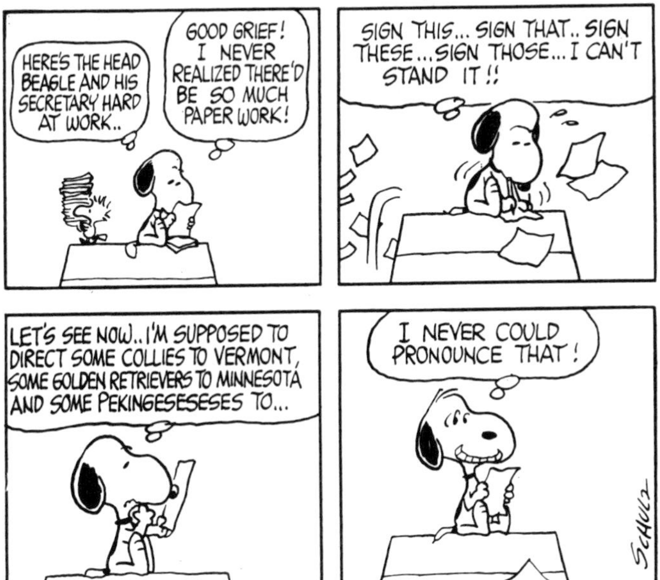
HERE'S THE HEAD BEAGLE AND HIS SECRETARY HARD AT WORK..
GOOD GRIEF! I NEVER REALIZED THERE'D BE SO MUCH PAPER WORK!
SIGN THIS... SIGN THAT.. SIGN THESE... SIGN THOSE... I CAN'T STAND IT!!
LET'S SEE NOW.. I'M SUPPOSED TO DIRECT SOME COLLIES TO VERMONT, SOME GOLDEN RETRIEVERS TO MINNESOTA AND SOME PEKINGESESESES TO...
I NEVER COULD PRONOUNCE THAT!
SCHULZ

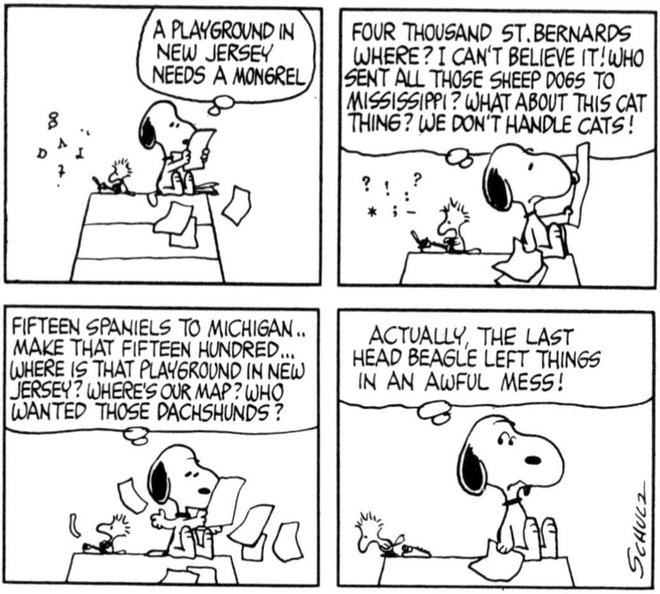
A PLAYGROUND IN NEW JERSEY NEEDS A MONGREL
FOUR THOUSAND ST. BERNARDS WHERE? I CAN'T BELIEVE IT! WHO SENT ALL THOSE SHEEP DOGS TO MISSISSIPPI? WHAT ABOUT THIS CAT THING? WE DON'T HANDLE CATS!
FIFTEEN SPANIELS TO MICHIGAN.. MAKE THAT FIFTEEN HUNDRED... WHERE IS THAT PLAYGROUND IN NEW JERSEY? WHERE'S OUR MAP? WHO WANTED THOSE DACHSHUNDS?
ACTUALLY, THE LAST HEAD BEAGLE LEFT THINGS IN AN AWFUL MESS!
SCHULZ

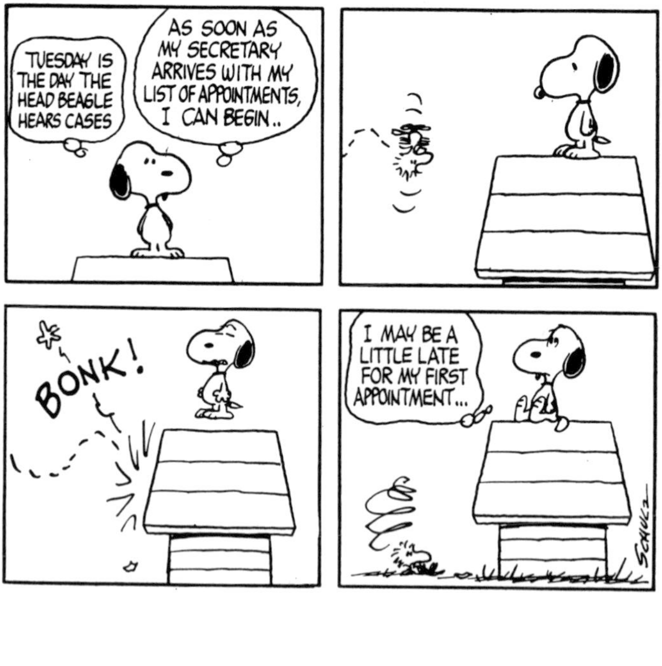
TUESDAY IS THE DAY THE HEAD BEAGLE HEARS CASES
AS SOON AS MY SECRETARY ARRIVES WITH MY LIST OF APPOINTMENTS, I CAN BEGIN..
BONK!
I MAY BE A LITTLE LATE FOR MY FIRST APPOINTMENT...
SCHULZ

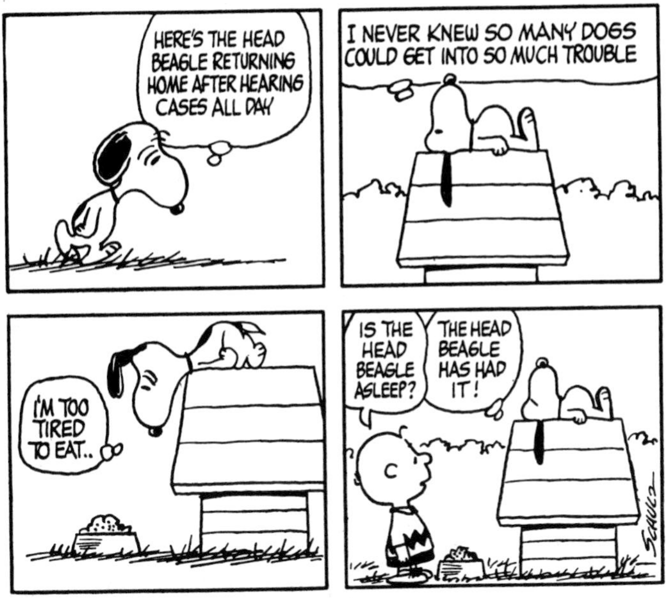
HERE'S THE HEAD BEAGLE RETURNING HOME AFTER HEARING CASES ALL DAY
I NEVER KNEW SO MANY DOGS COULD GET INTO SO MUCH TROUBLE
I'M TOO TIRED TO EAT..
IS THE HEAD BEAGLE ASLEEP?
THE HEAD BEAGLE HAS HAD IT!
SCHULZ

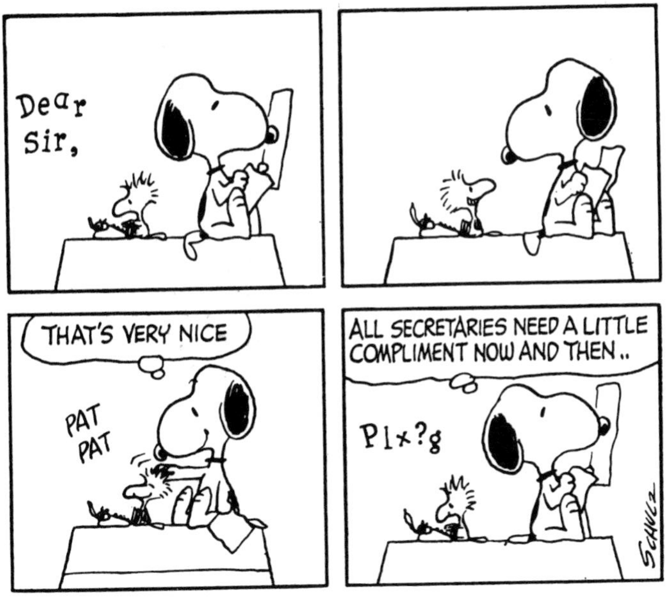
Dear Sir,
THAT'S VERY NICE
PAT PAT
ALL SECRETARIES NEED A LITTLE COMPLIMENT NOW AND THEN..
Plx?g
SCHULZ

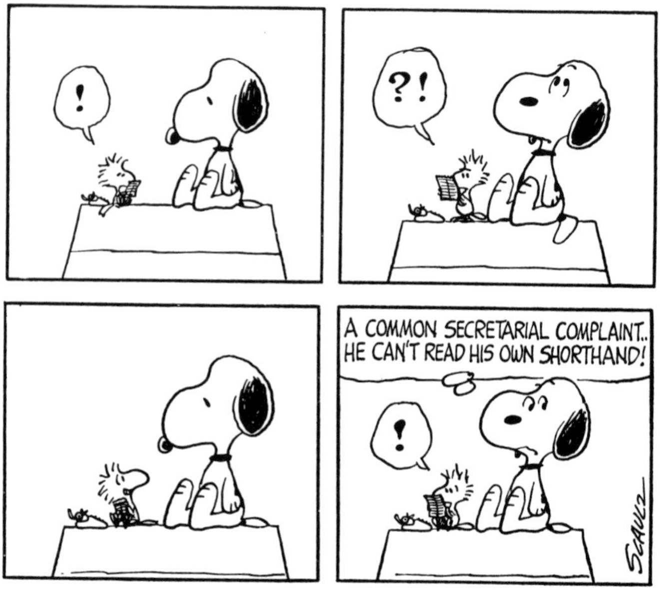
!
?!
A COMMON SECRETARIAL COMPLAINT..
HE CAN'T READ HIS OWN SHORTHAND!
!
SCHULZ

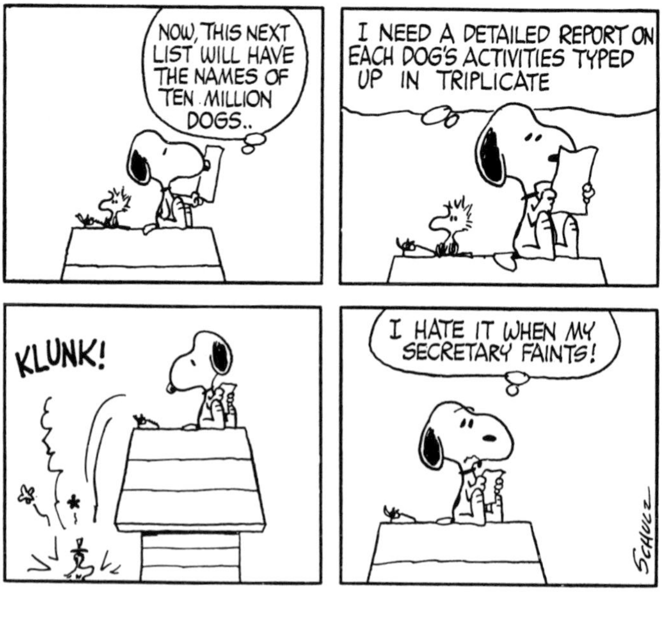
NOW, THIS NEXT LIST WILL HAVE THE NAMES OF TEN MILLION DOGS..
I NEED A DETAILED REPORT ON EACH DOG'S ACTIVITIES TYPED UP IN TRIPLICATE
KLUNK!
I HATE IT WHEN MY SECRETARY FAINTS!
SCHULZ

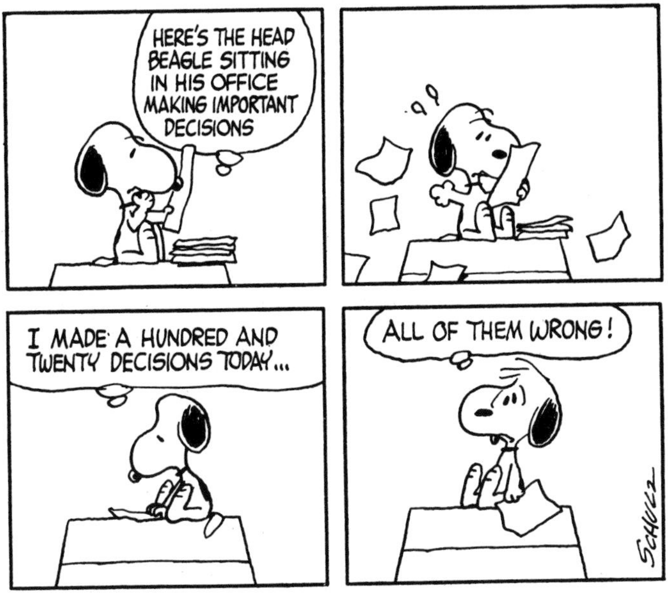
HERE'S THE HEAD BEAGLE SITTING IN HIS OFFICE MAKING IMPORTANT DECISIONS
I MADE A HUNDRED AND TWENTY DECISIONS TODAY...
ALL OF THEM WRONG!
SCHULZ

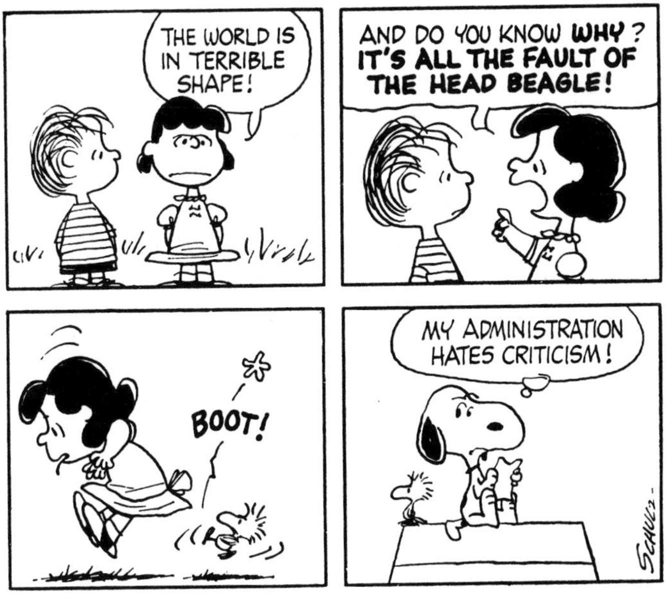
THE WORLD IS IN TERRIBLE SHAPE!
AND DO YOU KNOW **WHY**? **IT'S ALL THE FAULT OF THE HEAD BEAGLE!**
BOOT!
MY ADMINISTRATION HATES CRITICISM!
SCHULZ

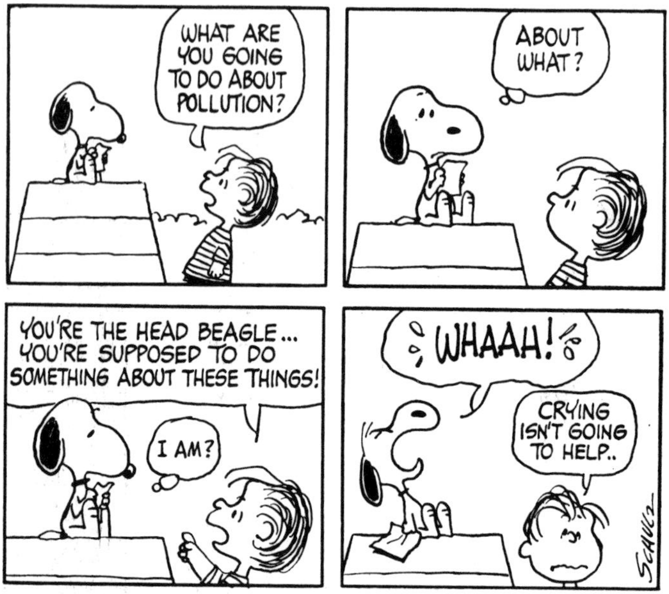
WHAT ARE YOU GOING TO DO ABOUT POLLUTION?
ABOUT WHAT?
YOU'RE THE HEAD BEAGLE... YOU'RE SUPPOSED TO DO SOMETHING ABOUT THESE THINGS!
I AM?
WHAAAH!
CRYING ISN'T GOING TO HELP..
SCHULZ

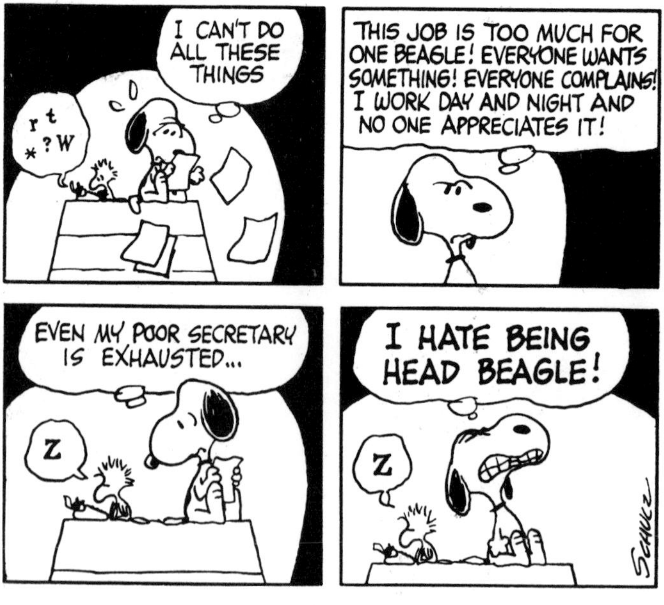
r t
* ? W
I CAN'T DO ALL THESE THINGS
THIS JOB IS TOO MUCH FOR ONE BEAGLE! EVERYONE WANTS SOMETHING! EVERYONE COMPLAINS! I WORK DAY AND NIGHT AND NO ONE APPRECIATES IT!
EVEN MY POOR SECRETARY IS EXHAUSTED...
Z
I HATE BEING HEAD BEAGLE!
Z
SCHULZ

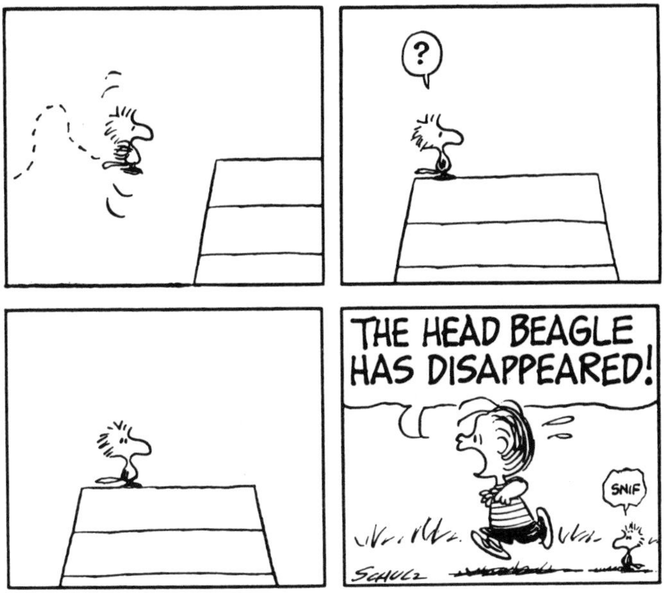
?
THE HEAD BEAGLE HAS DISAPPEARED!
SNIF
SCHULZ

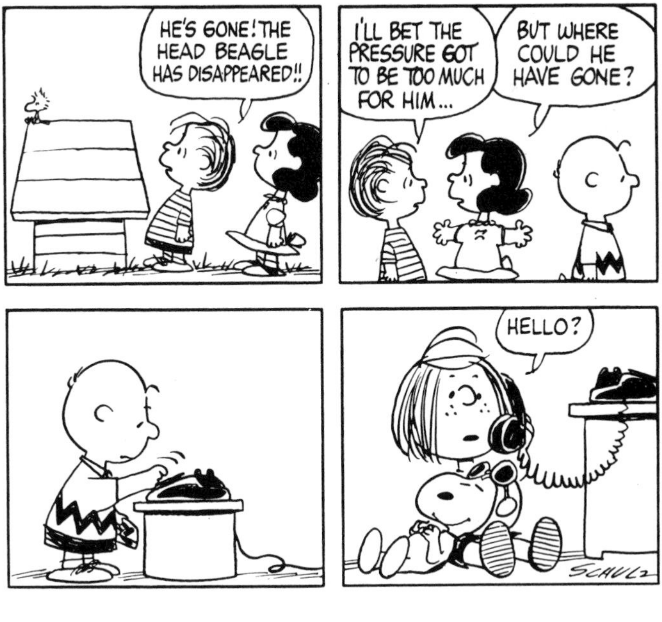
HE'S GONE! THE HEAD BEAGLE HAS DISAPPEARED!!
I'LL BET THE PRESSURE GOT TO BE TOO MUCH FOR HIM...
BUT WHERE COULD HE HAVE GONE?
HELLO?
SCHULZ

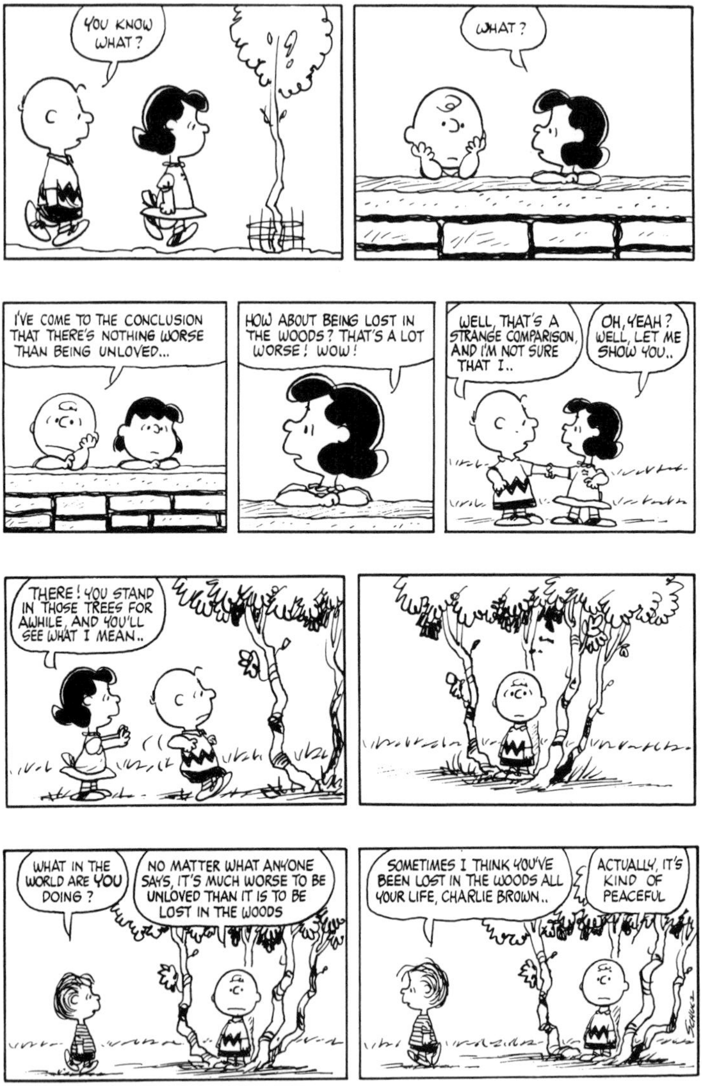
YOU KNOW WHAT?
WHAT?
I'VE COME TO THE CONCLUSION THAT THERE'S NOTHING WORSE THAN BEING UNLOVED...
HOW ABOUT BEING LOST IN THE WOODS? THAT'S A LOT WORSE! WOW!
WELL, THAT'S A STRANGE COMPARISON, AND I'M NOT SURE THAT I..
OH, YEAH? WELL, LET ME SHOW YOU..
THERE! YOU STAND IN THOSE TREES FOR AWHILE, AND YOU'LL SEE WHAT I MEAN..
WHAT IN THE WORLD ARE YOU DOING?
NO MATTER WHAT ANYONE SAYS, IT'S MUCH WORSE TO BE UNLOVED THAN IT IS TO BE LOST IN THE WOODS
SOMETIMES I THINK YOU'VE BEEN LOST IN THE WOODS ALL YOUR LIFE, CHARLIE BROWN..
ACTUALLY, IT'S KIND OF PEACEFUL
SCHULZ

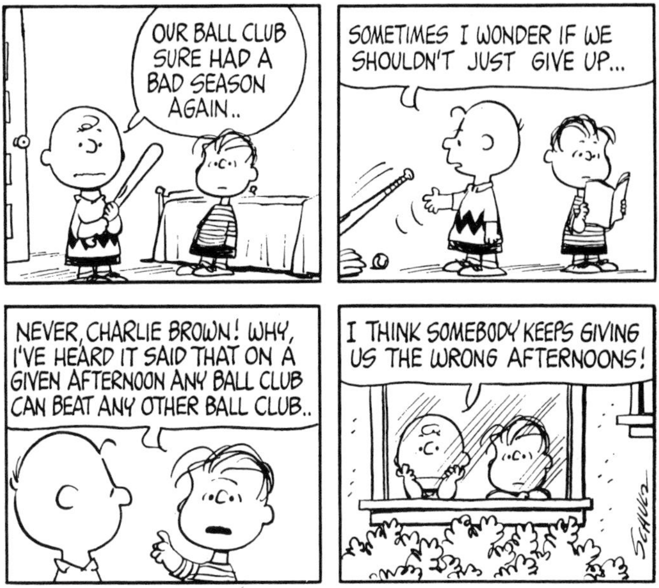
OUR BALL CLUB SURE HAD A BAD SEASON AGAIN..
SOMETIMES I WONDER IF WE SHOULDN'T JUST GIVE UP...
NEVER, CHARLIE BROWN! WHY, I'VE HEARD IT SAID THAT ON A GIVEN AFTERNOON ANY BALL CLUB CAN BEAT ANY OTHER BALL CLUB..
I THINK SOMEBODY KEEPS GIVING US THE WRONG AFTERNOONS!
SCHULZ

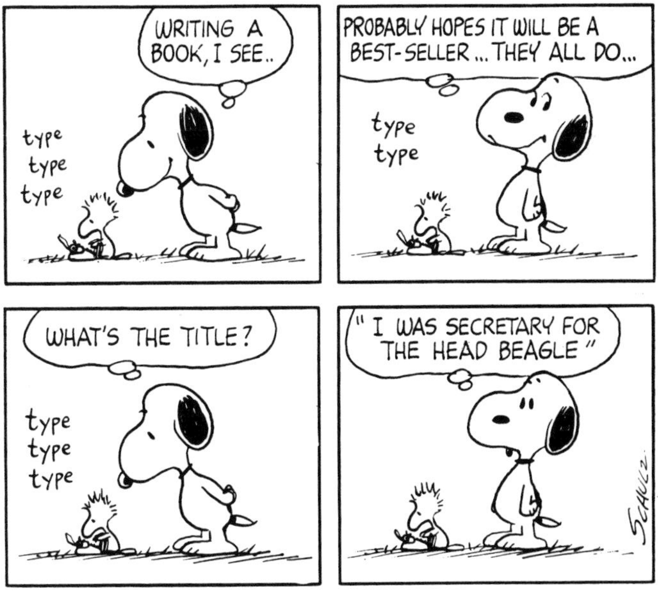
WRITING A BOOK, I SEE..
type type type
PROBABLY HOPES IT WILL BE A BEST-SELLER ... THEY ALL DO...
type type
WHAT'S THE TITLE?
type type type
" I WAS SECRETARY FOR THE HEAD BEAGLE "
SCHULZ

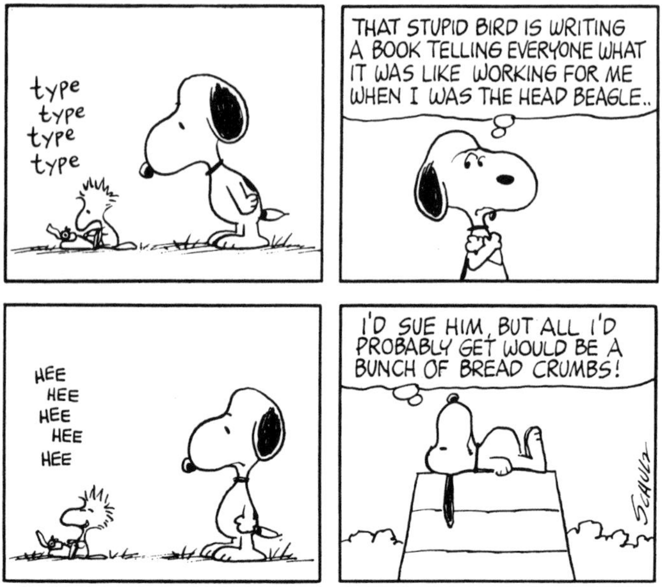
type
type
type
type
THAT STUPID BIRD IS WRITING A BOOK TELLING EVERYONE WHAT IT WAS LIKE WORKING FOR ME WHEN I WAS THE HEAD BEAGLE..
HEE
HEE
HEE
HEE
HEE
I'D SUE HIM, BUT ALL I'D PROBABLY GET WOULD BE A BUNCH OF BREAD CRUMBS!
SCHULZ

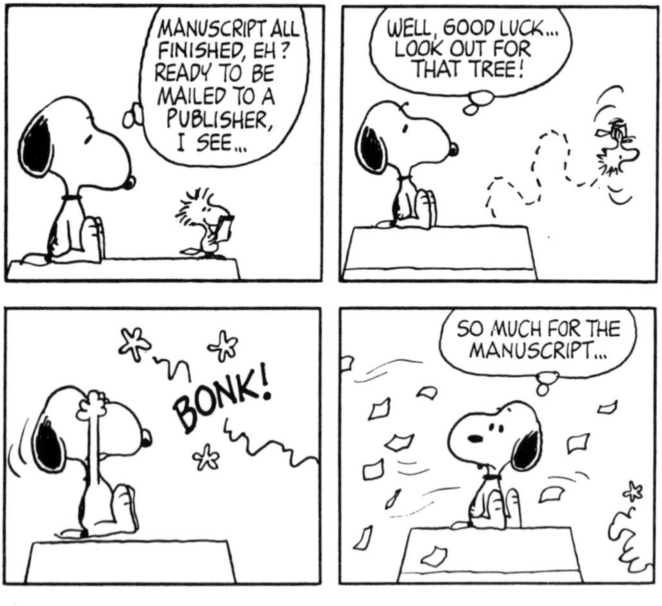
MANUSCRIPT ALL FINISHED, EH? READY TO BE MAILED TO A PUBLISHER, I SEE...
WELL, GOOD LUCK... LOOK OUT FOR THAT TREE!
BONK!
SO MUCH FOR THE MANUSCRIPT...

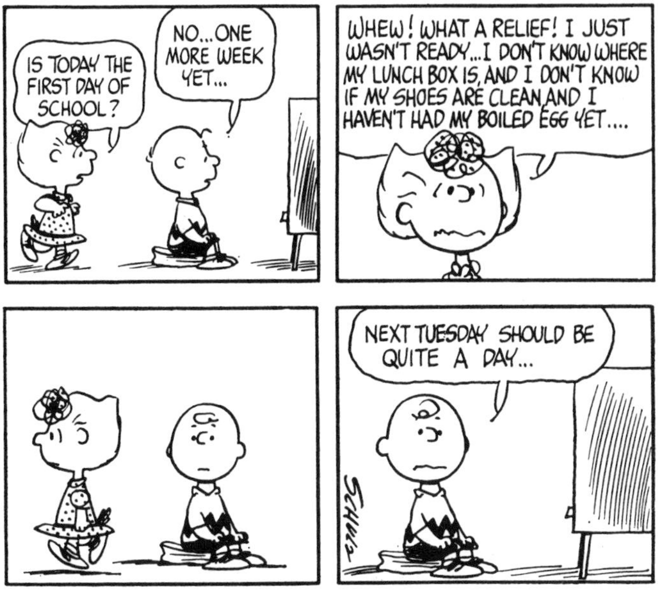
IS TODAY THE FIRST DAY OF SCHOOL?
NO...ONE MORE WEEK YET...
WHEW! WHAT A RELIEF! I JUST WASN'T READY...I DON'T KNOW WHERE MY LUNCH BOX IS, AND I DON'T KNOW IF MY SHOES ARE CLEAN AND I HAVEN'T HAD MY BOILED EGG YET....
NEXT TUESDAY SHOULD BE QUITE A DAY...
SCHULZ

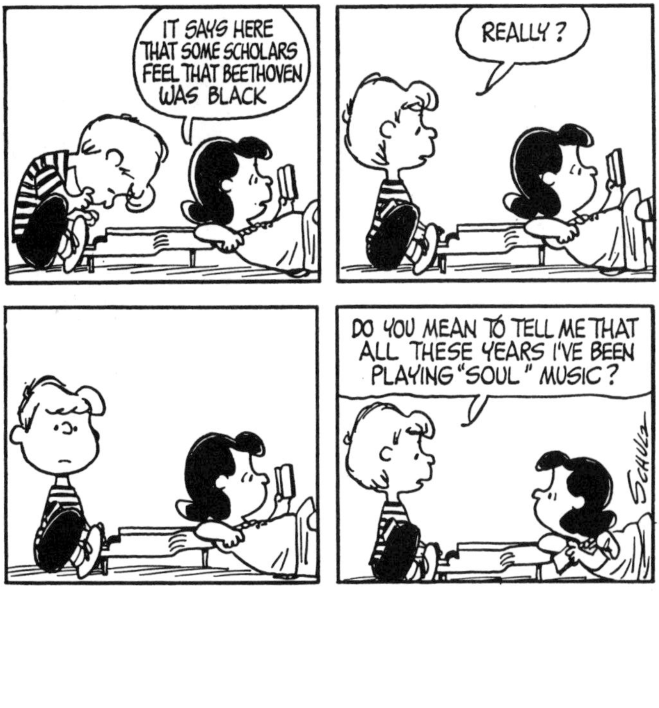
IT SAYS HERE THAT SOME SCHOLARS FEEL THAT BEETHOVEN WAS BLACK
REALLY?
DO YOU MEAN TO TELL ME THAT ALL THESE YEARS I'VE BEEN PLAYING "SOUL" MUSIC?
SCHULZ

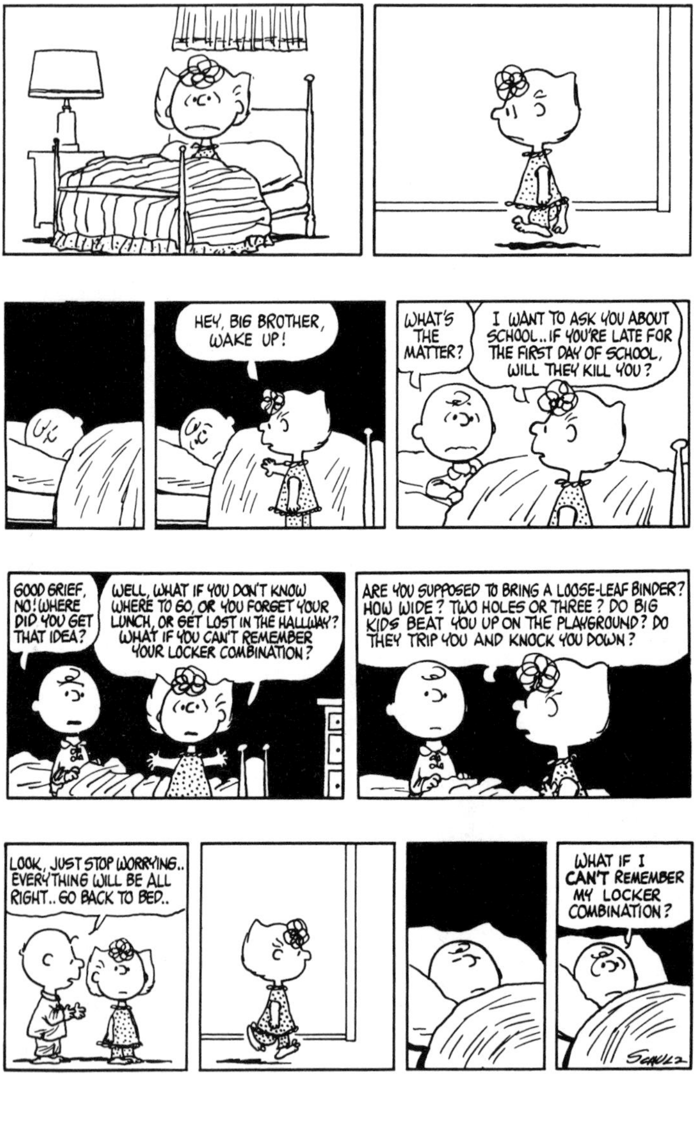
HEY, BIG BROTHER, WAKE UP!
WHAT'S THE MATTER?
I WANT TO ASK YOU ABOUT SCHOOL.. IF YOU'RE LATE FOR THE FIRST DAY OF SCHOOL, WILL THEY KILL YOU?
GOOD GRIEF, NO! WHERE DID YOU GET THAT IDEA?
WELL, WHAT IF YOU DON'T KNOW WHERE TO GO, OR YOU FORGET YOUR LUNCH, OR GET LOST IN THE HALLWAY? WHAT IF YOU CAN'T REMEMBER YOUR LOCKER COMBINATION?
ARE YOU SUPPOSED TO BRING A LOOSE-LEAF BINDER? HOW WIDE? TWO HOLES OR THREE? DO BIG KIDS BEAT YOU UP ON THE PLAYGROUND? DO THEY TRIP YOU AND KNOCK YOU DOWN?
LOOK, JUST STOP WORRYING.. EVERYTHING WILL BE ALL RIGHT.. GO BACK TO BED..
WHAT IF I **CAN'T** REMEMBER MY LOCKER COMBINATION?
SCHULZ

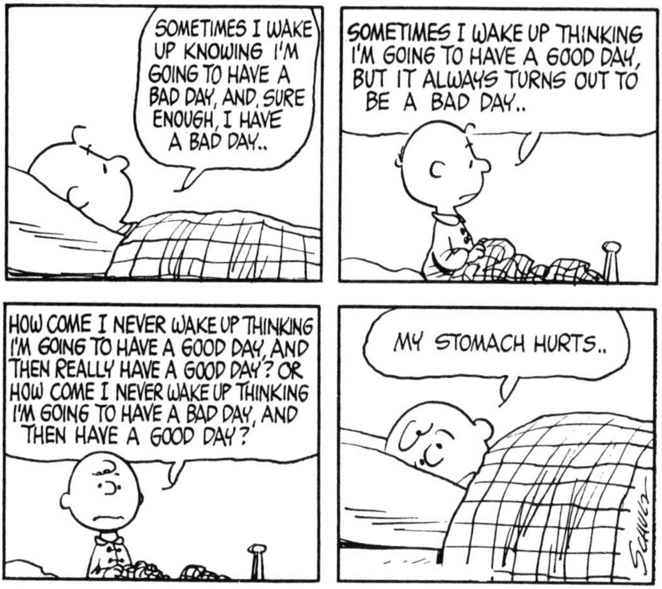
SOMETIMES I WAKE UP KNOWING I'M GOING TO HAVE A BAD DAY, AND, SURE ENOUGH, I HAVE A BAD DAY..
SOMETIMES I WAKE UP THINKING I'M GOING TO HAVE A GOOD DAY, BUT IT ALWAYS TURNS OUT TO BE A BAD DAY..
HOW COME I NEVER WAKE UP THINKING I'M GOING TO HAVE A GOOD DAY, AND THEN REALLY HAVE A GOOD DAY? OR HOW COME I NEVER WAKE UP THINKING I'M GOING TO HAVE A BAD DAY, AND THEN HAVE A GOOD DAY?
MY STOMACH HURTS..
SCHULZ

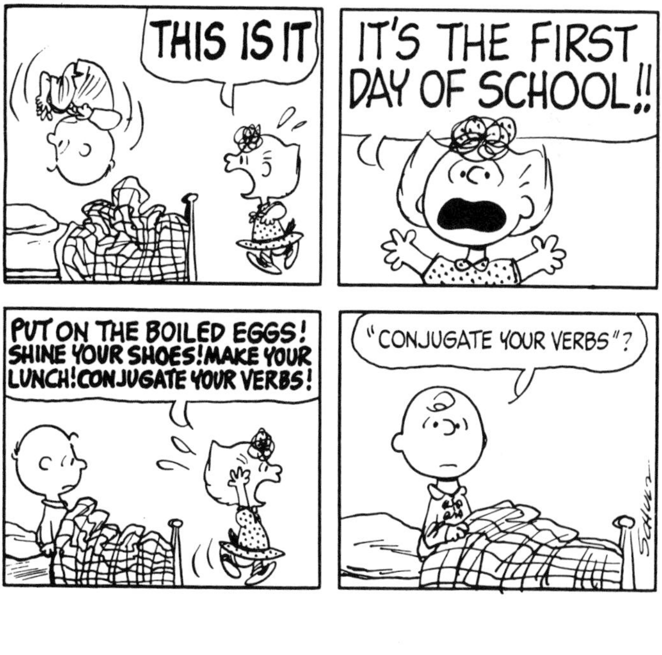
THIS IS IT
IT'S THE FIRST DAY OF SCHOOL!!
PUT ON THE BOILED EGGS! SHINE YOUR SHOES! MAKE YOUR LUNCH! CONJUGATE YOUR VERBS!
"CONJUGATE YOUR VERBS"?
SCHULZ

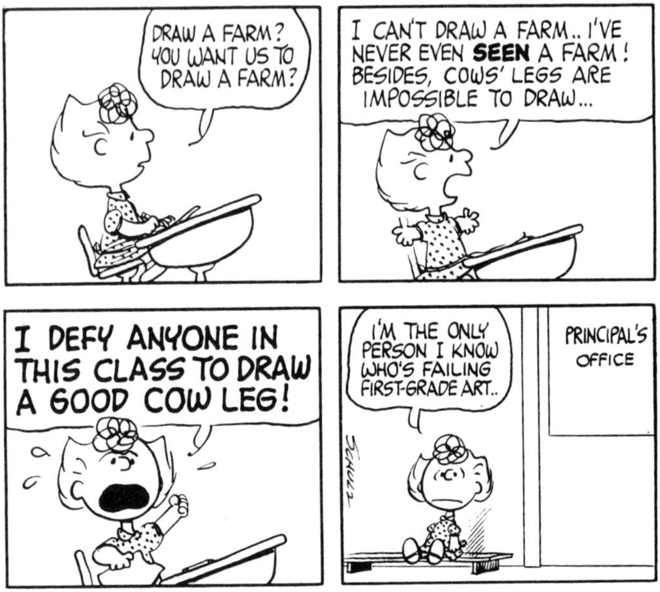
DRAW A FARM? YOU WANT US TO DRAW A FARM?
I CAN'T DRAW A FARM.. I'VE NEVER EVEN **SEEN** A FARM! BESIDES, COWS' LEGS ARE IMPOSSIBLE TO DRAW...
I DEFY ANYONE IN THIS CLASS TO DRAW A GOOD COW LEG!
I'M THE ONLY PERSON I KNOW WHO'S FAILING FIRST-GRADE ART..
PRINCIPAL'S OFFICE

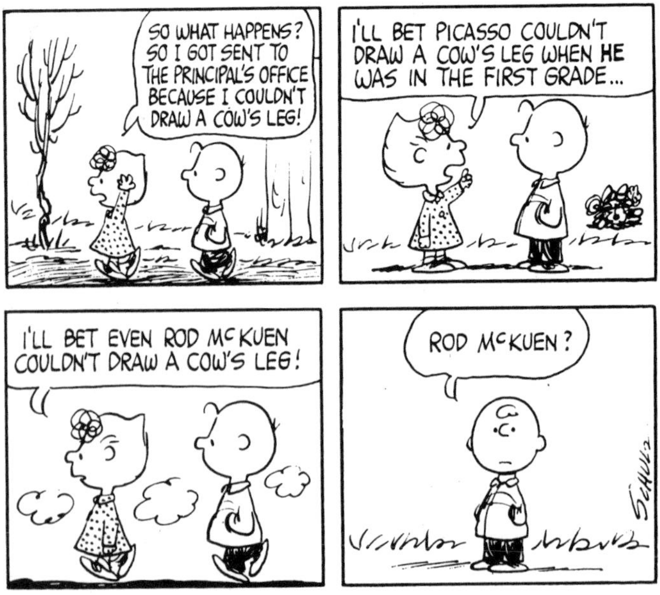
SO WHAT HAPPENS? SO I GOT SENT TO THE PRINCIPAL'S OFFICE BECAUSE I COULDN'T DRAW A COW'S LEG!
I'LL BET PICASSO COULDN'T DRAW A COW'S LEG WHEN **HE** WAS IN THE FIRST GRADE...
I'LL BET EVEN ROD McKUEN COULDN'T DRAW A COW'S LEG!
ROD McKUEN?

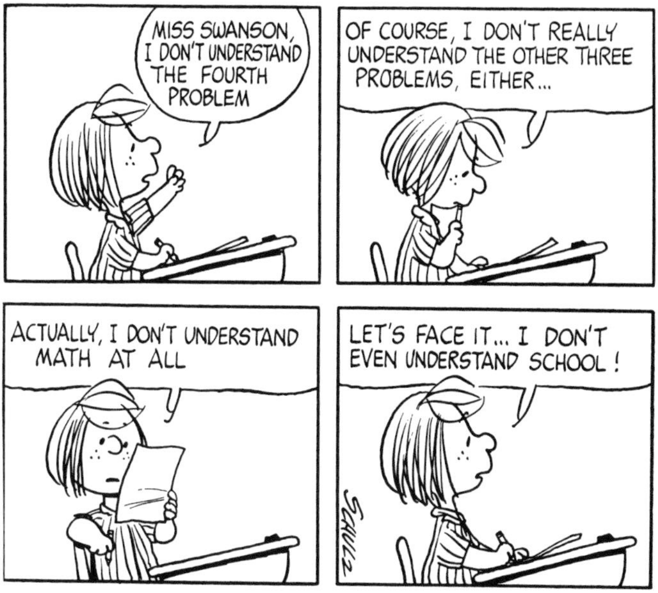
MISS SWANSON, I DON'T UNDERSTAND THE FOURTH PROBLEM
OF COURSE, I DON'T REALLY UNDERSTAND THE OTHER THREE PROBLEMS, EITHER...
ACTUALLY, I DON'T UNDERSTAND MATH AT ALL
LET'S FACE IT... I DON'T EVEN UNDERSTAND SCHOOL!
SCHULZ

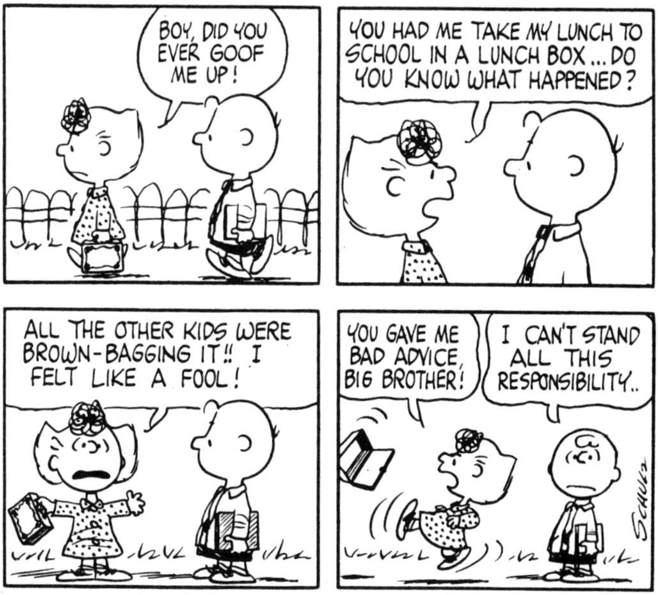
BOY, DID YOU EVER GOOF ME UP!
YOU HAD ME TAKE MY LUNCH TO SCHOOL IN A LUNCH BOX... DO YOU KNOW WHAT HAPPENED?
ALL THE OTHER KIDS WERE BROWN-BAGGING IT!! I FELT LIKE A FOOL!
YOU GAVE ME BAD ADVICE, BIG BROTHER!
I CAN'T STAND ALL THIS RESPONSIBILITY..
SCHULZ

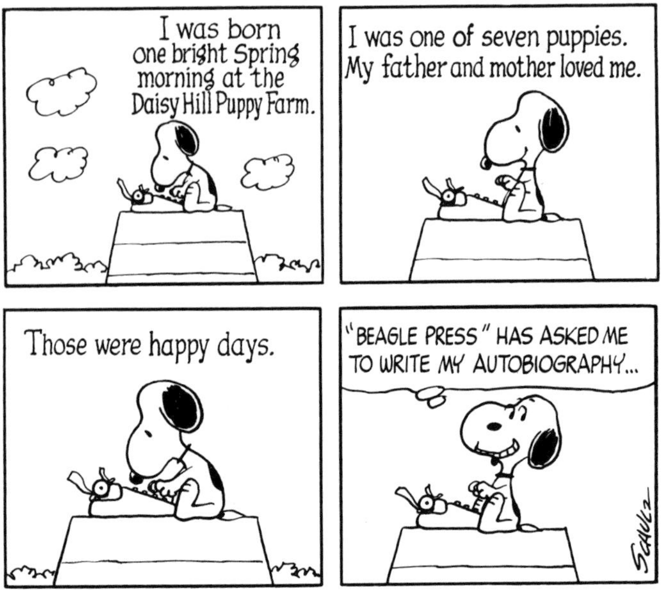
I was born one bright Spring morning at the Daisy Hill Puppy Farm.
I was one of seven puppies. My father and mother loved me.
Those were happy days.
"BEAGLE PRESS" HAS ASKED ME TO WRITE MY AUTOBIOGRAPHY...
SCHULZ

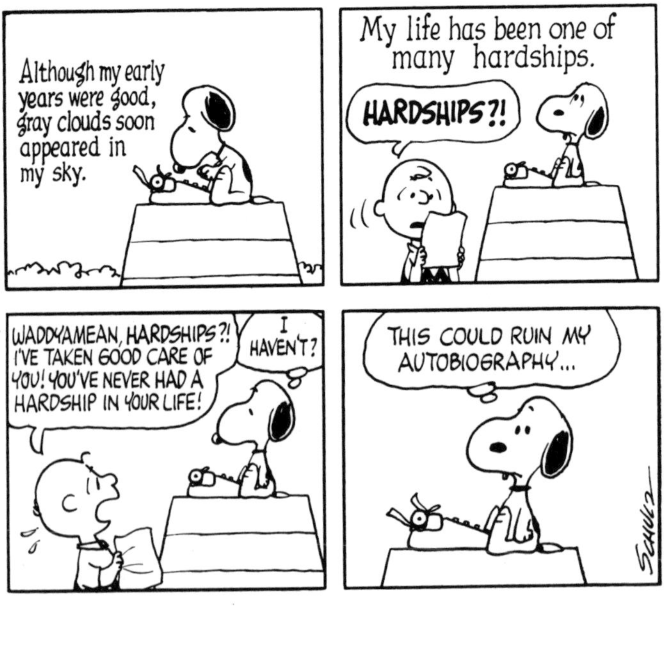
Although my early years were good, gray clouds soon appeared in my sky.
My life has been one of many hardships.
HARDSHIPS?!
WADDYAMEAN, HARDSHIPS?! I'VE TAKEN GOOD CARE OF YOU! YOU'VE NEVER HAD A HARDSHIP IN YOUR LIFE!
I HAVEN'T?
THIS COULD RUIN MY AUTOBIOGRAPHY...
SCHULZ

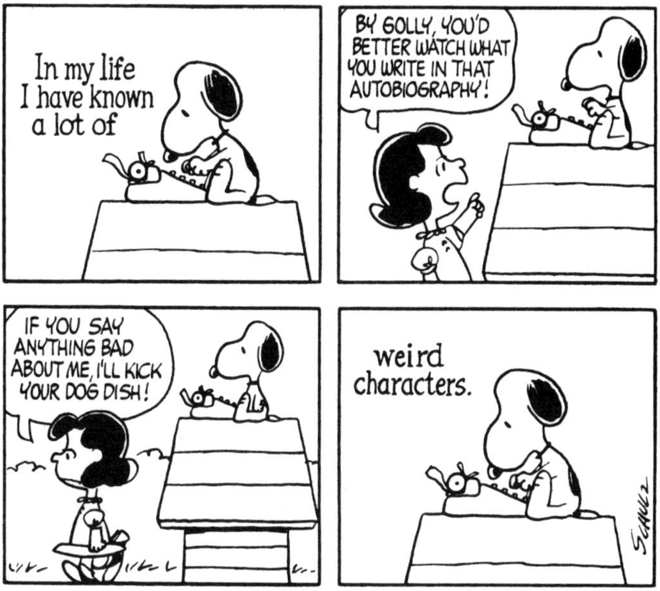
In my life I have known a lot of
BY GOLLY, YOU'D BETTER WATCH WHAT YOU WRITE IN THAT AUTOBIOGRAPHY!
IF YOU SAY ANYTHING BAD ABOUT ME, I'LL KICK YOUR DOG DISH!
weird characters.
SCHULZ

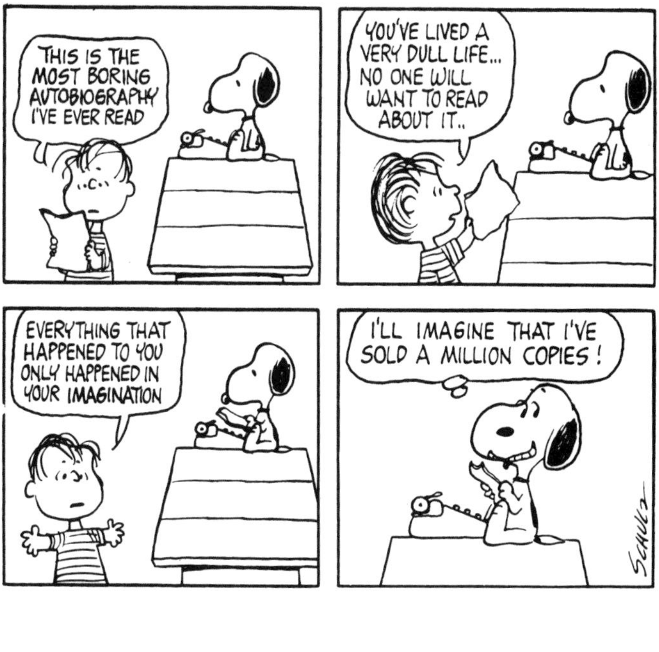
THIS IS THE MOST BORING AUTOBIOGRAPHY I'VE EVER READ
YOU'VE LIVED A VERY DULL LIFE... NO ONE WILL WANT TO READ ABOUT IT..
EVERYTHING THAT HAPPENED TO YOU ONLY HAPPENED IN YOUR IMAGINATION
I'LL IMAGINE THAT I'VE SOLD A MILLION COPIES!
SCHULZ

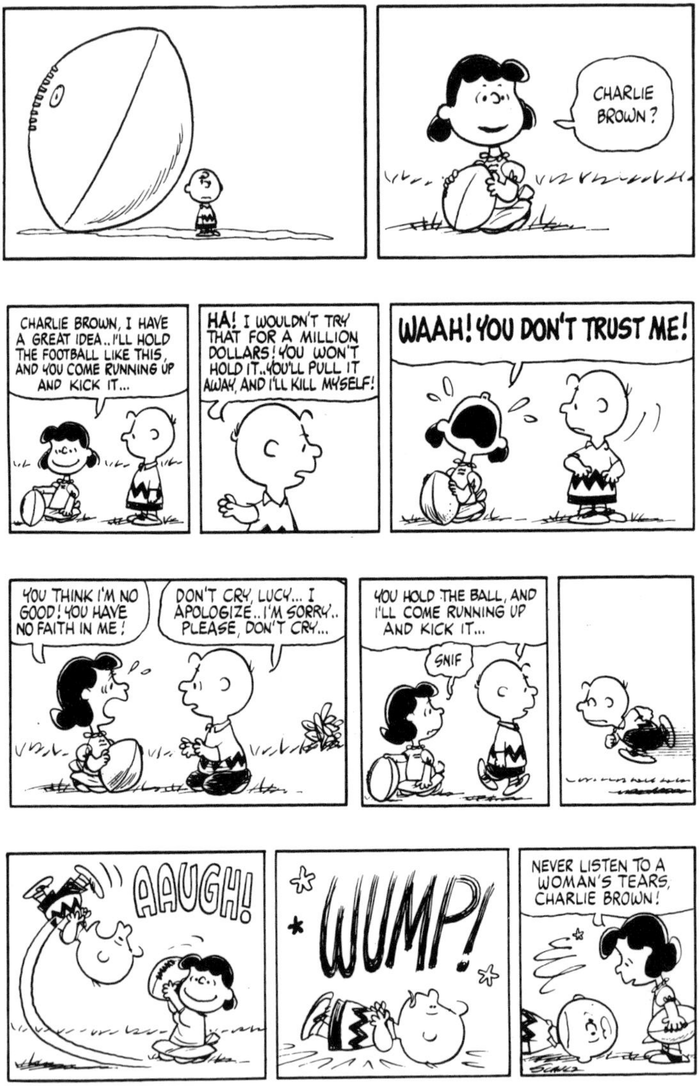

CHARLIE BROWN ?
CHARLIE BROWN, I HAVE A GREAT IDEA.. I'LL HOLD THE FOOTBALL LIKE THIS, AND YOU COME RUNNING UP AND KICK IT...
HA! I WOULDN'T TRY THAT FOR A MILLION DOLLARS! YOU WON'T HOLD IT..YOU'LL PULL IT AWAY, AND I'LL KILL MYSELF!
WAAH! YOU DON'T TRUST ME!
YOU THINK I'M NO GOOD! YOU HAVE NO FAITH IN ME!
DON'T CRY, LUCY... I APOLOGIZE.. I'M SORRY.. PLEASE, DON'T CRY...
YOU HOLD THE BALL, AND I'LL COME RUNNING UP AND KICK IT...
SNIF
AAUGH!
WUMP!
NEVER LISTEN TO A WOMAN'S TEARS, CHARLIE BROWN!

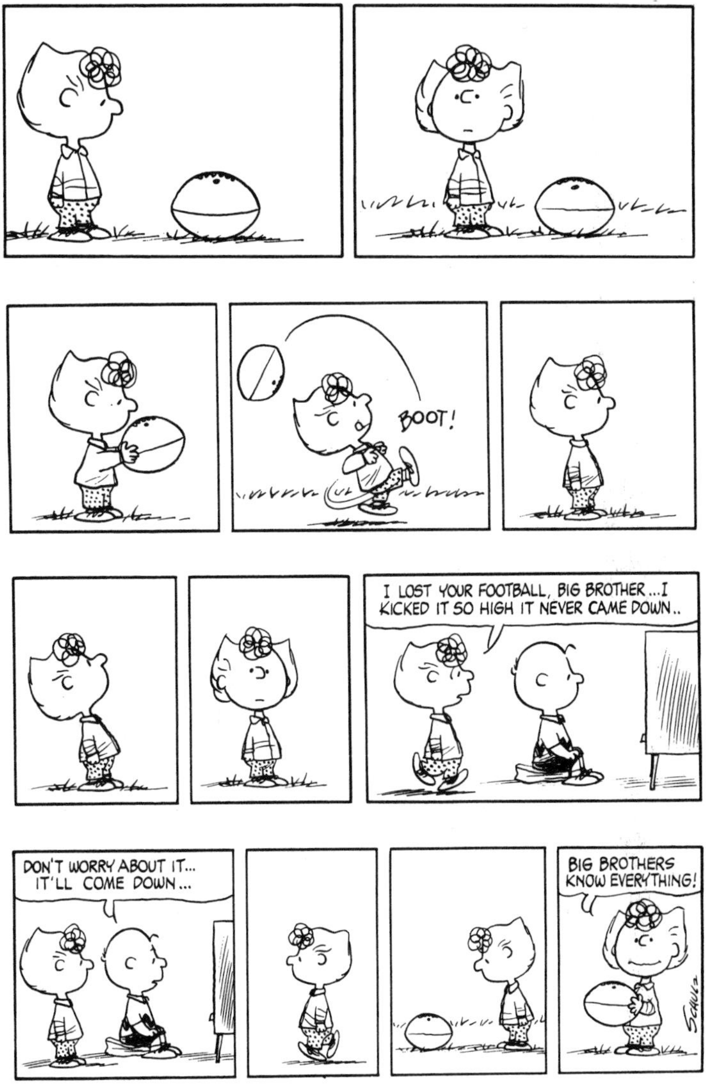
BOOT!
I LOST YOUR FOOTBALL, BIG BROTHER...I KICKED IT SO HIGH IT NEVER CAME DOWN..
DON'T WORRY ABOUT IT... IT'LL COME DOWN...
BIG BROTHERS KNOW EVERYTHING!
SCHULZ

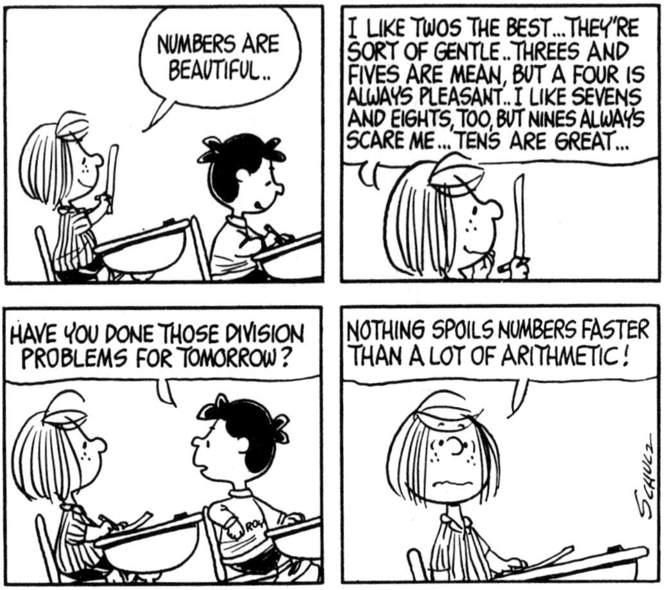
NUMBERS ARE BEAUTIFUL..
I LIKE TWOS THE BEST...THEY'RE SORT OF GENTLE..THREES AND FIVES ARE MEAN, BUT A FOUR IS ALWAYS PLEASANT..I LIKE SEVENS AND EIGHTS, TOO, BUT NINES ALWAYS SCARE ME...TENS ARE GREAT...
HAVE YOU DONE THOSE DIVISION PROBLEMS FOR TOMORROW?
NOTHING SPOILS NUMBERS FASTER THAN A LOT OF ARITHMETIC!
SCHULZ

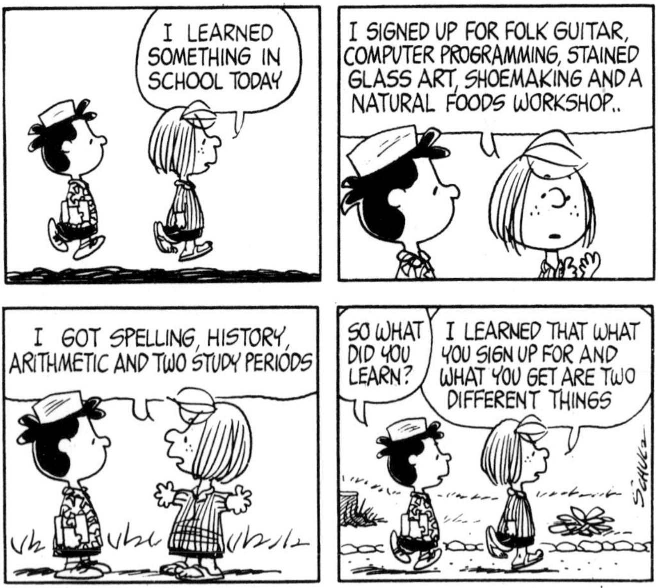
I LEARNED SOMETHING IN SCHOOL TODAY
I SIGNED UP FOR FOLK GUITAR, COMPUTER PROGRAMMING, STAINED GLASS ART, SHOEMAKING AND A NATURAL FOODS WORKSHOP..
I GOT SPELLING, HISTORY, ARITHMETIC AND TWO STUDY PERIODS
SO WHAT DID YOU LEARN?
I LEARNED THAT WHAT YOU SIGN UP FOR AND WHAT YOU GET ARE TWO DIFFERENT THINGS
SCHULZ

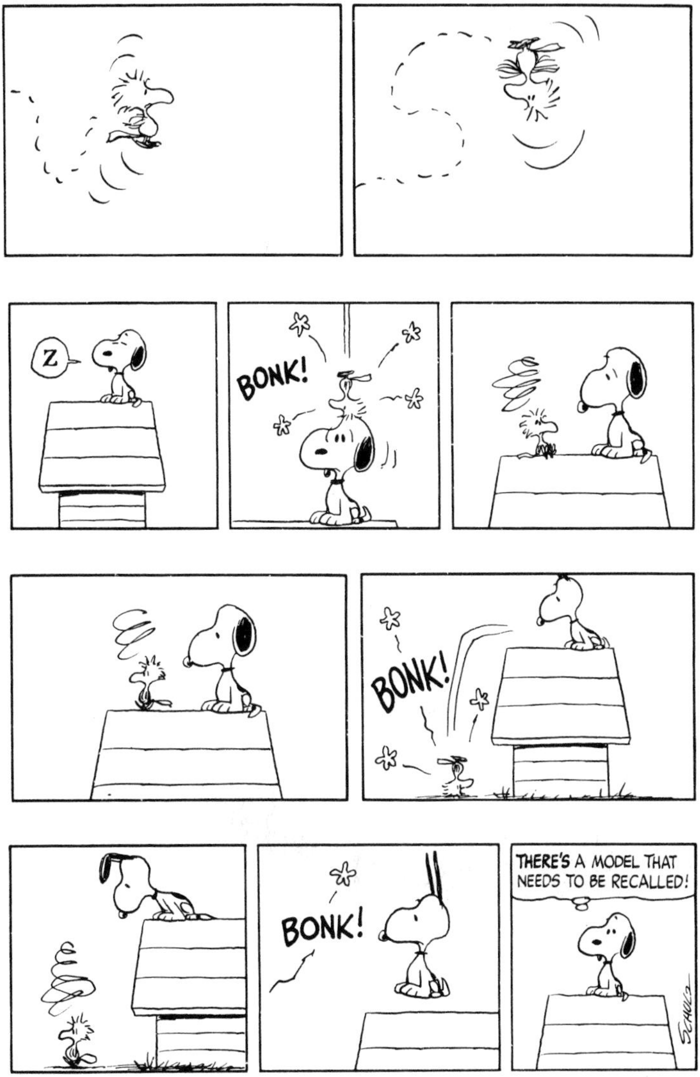
Z
BONK!
BONK!
BONK!
THERE'S A MODEL THAT NEEDS TO BE RECALLED!
SCHULZ

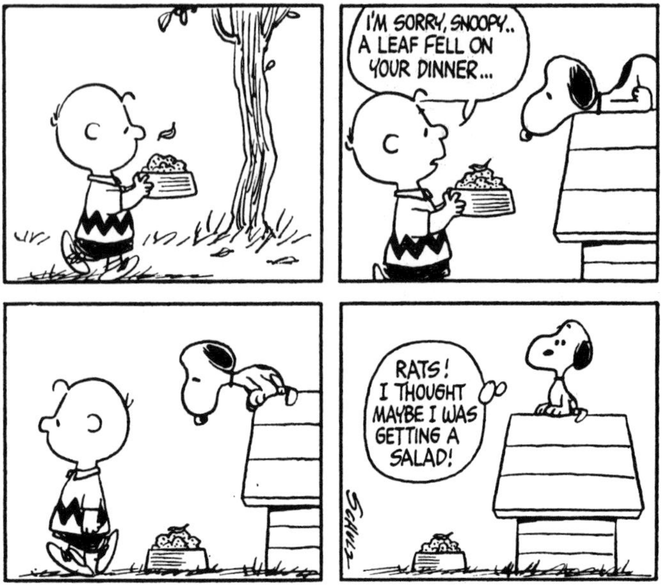
I'M SORRY, SNOOPY.. A LEAF FELL ON YOUR DINNER...
RATS! I THOUGHT MAYBE I WAS GETTING A SALAD!
SCHULZ

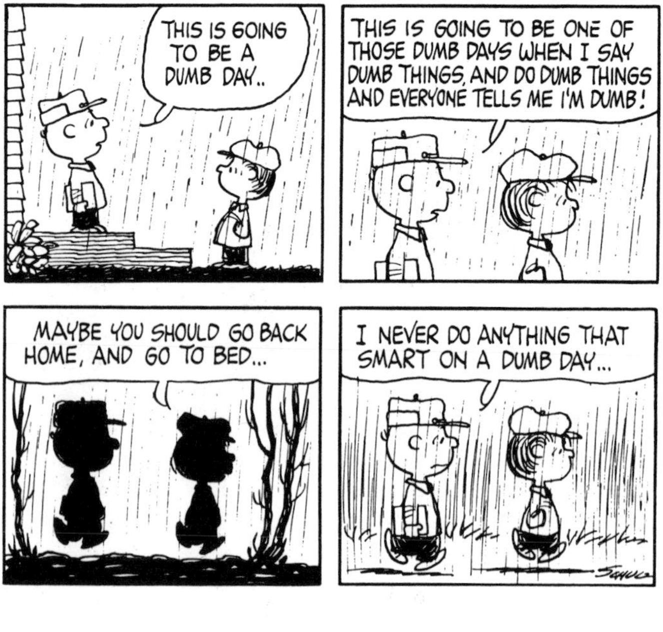
THIS IS GOING TO BE A DUMB DAY..
THIS IS GOING TO BE ONE OF THOSE DUMB DAYS WHEN I SAY DUMB THINGS, AND DO DUMB THINGS AND EVERYONE TELLS ME I'M DUMB!
MAYBE YOU SHOULD GO BACK HOME, AND GO TO BED...
I NEVER DO ANYTHING THAT SMART ON A DUMB DAY...
SCHULZ

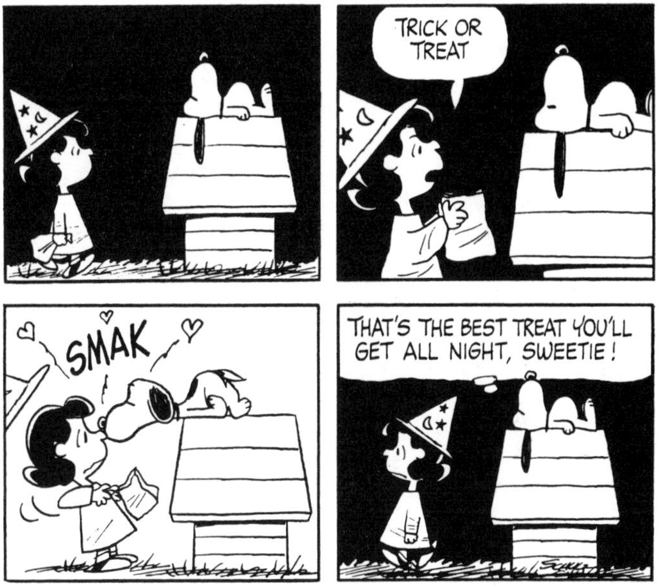
TRICK OR TREAT
SMAK
THAT'S THE BEST TREAT YOU'LL GET ALL NIGHT, SWEETIE!

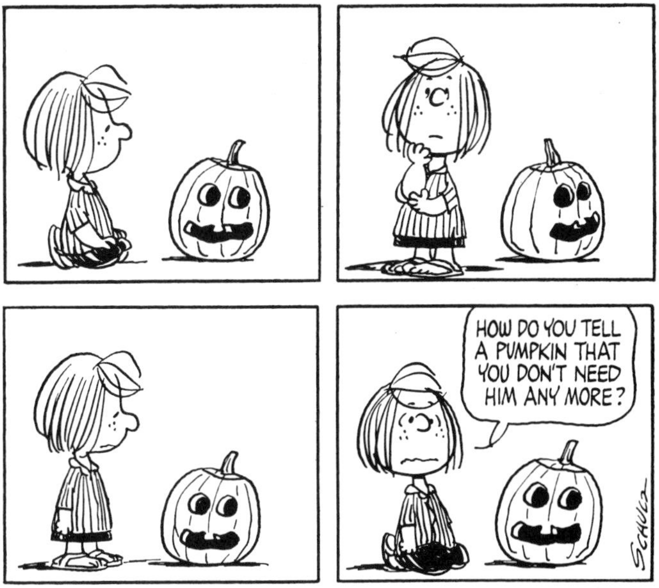
HOW DO YOU TELL A PUMPKIN THAT YOU DON'T NEED HIM ANY MORE?

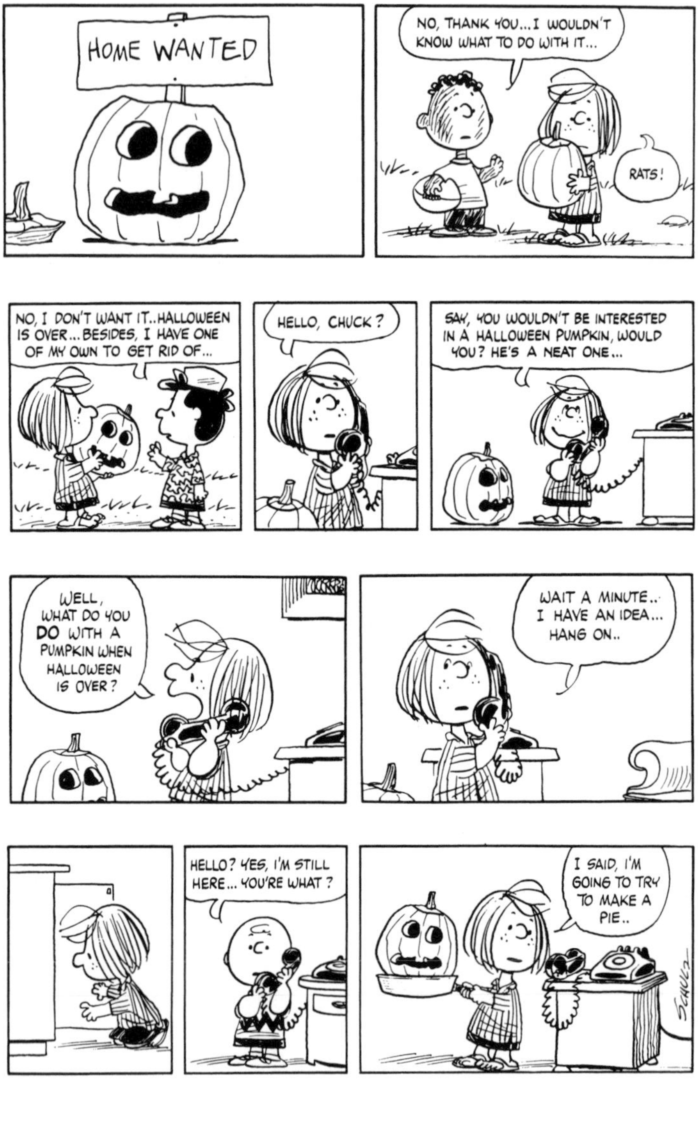
HOME WANTED
NO, THANK YOU...I WOULDN'T KNOW WHAT TO DO WITH IT...
RATS!
NO, I DON'T WANT IT..HALLOWEEN IS OVER...BESIDES, I HAVE ONE OF MY OWN TO GET RID OF...
HELLO, CHUCK?
SAY, YOU WOULDN'T BE INTERESTED IN A HALLOWEEN PUMPKIN, WOULD YOU? HE'S A NEAT ONE...
WELL, WHAT DO YOU DO WITH A PUMPKIN WHEN HALLOWEEN IS OVER?
WAIT A MINUTE.. I HAVE AN IDEA... HANG ON..
HELLO? YES, I'M STILL HERE... YOU'RE WHAT?
I SAID, I'M GOING TO TRY TO MAKE A PIE..
SCHULZ

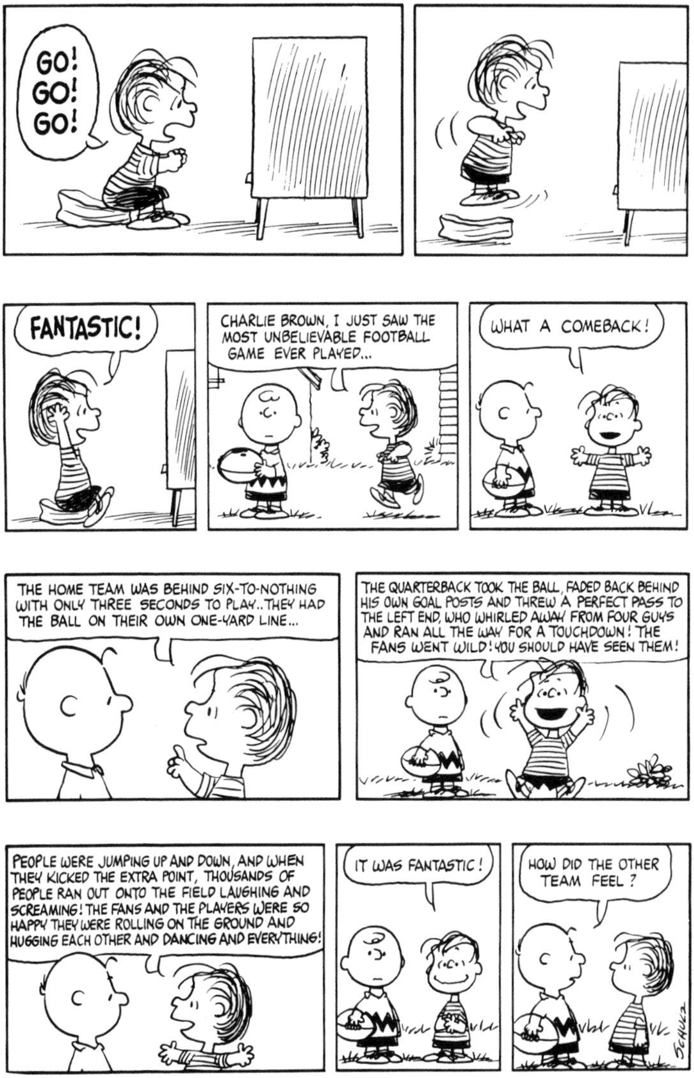
GO! GO! GO!
FANTASTIC!
CHARLIE BROWN, I JUST SAW THE MOST UNBELIEVABLE FOOTBALL GAME EVER PLAYED...
WHAT A COMEBACK!
THE HOME TEAM WAS BEHIND SIX-TO-NOTHING WITH ONLY THREE SECONDS TO PLAY..THEY HAD THE BALL ON THEIR OWN ONE-YARD LINE...
THE QUARTERBACK TOOK THE BALL, FADED BACK BEHIND HIS OWN GOAL POSTS AND THREW A PERFECT PASS TO THE LEFT END, WHO WHIRLED AWAY FROM FOUR GUYS AND RAN ALL THE WAY FOR A TOUCHDOWN! THE FANS WENT WILD! YOU SHOULD HAVE SEEN THEM!
PEOPLE WERE JUMPING UP AND DOWN, AND WHEN THEY KICKED THE EXTRA POINT, THOUSANDS OF PEOPLE RAN OUT ONTO THE FIELD LAUGHING AND SCREAMING! THE FANS AND THE PLAYERS WERE SO HAPPY THEY WERE ROLLING ON THE GROUND AND HUGGING EACH OTHER AND DANCING AND EVERYTHING!
IT WAS FANTASTIC!
HOW DID THE OTHER TEAM FEEL?
SCHULZ

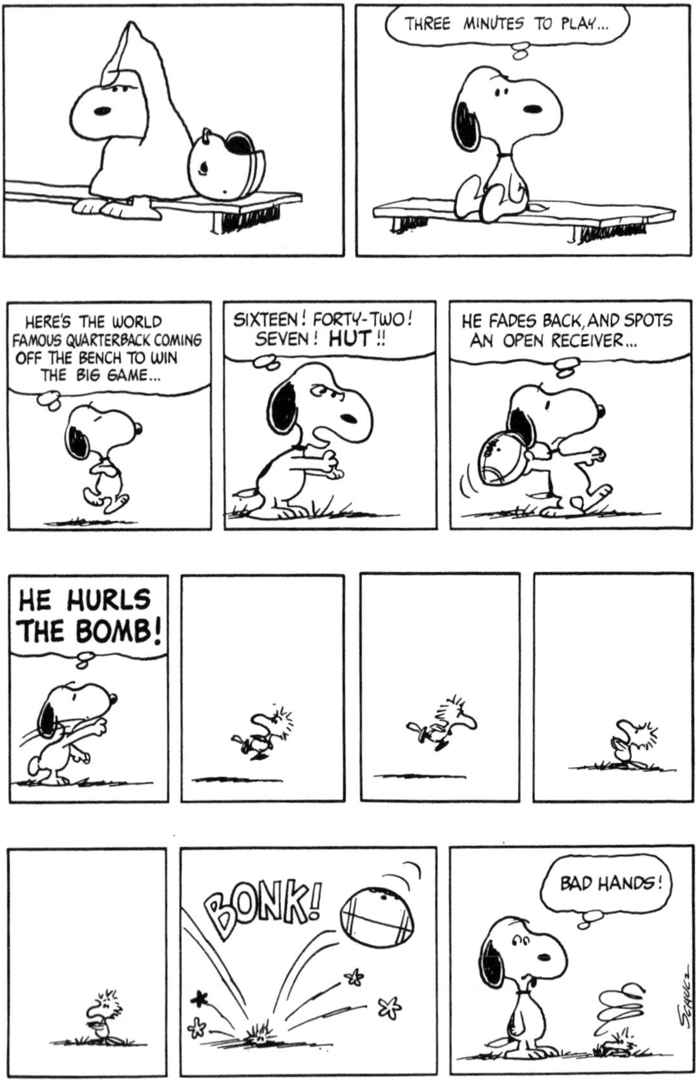

THREE MINUTES TO PLAY...
HERE'S THE WORLD FAMOUS QUARTERBACK COMING OFF THE BENCH TO WIN THE BIG GAME...
SIXTEEN! FORTY-TWO! SEVEN! HUT!!
HE FADES BACK, AND SPOTS AN OPEN RECEIVER...
HE HURLS THE BOMB!
BONK!
BAD HANDS!
SCHULZ

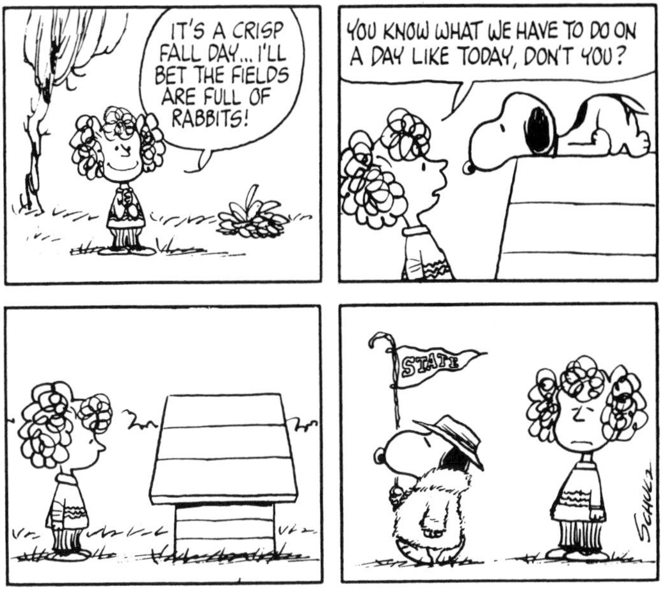
IT'S A CRISP FALL DAY... I'LL BET THE FIELDS ARE FULL OF RABBITS!
YOU KNOW WHAT WE HAVE TO DO ON A DAY LIKE TODAY, DON'T YOU?
STATE
SCHULZ

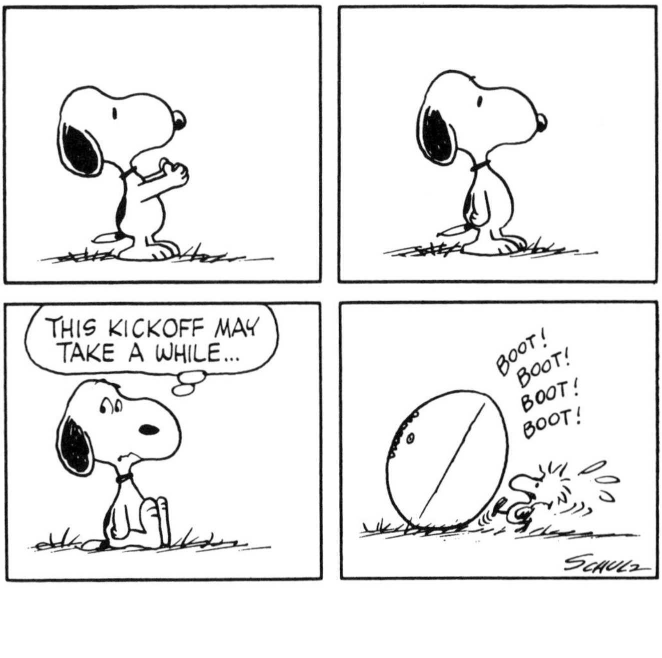
THIS KICKOFF MAY TAKE A WHILE...
BOOT! BOOT! BOOT! BOOT!
SCHULZ

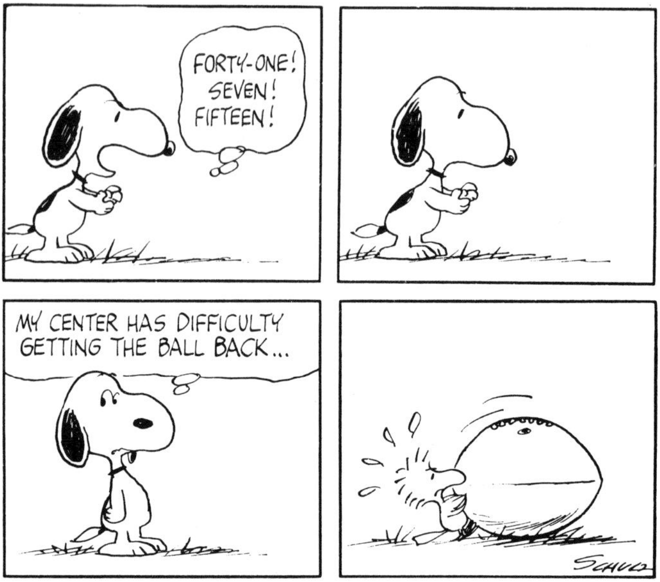
FORTY-ONE! SEVEN! FIFTEEN!
MY CENTER HAS DIFFICULTY GETTING THE BALL BACK...
SCHULZ

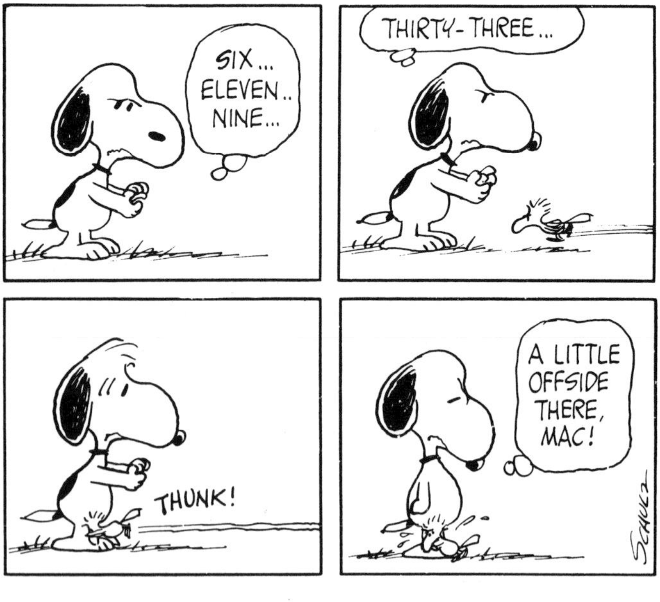
SIX... ELEVEN.. NINE...
THIRTY-THREE...
THUNK!
A LITTLE OFFSIDE THERE, MAC!
SCHULZ

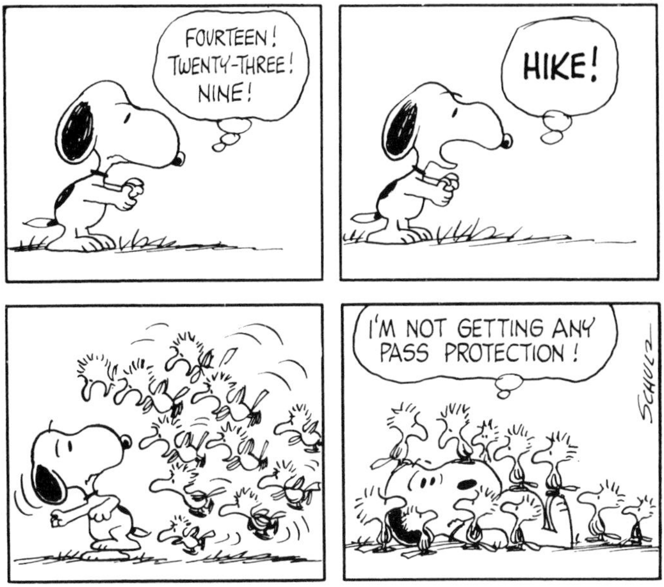
FOURTEEN! TWENTY-THREE! NINE!
HIKE!
I'M NOT GETTING ANY PASS PROTECTION!
SCHULZ

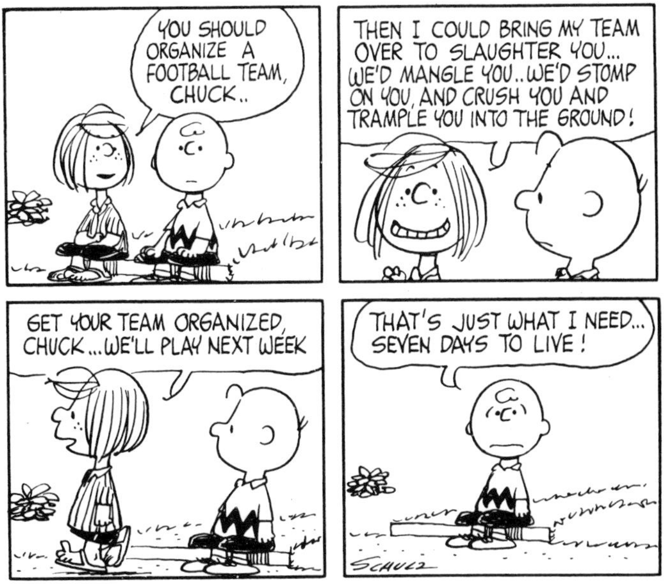
YOU SHOULD ORGANIZE A FOOTBALL TEAM, CHUCK..
THEN I COULD BRING MY TEAM OVER TO SLAUGHTER YOU... WE'D MANGLE YOU..WE'D STOMP ON YOU, AND CRUSH YOU AND TRAMPLE YOU INTO THE GROUND!
GET YOUR TEAM ORGANIZED, CHUCK...WE'LL PLAY NEXT WEEK
THAT'S JUST WHAT I NEED... SEVEN DAYS TO LIVE!
SCHULZ

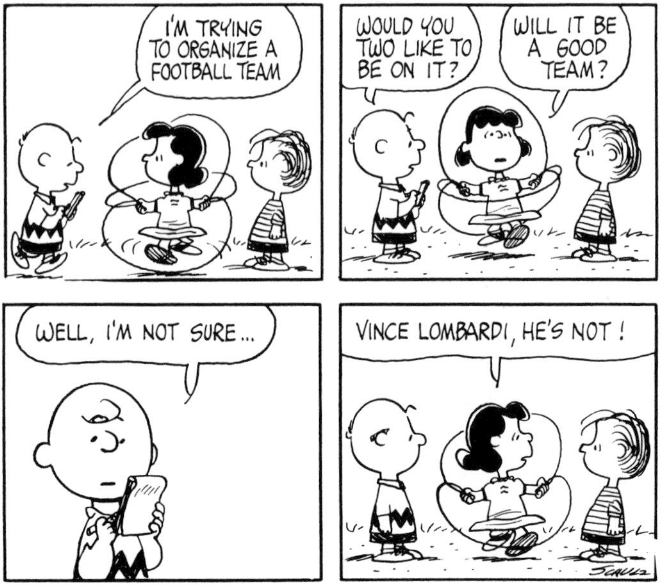
I'M TRYING TO ORGANIZE A FOOTBALL TEAM
WOULD YOU TWO LIKE TO BE ON IT?
WILL IT BE A GOOD TEAM?
WELL, I'M NOT SURE...
VINCE LOMBARDI, HE'S NOT!
SCHULZ

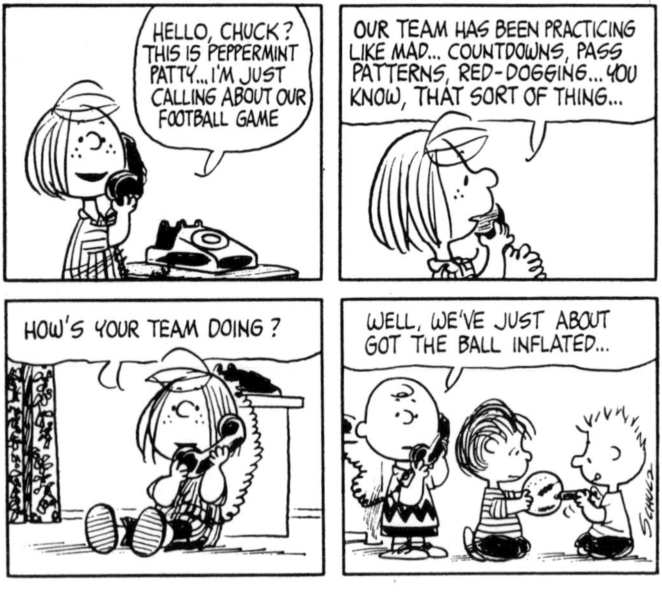
HELLO, CHUCK? THIS IS PEPPERMINT PATTY... I'M JUST CALLING ABOUT OUR FOOTBALL GAME
OUR TEAM HAS BEEN PRACTICING LIKE MAD... COUNTDOWNS, PASS PATTERNS, RED-DOGGING... YOU KNOW, THAT SORT OF THING...
HOW'S YOUR TEAM DOING?
WELL, WE'VE JUST ABOUT GOT THE BALL INFLATED...
SCHULZ

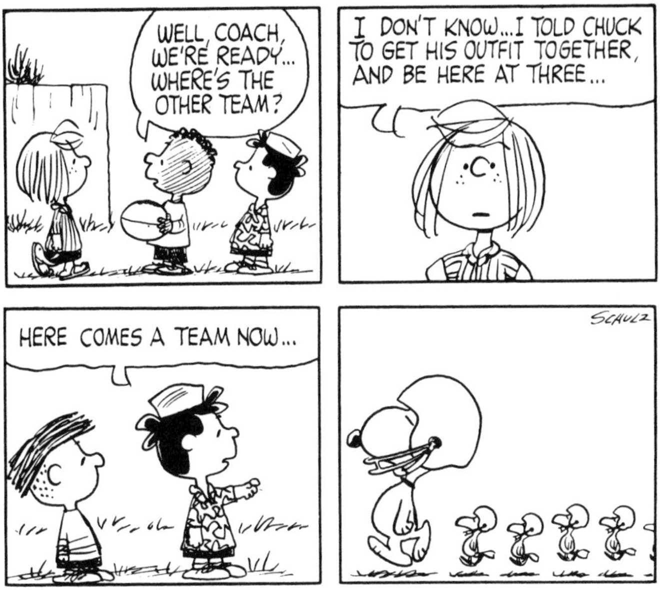
WELL, COACH, WE'RE READY... WHERE'S THE OTHER TEAM?
I DON'T KNOW...I TOLD CHUCK TO GET HIS OUTFIT TOGETHER, AND BE HERE AT THREE...
HERE COMES A TEAM NOW...
SCHULZ

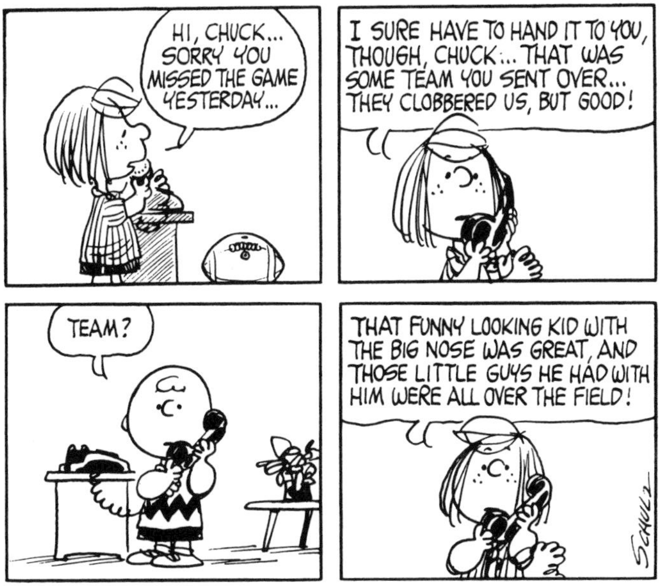
HI, CHUCK... SORRY YOU MISSED THE GAME YESTERDAY...
I SURE HAVE TO HAND IT TO YOU, THOUGH, CHUCK... THAT WAS SOME TEAM YOU SENT OVER... THEY CLOBBERED US, BUT GOOD!
TEAM?
THAT FUNNY LOOKING KID WITH THE BIG NOSE WAS GREAT, AND THOSE LITTLE GUYS HE HAD WITH HIM WERE ALL OVER THE FIELD!
SCHULZ

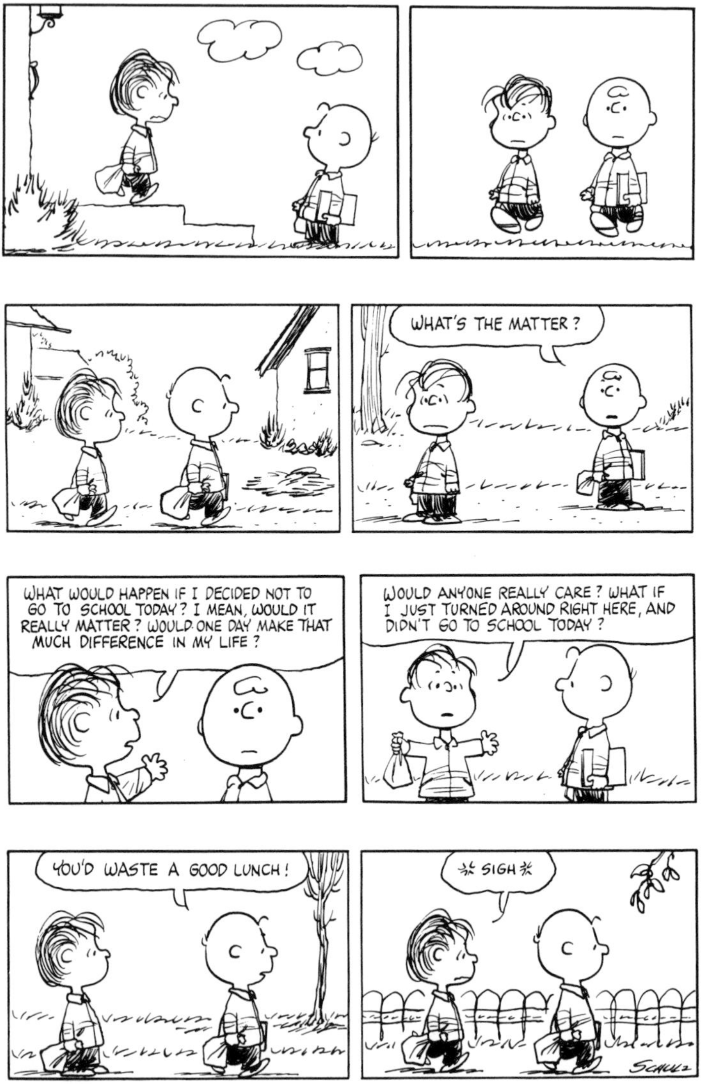
WHAT'S THE MATTER?
WHAT WOULD HAPPEN IF I DECIDED NOT TO GO TO SCHOOL TODAY? I MEAN, WOULD IT REALLY MATTER? WOULD ONE DAY MAKE THAT MUCH DIFFERENCE IN MY LIFE?
WOULD ANYONE REALLY CARE? WHAT IF I JUST TURNED AROUND RIGHT HERE, AND DIDN'T GO TO SCHOOL TODAY?
YOU'D WASTE A GOOD LUNCH!
SIGH
SCHULZ

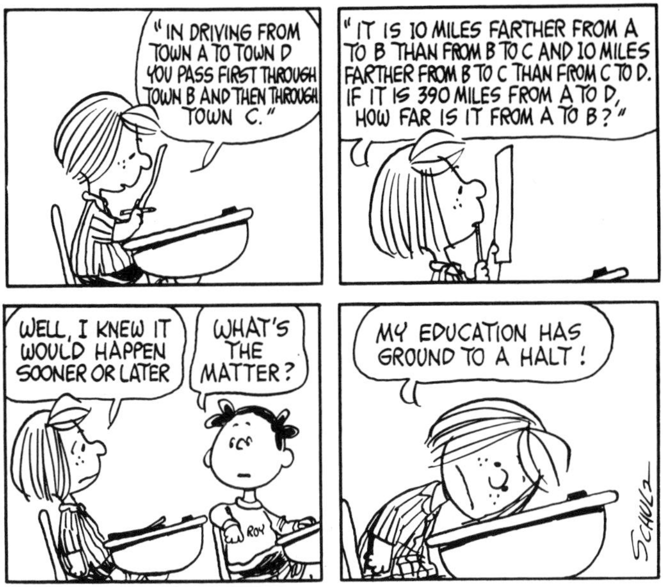
"IN DRIVING FROM TOWN A TO TOWN D YOU PASS FIRST THROUGH TOWN B AND THEN THROUGH TOWN C."
"IT IS 10 MILES FARTHER FROM A TO B THAN FROM B TO C AND 10 MILES FARTHER FROM B TO C THAN FROM C TO D. IF IT IS 390 MILES FROM A TO D, HOW FAR IS IT FROM A TO B?"
WELL, I KNEW IT WOULD HAPPEN SOONER OR LATER
WHAT'S THE MATTER?
ROY
MY EDUCATION HAS GROUND TO A HALT!
SCHULZ

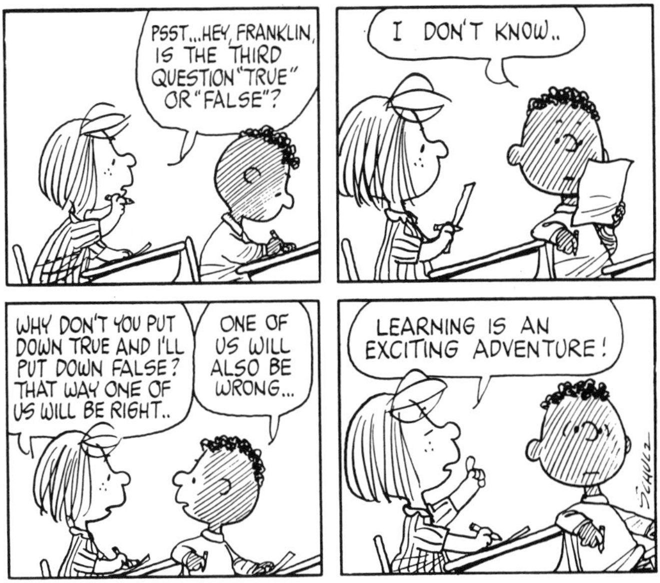
PSST...HEY, FRANKLIN, IS THE THIRD QUESTION "TRUE" OR "FALSE"?
I DON'T KNOW..
WHY DON'T YOU PUT DOWN TRUE AND I'LL PUT DOWN FALSE? THAT WAY ONE OF US WILL BE RIGHT..
ONE OF US WILL ALSO BE WRONG...
LEARNING IS AN EXCITING ADVENTURE!
SCHULZ

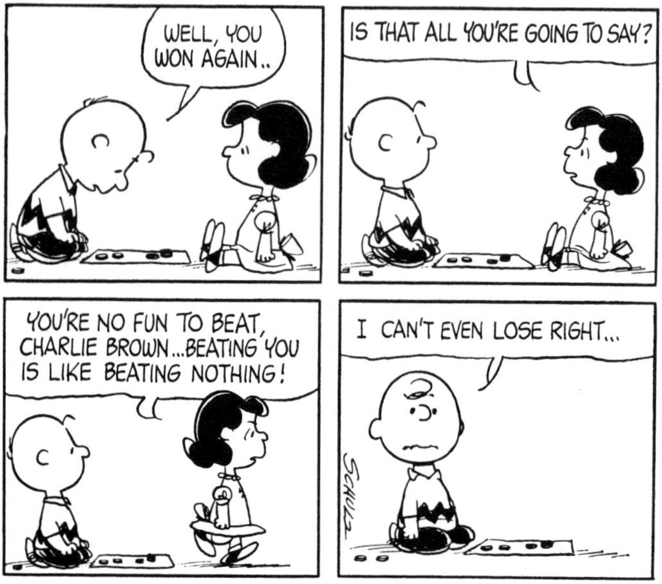
WELL, YOU WON AGAIN..
IS THAT ALL YOU'RE GOING TO SAY?
YOU'RE NO FUN TO BEAT, CHARLIE BROWN...BEATING YOU IS LIKE BEATING NOTHING!
I CAN'T EVEN LOSE RIGHT...
SCHULZ

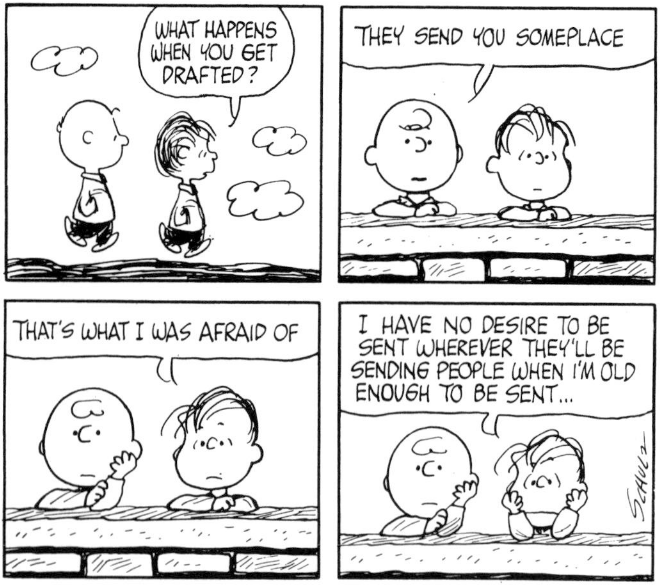
WHAT HAPPENS WHEN YOU GET DRAFTED?
THEY SEND YOU SOMEPLACE
THAT'S WHAT I WAS AFRAID OF
I HAVE NO DESIRE TO BE SENT WHEREVER THEY'LL BE SENDING PEOPLE WHEN I'M OLD ENOUGH TO BE SENT...
SCHULZ

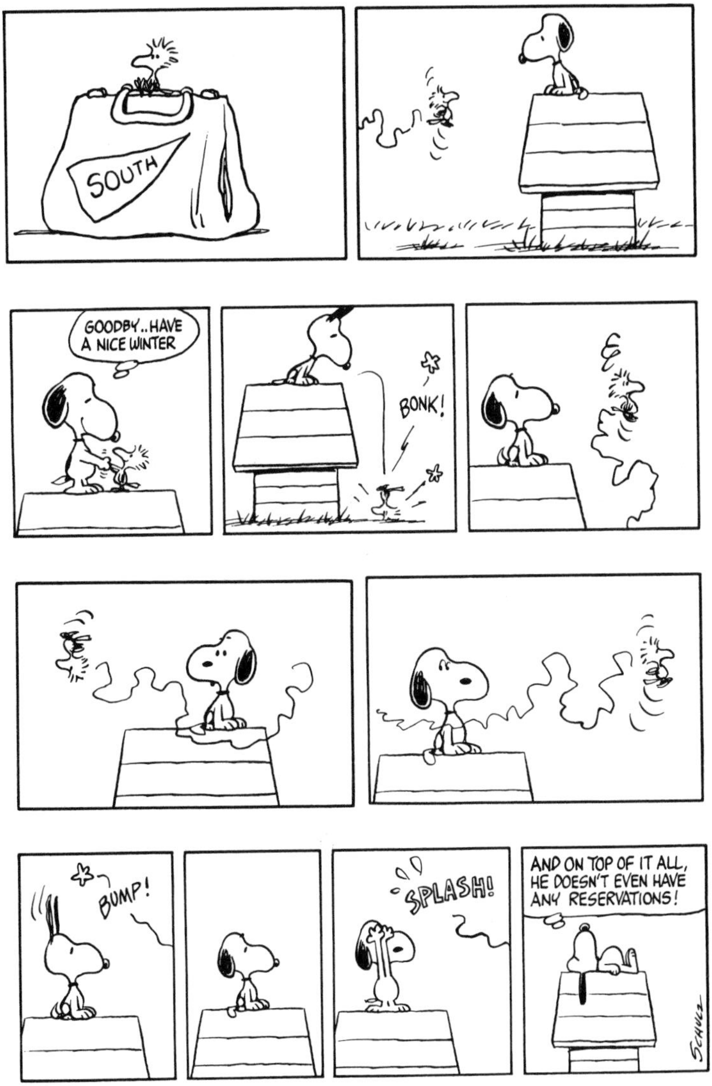
SOUTH
GOODBY.. HAVE A NICE WINTER
BONK!
BUMP!
SPLASH!
AND ON TOP OF IT ALL, HE DOESN'T EVEN HAVE ANY RESERVATIONS!
SCHULZ

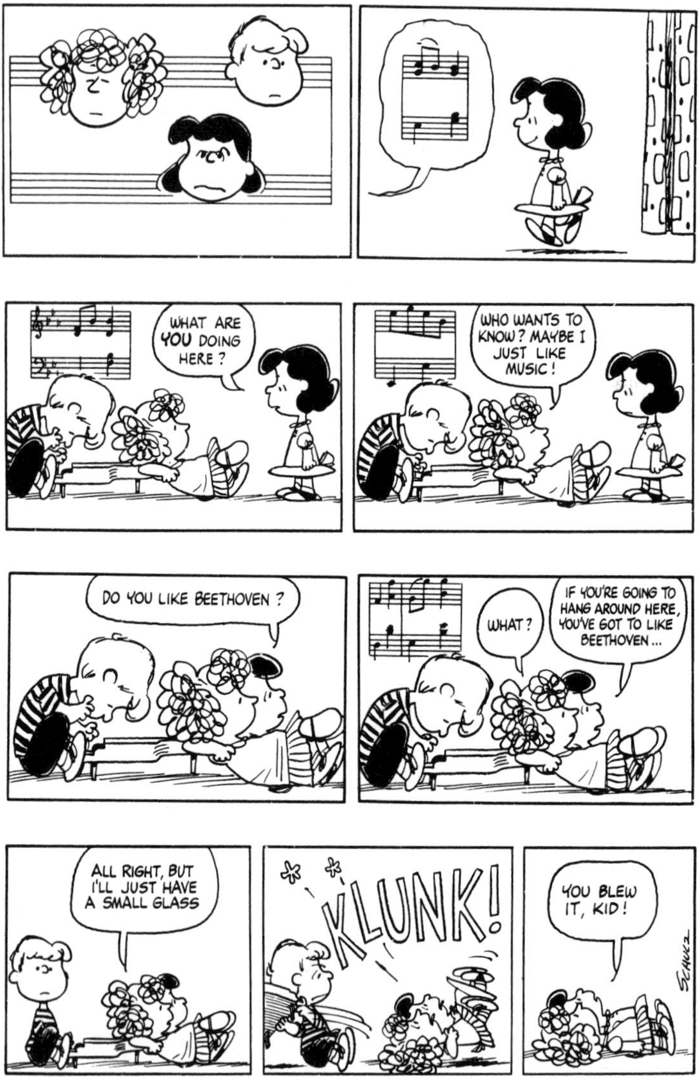
WHAT ARE YOU DOING HERE ?
WHO WANTS TO KNOW ? MAYBE I JUST LIKE MUSIC !
DO YOU LIKE BEETHOVEN ?
WHAT ?
IF YOU'RE GOING TO HANG AROUND HERE, YOU'VE GOT TO LIKE BEETHOVEN ...
ALL RIGHT, BUT I'LL JUST HAVE A SMALL GLASS
KLUNK!
YOU BLEW IT, KID !
SCHULZ

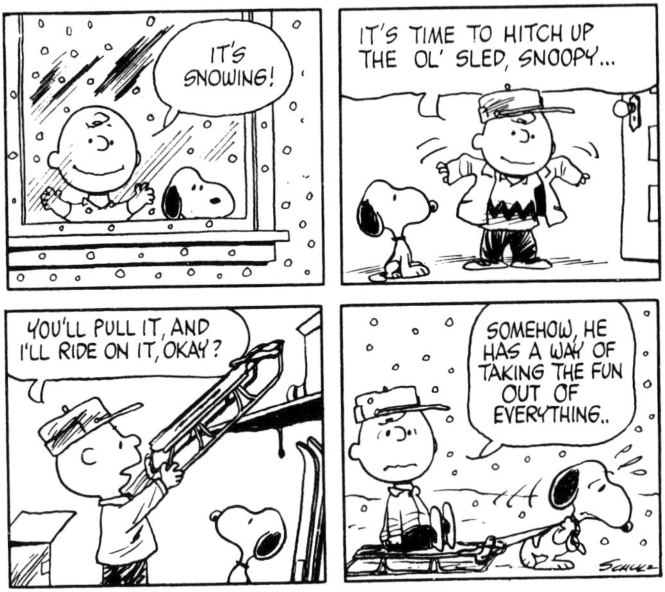
IT'S SNOWING!
IT'S TIME TO HITCH UP THE OL' SLED, SNOOPY...
YOU'LL PULL IT, AND I'LL RIDE ON IT, OKAY?
SOMEHOW, HE HAS A WAY OF TAKING THE FUN OUT OF EVERYTHING..
SCHULZ

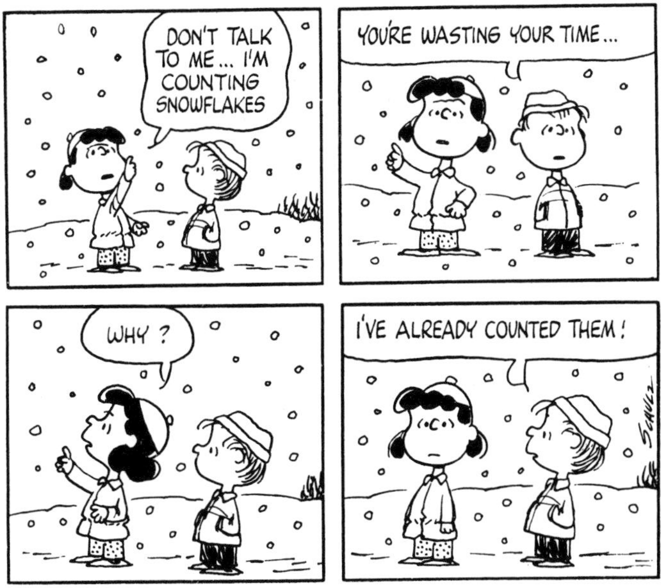
DON'T TALK TO ME... I'M COUNTING SNOWFLAKES
YOU'RE WASTING YOUR TIME...
WHY?
I'VE ALREADY COUNTED THEM!
SCHULZ

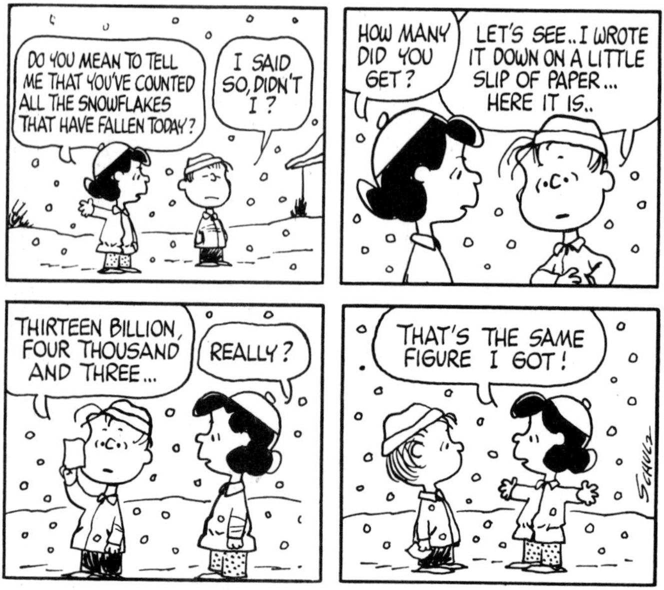
DO YOU MEAN TO TELL ME THAT YOU'VE COUNTED ALL THE SNOWFLAKES THAT HAVE FALLEN TODAY?
I SAID SO, DIDN'T I?
HOW MANY DID YOU GET?
LET'S SEE.. I WROTE IT DOWN ON A LITTLE SLIP OF PAPER... HERE IT IS..
THIRTEEN BILLION, FOUR THOUSAND AND THREE...
REALLY?
THAT'S THE SAME FIGURE I GOT!
SCHULZ

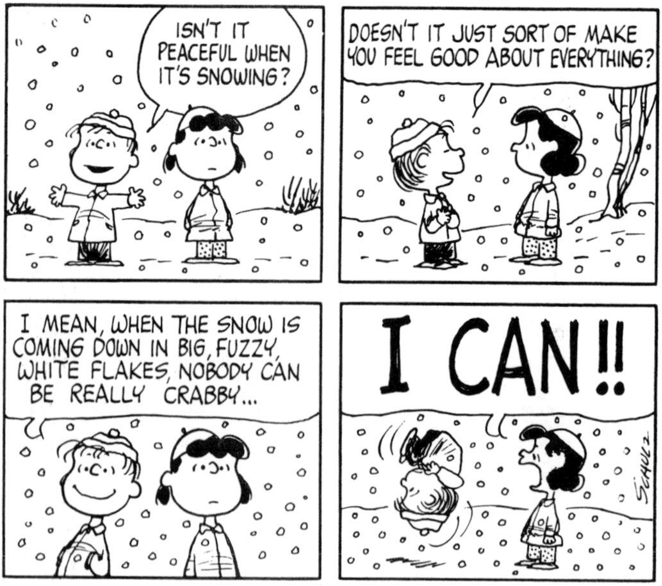
ISN'T IT PEACEFUL WHEN IT'S SNOWING?
DOESN'T IT JUST SORT OF MAKE YOU FEEL GOOD ABOUT EVERYTHING?
I MEAN, WHEN THE SNOW IS COMING DOWN IN BIG, FUZZY, WHITE FLAKES, NOBODY CAN BE REALLY CRABBY...
I CAN!!
SCHULZ

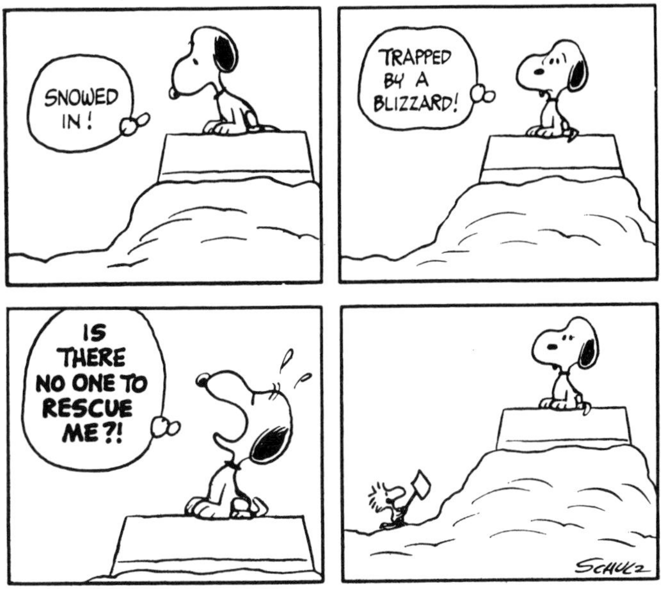
SNOWED IN!
TRAPPED BY A BLIZZARD!
IS THERE NO ONE TO RESCUE ME?!

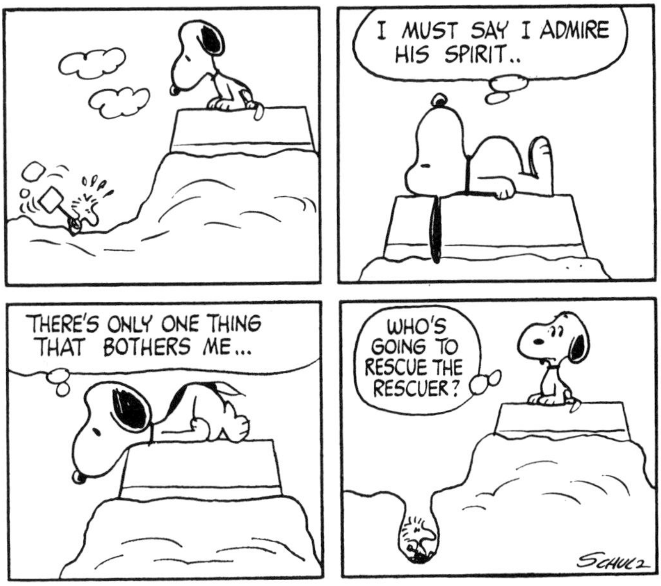
I MUST SAY I ADMIRE HIS SPIRIT..
THERE'S ONLY ONE THING THAT BOTHERS ME...
WHO'S GOING TO RESCUE THE RESCUER?

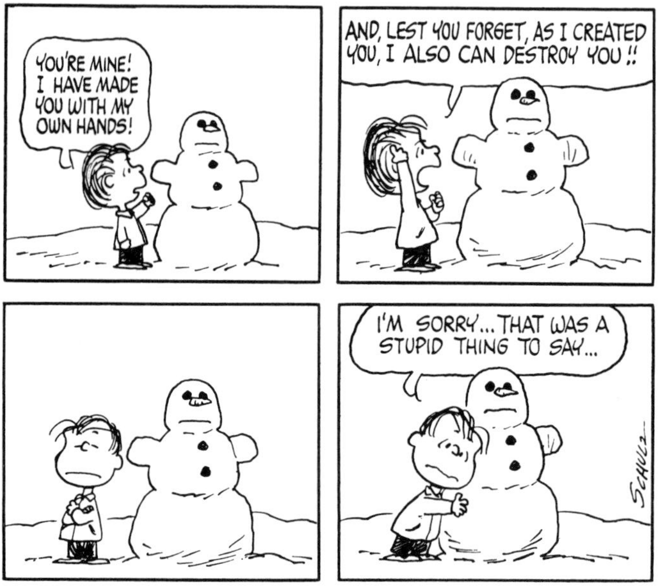
YOU'RE MINE! I HAVE MADE YOU WITH MY OWN HANDS!
AND, LEST YOU FORGET, AS I CREATED YOU, I ALSO CAN DESTROY YOU!!
I'M SORRY... THAT WAS A STUPID THING TO SAY...
SCHULZ

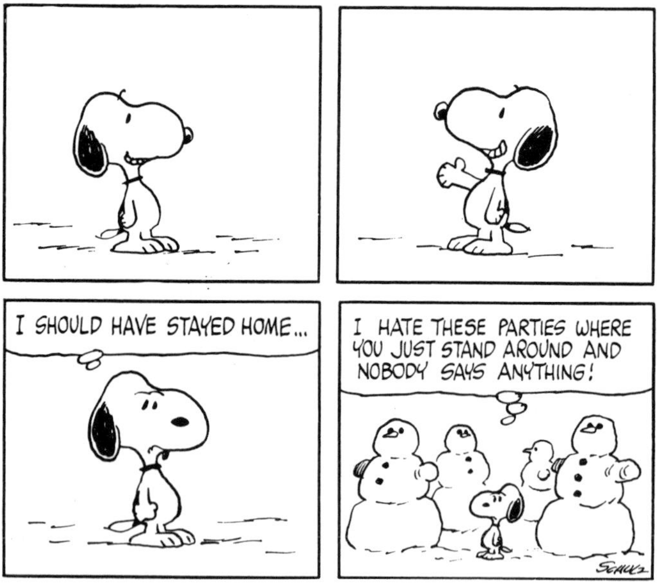
I SHOULD HAVE STAYED HOME...
I HATE THESE PARTIES WHERE YOU JUST STAND AROUND AND NOBODY SAYS ANYTHING!
SCHULZ

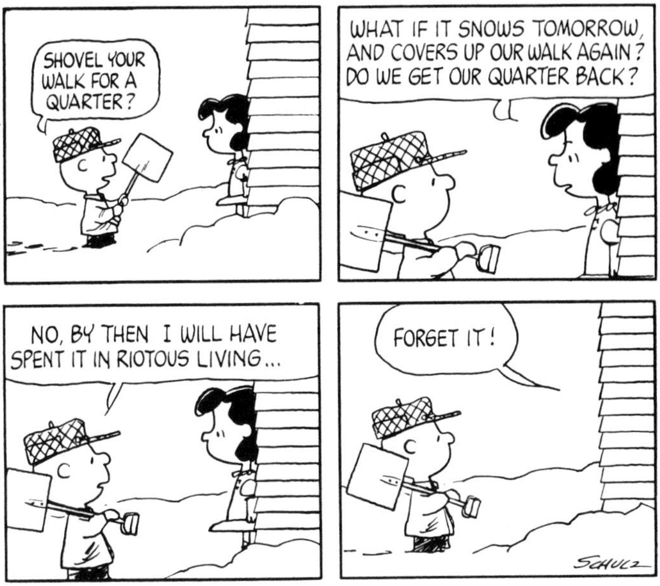
SHOVEL YOUR WALK FOR A QUARTER?
WHAT IF IT SNOWS TOMORROW, AND COVERS UP OUR WALK AGAIN? DO WE GET OUR QUARTER BACK?
NO, BY THEN I WILL HAVE SPENT IT IN RIOTOUS LIVING...
FORGET IT!
SCHULZ

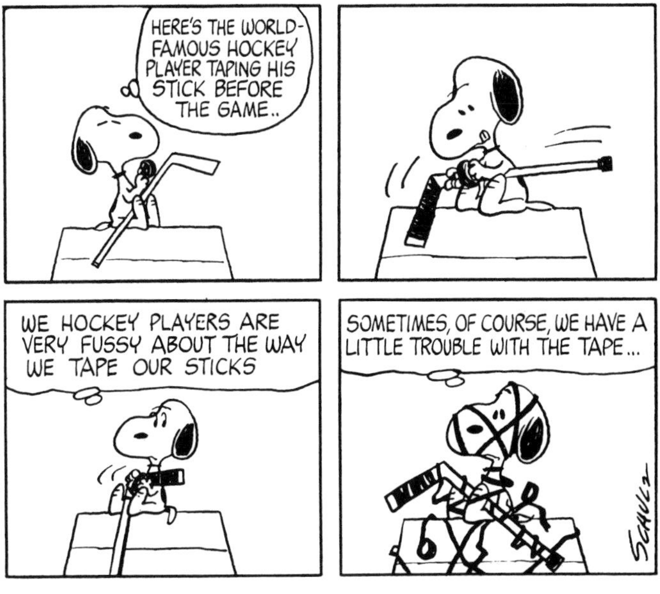
HERE'S THE WORLD-FAMOUS HOCKEY PLAYER TAPING HIS STICK BEFORE THE GAME..
WE HOCKEY PLAYERS ARE VERY FUSSY ABOUT THE WAY WE TAPE OUR STICKS
SOMETIMES, OF COURSE, WE HAVE A LITTLE TROUBLE WITH THE TAPE...
SCHULZ

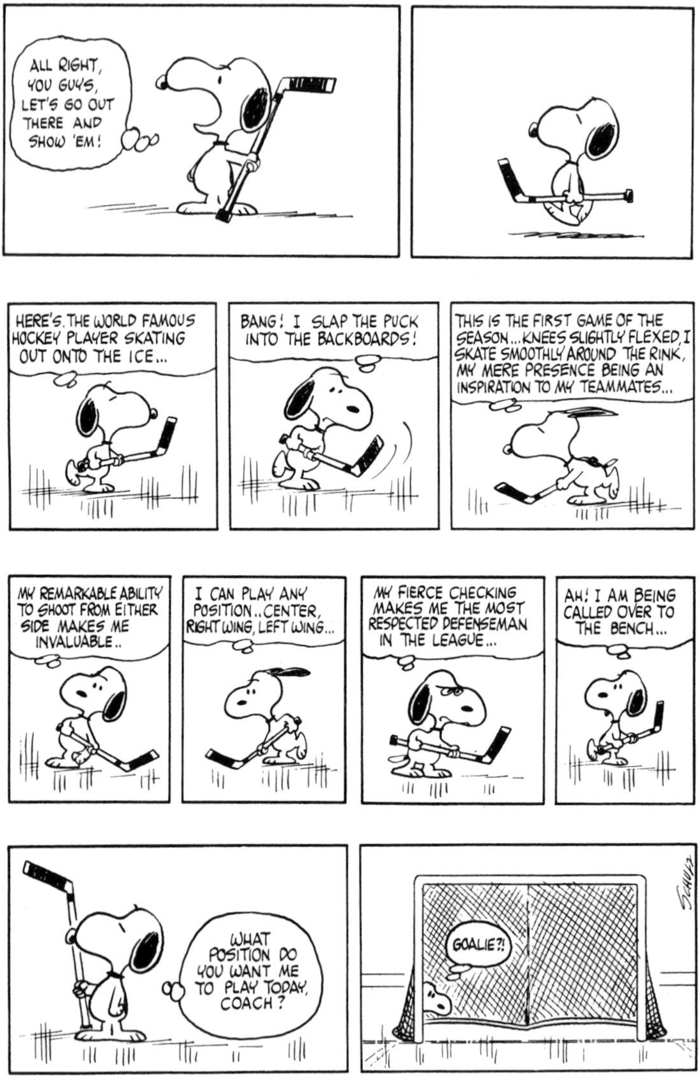

ALL RIGHT, YOU GUYS, LET'S GO OUT THERE AND SHOW 'EM!
HERE'S THE WORLD FAMOUS HOCKEY PLAYER SKATING OUT ONTO THE ICE...
BANG! I SLAP THE PUCK INTO THE BACKBOARDS!
THIS IS THE FIRST GAME OF THE SEASON...KNEES SLIGHTLY FLEXED, I SKATE SMOOTHLY AROUND THE RINK, MY MERE PRESENCE BEING AN INSPIRATION TO MY TEAMMATES...
MY REMARKABLE ABILITY TO SHOOT FROM EITHER SIDE MAKES ME INVALUABLE..
I CAN PLAY ANY POSITION..CENTER, RIGHT WING, LEFT WING...
MY FIERCE CHECKING MAKES ME THE MOST RESPECTED DEFENSEMAN IN THE LEAGUE...
AH! I AM BEING CALLED OVER TO THE BENCH...
WHAT POSITION DO YOU WANT ME TO PLAY TODAY, COACH?
GOALIE?!
SCHULZ

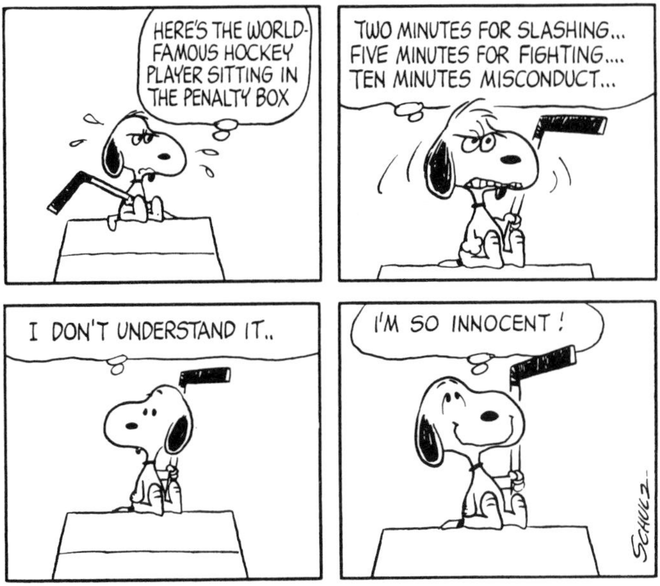
HERE'S THE WORLD-FAMOUS HOCKEY PLAYER SITTING IN THE PENALTY BOX
TWO MINUTES FOR SLASHING... FIVE MINUTES FOR FIGHTING.... TEN MINUTES MISCONDUCT...
I DON'T UNDERSTAND IT..
I'M SO INNOCENT!
SCHULZ

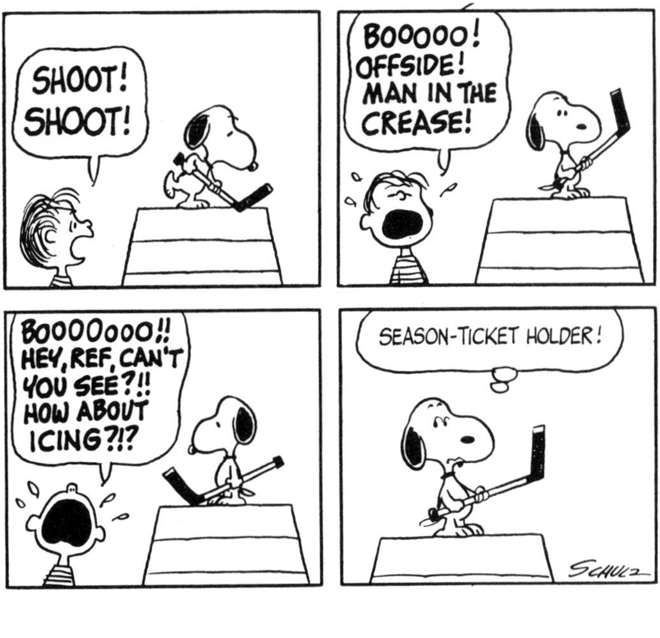
SHOOT! SHOOT!
BOOOOO! OFFSIDE! MAN IN THE CREASE!
BOOOOooo!! HEY, REF, CAN'T YOU SEE?!! HOW ABOUT ICING?!?
SEASON-TICKET HOLDER!
SCHULZ

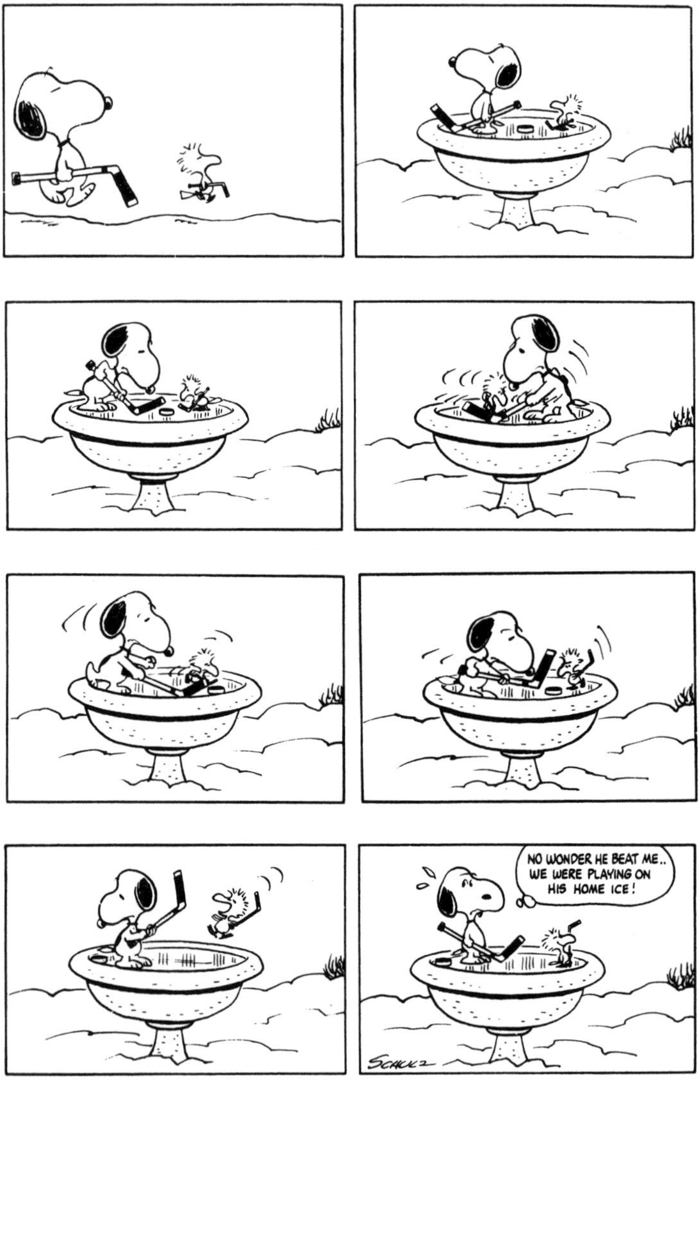
NO WONDER HE BEAT ME..
WE WERE PLAYING ON
HIS HOME ICE!
SCHULZ

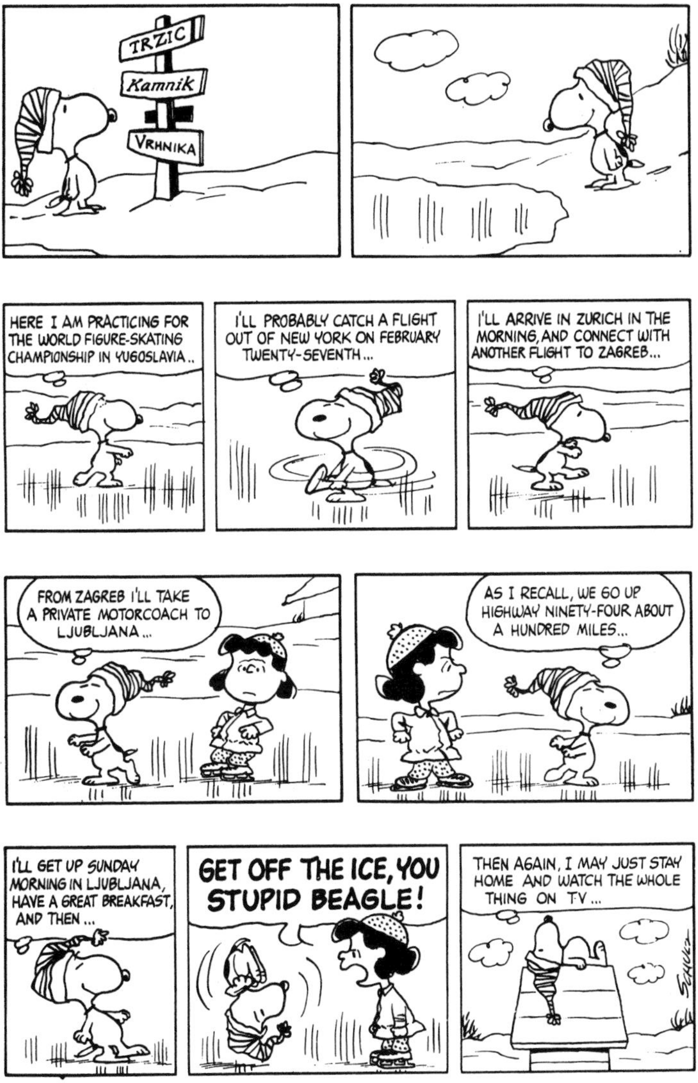

TRZIC
Kamnik
VRHNIKA
HERE I AM PRACTICING FOR THE WORLD FIGURE-SKATING CHAMPIONSHIP IN YUGOSLAVIA..
I'LL PROBABLY CATCH A FLIGHT OUT OF NEW YORK ON FEBRUARY TWENTY-SEVENTH...
I'LL ARRIVE IN ZURICH IN THE MORNING, AND CONNECT WITH ANOTHER FLIGHT TO ZAGREB...
FROM ZAGREB I'LL TAKE A PRIVATE MOTORCOACH TO LJUBLJANA...
AS I RECALL, WE GO UP HIGHWAY NINETY-FOUR ABOUT A HUNDRED MILES...
I'LL GET UP SUNDAY MORNING IN LJUBLJANA, HAVE A GREAT BREAKFAST, AND THEN...
GET OFF THE ICE, YOU STUPID BEAGLE!
THEN AGAIN, I MAY JUST STAY HOME AND WATCH THE WHOLE THING ON TV...
SCHULZ

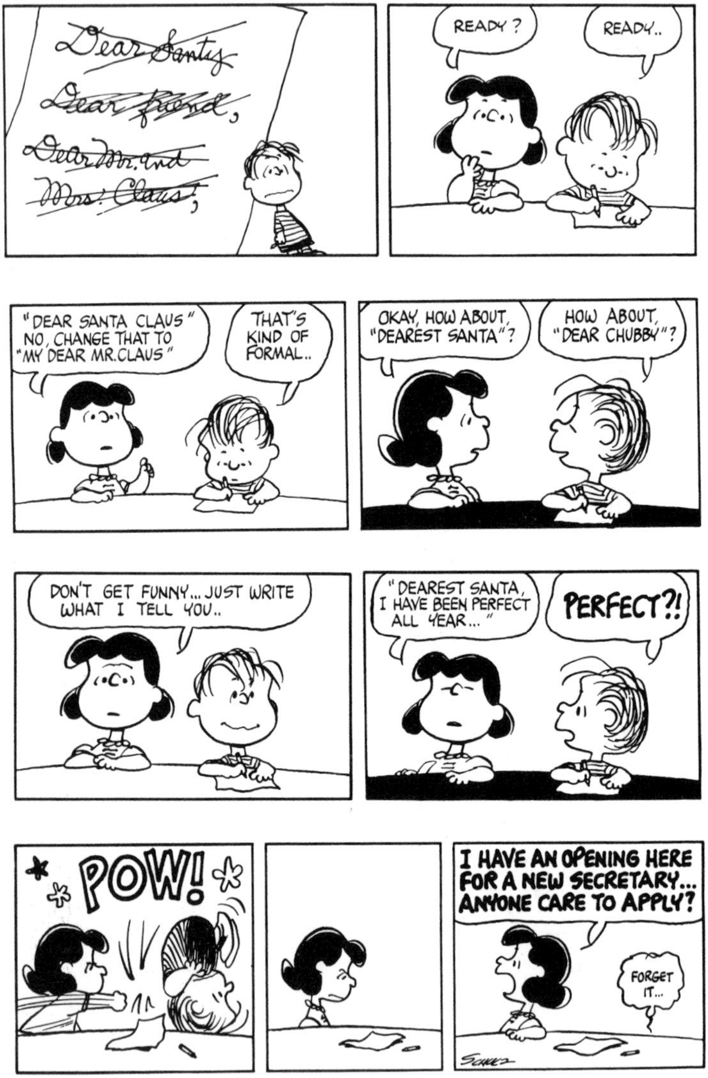
Dear Santy
Dear Friend,
Dear Mr. and Mrs. Claus,
READY?
READY..
"DEAR SANTA CLAUS" NO, CHANGE THAT TO "MY DEAR MR. CLAUS"
THAT'S KIND OF FORMAL..
OKAY, HOW ABOUT, "DEAREST SANTA"?
HOW ABOUT, "DEAR CHUBBY"?
DON'T GET FUNNY... JUST WRITE WHAT I TELL YOU..
"DEAREST SANTA, I HAVE BEEN PERFECT ALL YEAR..."
PERFECT?!
POW!
I HAVE AN OPENING HERE FOR A NEW SECRETARY... ANYONE CARE TO APPLY?
FORGET IT...

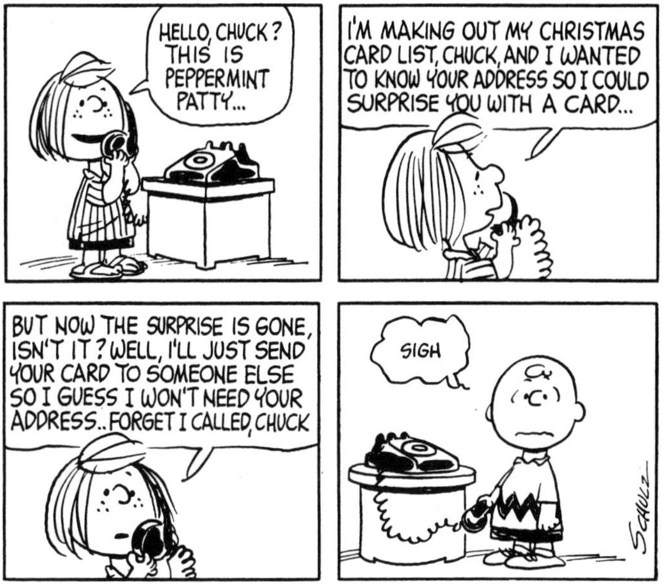
HELLO, CHUCK? THIS IS PEPPERMINT PATTY...
I'M MAKING OUT MY CHRISTMAS CARD LIST, CHUCK, AND I WANTED TO KNOW YOUR ADDRESS SO I COULD SURPRISE YOU WITH A CARD...
BUT NOW THE SURPRISE IS GONE, ISN'T IT? WELL, I'LL JUST SEND YOUR CARD TO SOMEONE ELSE SO I GUESS I WON'T NEED YOUR ADDRESS.. FORGET I CALLED, CHUCK
SIGH
SCHULZ

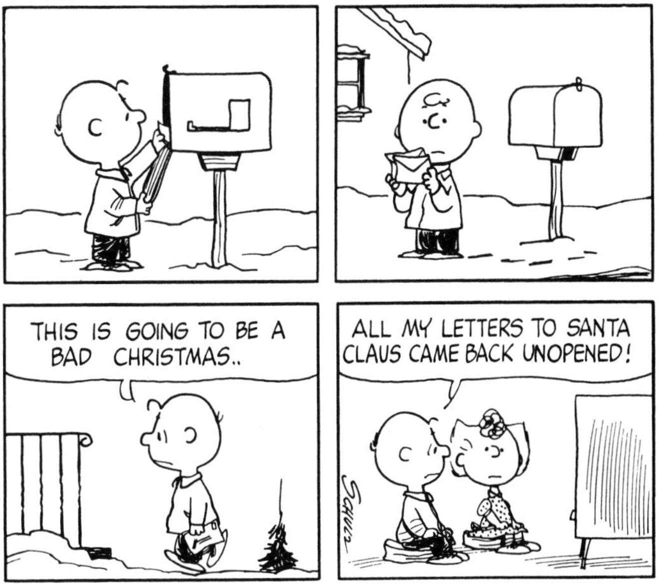
THIS IS GOING TO BE A BAD CHRISTMAS..
ALL MY LETTERS TO SANTA CLAUS CAME BACK UNOPENED!
SCHULZ

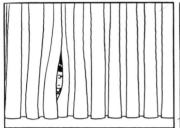

DO YOU KNOW WHAT YOU'RE GOING TO SAY?

OF COURSE, I KNOW WHAT I'M GOING TO SAY

OKAY, YOU'RE ON!

"THE BOOK OF THE GENERATION OF JESUS CHRIST, THE SON OF DAVID, THE SON OF ABRAHAM"

"ABRAHAM BEGAT ISAAC; AND ISAAC BEGAT JACOB; AND JACOB BEGAT JUDAS AND HIS BRETHREN; AND JUDAS BEGAT PHARES AND ZARA OF THAMAR; AND PHARES BEGAT ESROM; AND ESROM BEGAT ARAM..."

"..AND JESSE BEGAT DAVID THE KING; AND DAVID THE KING BEGAT SOLOMON OF HER THAT HAD BEEN THE WIFE OF URIAS; AND SOLOMON BEGAT ROBOAM; AND ROBOAM BEGAT ABIA; AND ABIA BEGAT ASA..."

"..AND JACOB BEGAT JOSEPH THE HUSBAND OF MARY, OF WHOM WAS BORN JESUS, WHO IS CALLED CHRIST. SO ALL THE GENERATIONS FROM ABRAHAM TO DAVID ARE FOURTEEN GENERATIONS..."

"NOW THE BIRTH OF JESUS CHRIST WAS ON THIS WISE.."

WHY DIDN'T YOU JUST START WITH THE FIRST CHAPTER OF GENESIS WHILE YOU WERE AT IT?

DON'T BE SARCASTIC.. "'TIS THE SEASON TO BE JOLLY!"

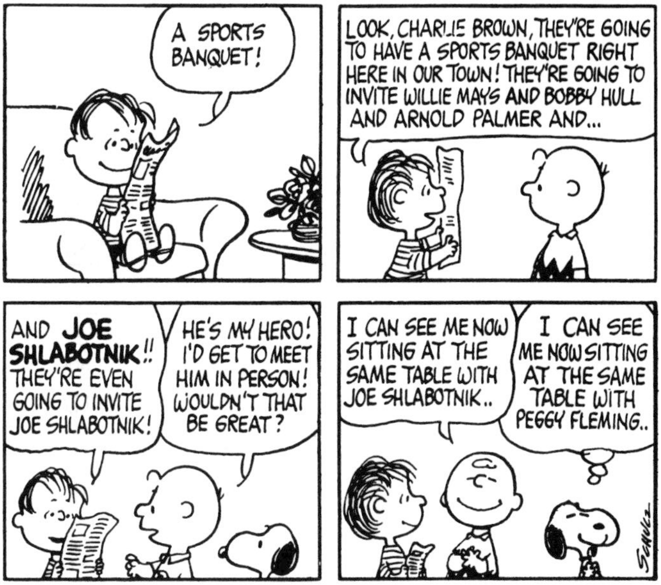
A SPORTS BANQUET!
LOOK, CHARLIE BROWN, THEY'RE GOING TO HAVE A SPORTS BANQUET RIGHT HERE IN OUR TOWN! THEY'RE GOING TO INVITE WILLIE MAYS AND BOBBY HULL AND ARNOLD PALMER AND...
AND JOE SHLABOTNIK!! THEY'RE EVEN GOING TO INVITE JOE SHLABOTNIK!
HE'S MY HERO! I'D GET TO MEET HIM IN PERSON! WOULDN'T THAT BE GREAT?
I CAN SEE ME NOW SITTING AT THE SAME TABLE WITH JOE SHLABOTNIK..
I CAN SEE ME NOW SITTING AT THE SAME TABLE WITH PEGGY FLEMING..
SCHULZ

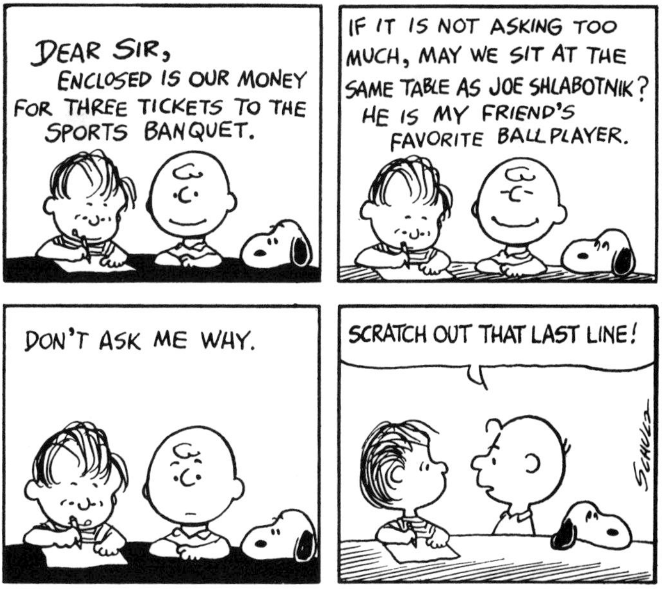
DEAR SIR,
ENCLOSED IS OUR MONEY FOR THREE TICKETS TO THE SPORTS BANQUET.
IF IT IS NOT ASKING TOO MUCH, MAY WE SIT AT THE SAME TABLE AS JOE SHLABOTNIK? HE IS MY FRIEND'S FAVORITE BALLPLAYER.
DON'T ASK ME WHY.
SCRATCH OUT THAT LAST LINE!
SCHULZ

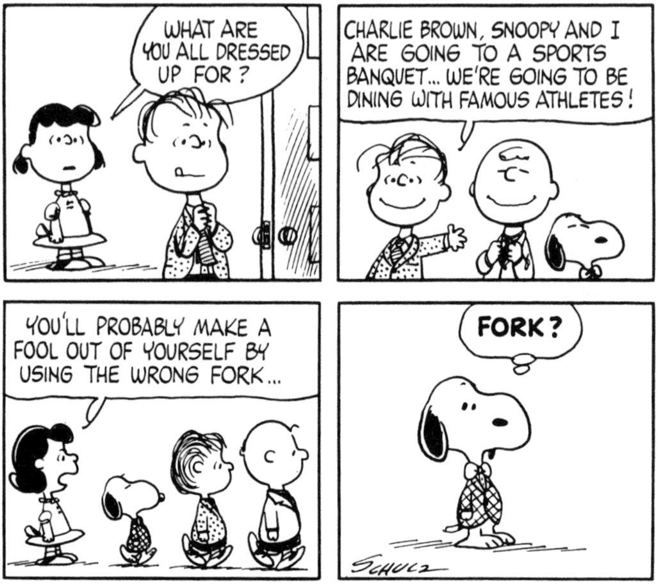
WHAT ARE YOU ALL DRESSED UP FOR ?
CHARLIE BROWN, SNOOPY AND I ARE GOING TO A SPORTS BANQUET... WE'RE GOING TO BE DINING WITH FAMOUS ATHLETES !
YOU'LL PROBABLY MAKE A FOOL OUT OF YOURSELF BY USING THE WRONG FORK...
FORK ?
SCHULZ

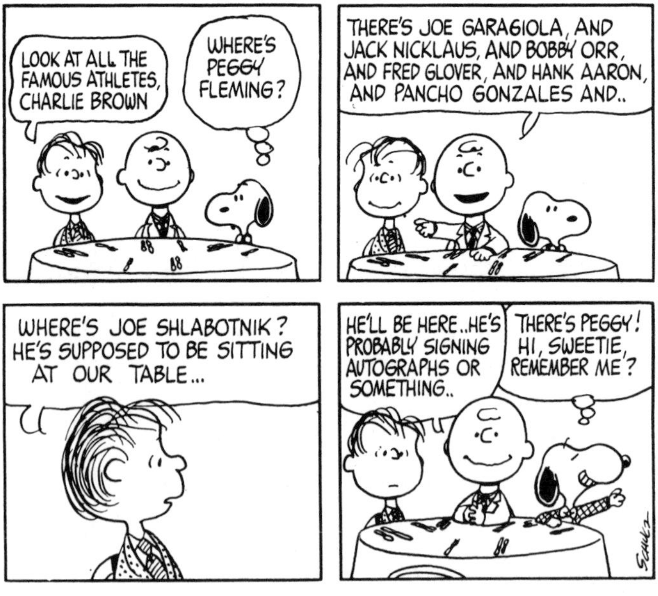
LOOK AT ALL THE FAMOUS ATHLETES, CHARLIE BROWN
WHERE'S PEGGY FLEMING ?
THERE'S JOE GARAGIOLA, AND JACK NICKLAUS, AND BOBBY ORR, AND FRED GLOVER, AND HANK AARON, AND PANCHO GONZALES AND..
WHERE'S JOE SHLABOTNIK ? HE'S SUPPOSED TO BE SITTING AT OUR TABLE...
HE'LL BE HERE..HE'S PROBABLY SIGNING AUTOGRAPHS OR SOMETHING..
THERE'S PEGGY ! HI, SWEETIE, REMEMBER ME ?
SCHULZ

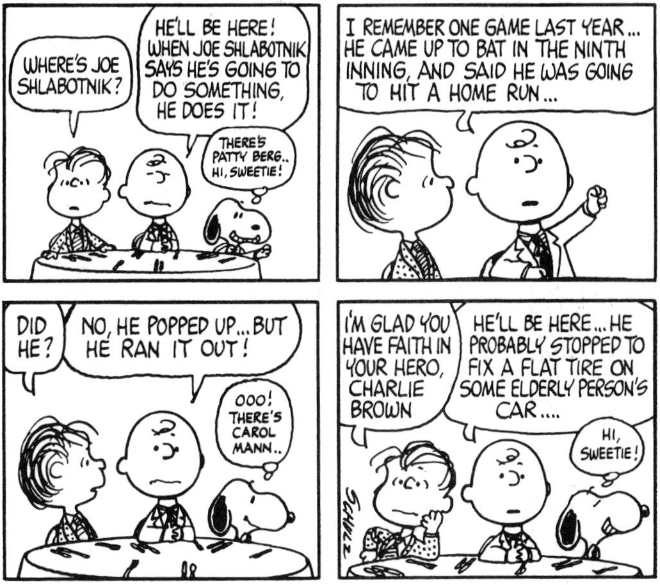
WHERE'S JOE SHLABOTNIK?
HE'LL BE HERE! WHEN JOE SHLABOTNIK SAYS HE'S GOING TO DO SOMETHING, HE DOES IT!
THERE'S PATTY BERG.. HI, SWEETIE!
I REMEMBER ONE GAME LAST YEAR... HE CAME UP TO BAT IN THE NINTH INNING, AND SAID HE WAS GOING TO HIT A HOME RUN...
DID HE?
NO, HE POPPED UP... BUT HE RAN IT OUT!
OOO! THERE'S CAROL MANN..
I'M GLAD YOU HAVE FAITH IN YOUR HERO, CHARLIE BROWN
HE'LL BE HERE... HE PROBABLY STOPPED TO FIX A FLAT TIRE ON SOME ELDERLY PERSON'S CAR....
HI, SWEETIE!

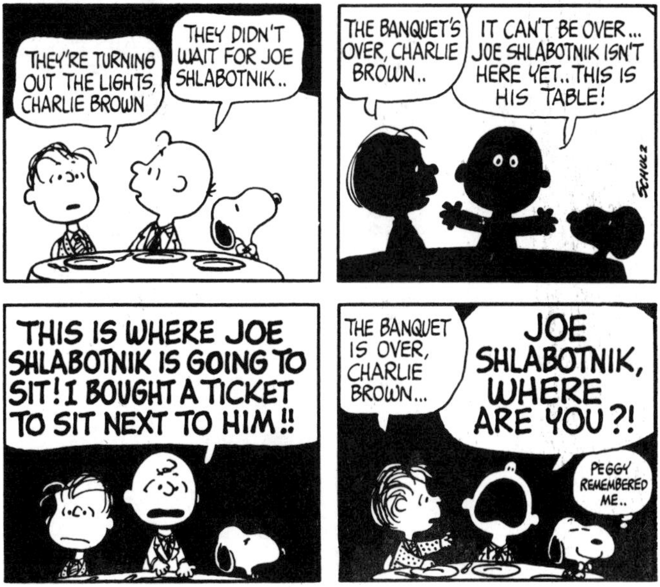
THEY'RE TURNING OUT THE LIGHTS, CHARLIE BROWN
THEY DIDN'T WAIT FOR JOE SHLABOTNIK..
THE BANQUET'S OVER, CHARLIE BROWN..
IT CAN'T BE OVER... JOE SHLABOTNIK ISN'T HERE YET.. THIS IS HIS TABLE!
THIS IS WHERE JOE SHLABOTNIK IS GOING TO SIT! I BOUGHT A TICKET TO SIT NEXT TO HIM!!
THE BANQUET IS OVER, CHARLIE BROWN...
JOE SHLABOTNIK, WHERE ARE YOU?!
PEGGY REMEMBERED ME..

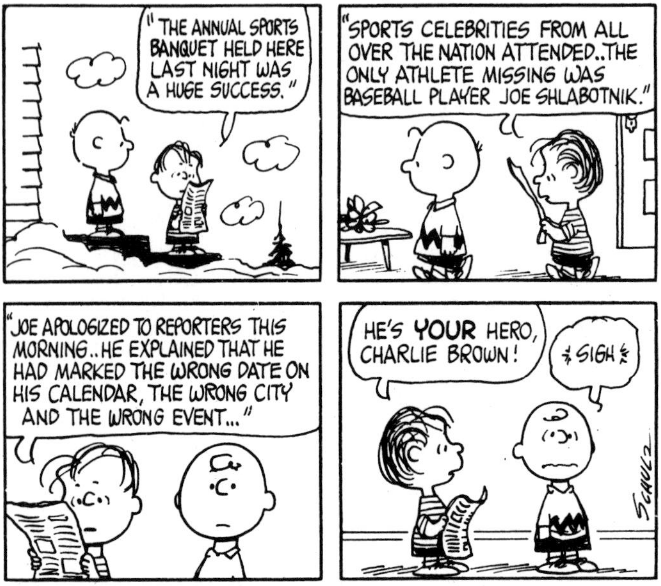
"THE ANNUAL SPORTS BANQUET HELD HERE LAST NIGHT WAS A HUGE SUCCESS."
"SPORTS CELEBRITIES FROM ALL OVER THE NATION ATTENDED..THE ONLY ATHLETE MISSING WAS BASEBALL PLAYER JOE SHLABOTNIK."
"JOE APOLOGIZED TO REPORTERS THIS MORNING..HE EXPLAINED THAT HE HAD MARKED THE WRONG DATE ON HIS CALENDAR, THE WRONG CITY AND THE WRONG EVENT..."
HE'S **YOUR** HERO, CHARLIE BROWN!
SIGH
SCHULZ

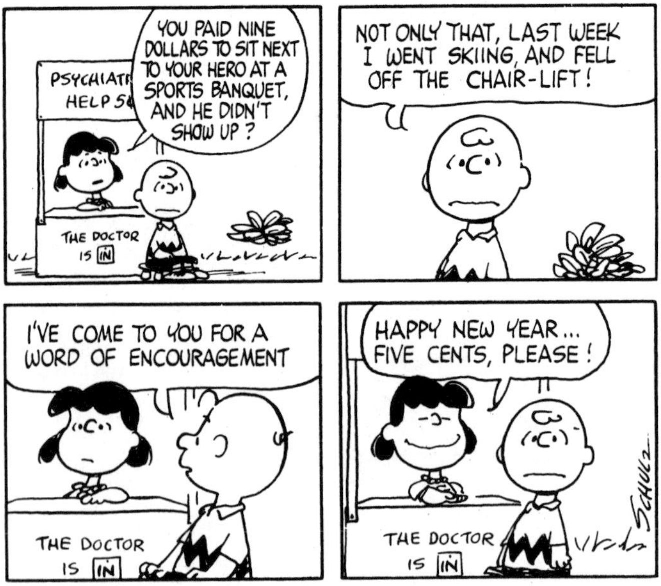
PSYCHIATR
HELP 5
YOU PAID NINE DOLLARS TO SIT NEXT TO YOUR HERO AT A SPORTS BANQUET, AND HE DIDN'T SHOW UP?
THE DOCTOR IS IN
NOT ONLY THAT, LAST WEEK I WENT SKIING, AND FELL OFF THE CHAIR-LIFT!
I'VE COME TO YOU FOR A WORD OF ENCOURAGEMENT
THE DOCTOR IS IN
HAPPY NEW YEAR... FIVE CENTS, PLEASE!
THE DOCTOR IS IN
SCHULZ